# DISCO DEATHTRAP

a novel of slasher horror
**by CAMERON ROUBIQUE**

Copyright © Cameron Roubique, 2016

Cover Art © Cameron Roubique, 2016

All rights reserved, including the right to reproduce this book or portions thereof in any form whatsoever.

This book is a work of fiction. Any references to historical events, real people, or real places are used fictitiously. Other names, characters, places, and events are products of the author's imagination, and any resemblance to actual events or places or persons, living or dead, is entirely coincidental.

ISBN 9781729122983

This book is for three of
my best friends:

Tim Taylor,
Ory Newman,
and
L.J. Dougherty

**Contents:**

Prologue ... 1

### Part One: New Year's Eve
### December 31, 1980

Chapter One: The Black Rose ... 4

Chapter Two: Picked Up ... 14

Chapter Three: Locked In ... 38

Chapter Four: Couples Only ... 61

Chapter Five: Disco King and Queen ... 84

Chapter Six: The Countdown ... 95

### Part Two: The Year of Blood
### January 1, 1981

Chapter Seven: The Death of Disco ... 106

Chapter Eight: Playing Dead ... 127

Chapter Nine: Whispers in the Pantry ... 147

Chapter Ten: The Ceiling ... 158

Chapter Eleven: Bus Ride ... 181

## Part Three: Resolutions
## January 1, 1981

Chapter Twelve: Under the Rink ... 216

Chapter Thirteen: Dropped ... 257

Epilogue ... 281

Afterword ... 284

# Prologue:

Almost no one knew about the bodies lying less than four feet beneath the polished hardwood floor of the Rollerville Disco Skating Rink. Every day the driving disco beat would start up, pound relentlessly for hours, and stop just after midnight. Inside the warped old coffins, tattered remnants of funeral suits and dresses would flutter and vibrate. Occasionally, a rotten, dried flap of skin, perhaps from a long dead cheek or rib-cage, would collapse from the constant vibration and send up a puff of stale mummy dust.

Their decades long peaceful rest ended on an autumn day in 1979 when they began to build Rollerville over a remote, supposedly unoccupied, corner of the Hart Hill Cemetery. KMZ Construction, the company who had been contracted to build the skating rink, found out about the bodies when a few of the undocumented Mexican workers were digging the foundation. They had started to get nervous when their front loaders began to scrape against the crumbling brick walls of what looked like a small buried crypt. They were scared once they climbed down in the hole and started to unearth what looked like white scraps of bones. As soon as they dug up three skulls in quick succession, they dropped their tools and ran screaming for the foreman.

The beefy foreman rushed over, took one look at the skeletons, and saw his end-of-the-year bonus check for completing the job earlier than scheduled swirling down the drain. He discreetly handed each of the workers an extra twenty dollar bill and said, "No le digan a nadie sobre esto. Sigan trabajando." *Don't tell anyone about this. Keep working.* And that was that.

Now the construction workers were hundreds of miles away working on some other job in another part of the country. They had spent their hush money long ago, and had all but forgotten about the incident. A few old timers in town may have known about the old fallen down crypt and the bodies, but they paid little attention to new things like roller disco. Some of the older members of the extensive Hart family may have known about them, but they had businesses to run and retirements to enjoy. Of course Charlie Hart, the cemetery's caretaker and black sheep of the family, knew about them, but he was a crazy old drunk, and no one had seen much of him around town over the past year or so.

Rollerville opened in January of 1980, and for a year, it did pretty well financially, despite the so called "death of disco." A lot of the local teens liked the fun atmosphere of the place even if they had little interest in skating, and it became a popular Friday and Saturday night hangout spot. Some nights, the rink was so packed with laughing, joking teens that it was hard to find space to skate. The living had taken what was once a place of death and made it a place of their own.

On January 1st, 1981, death took it back.

**Part One:**

**New Year's Eve**

**December 31, 1980**

# Chapter One:

## The Black Rose

### 1

A thousand small spots of light reflected off the big, sparkling disco ball as it spun lazily over the middle of the empty skating rink. Two dozen colored spotlights and two dozen more colored lights inside decorative translucent white globes the size of beach balls hung from the ceiling, casting spots of bright color everywhere. From the far front wall of Rollerville, the rink looked like a glittering red, blue, and purple jewel. The twenty-four inch disco ball was the glimmering diamond at its heart.

Denise rolled out onto the rink in her white skates with pink wheels. In one hand, she held the wide, flat mop that they used to sweep away the litter scattered across the rink from the last public skating session. It had ended less than five minutes earlier and the last straggling kids had already cleared off the rink. It had been a slow day, at least that was what Denise had been told by Diane, the day shift concessions counter girl.

Most likely the weather had kept people away, huddled up in their warm houses, awaiting the giant blizzard that was supposedly heading their way. Denise shivered at the thought of the storm, she absolutely hated the snow.

She slapped the mop down on the wood floor and began to skate forward, pushing it in front of her with both hands. She rolled around the outer edge of the rink with the mop tilted inwards, and spiraled towards the middle. Sweeping the rink wasn't normally her job. Usually Reggie, or one of the other skate monitors was supposed to do it, but Denise didn't mind. It was just nice to get away from the hot, cramped space behind the snack counter once in a while. She liked sweeping the rink because it somehow seemed to clear her mind from all the thoughts of blizzards, her asshole ex-boyfriend, the never-ending car trouble that seemed to plague her clunky old Ford Thunderbird, and the money she was trying to save to move out of this boring, snowbound, suburban town. The money never seemed to build up in her bank account very fast, something else was always chipping away at it. When she had enough saved, she planned on moving somewhere that was warm all year round, preferably near the ocean. But when she was skating, all those thoughts got left behind, whipped away in the breeze behind her flipped out, shoulder-length, auburn hair.

Denise passed the carpet-covered, elevated DJ booth and saw Freddy Atkinson, the night shift DJ, just sitting down for the night. He had gotten the job because his uncle, Geno Atkinson, was the manager. He wore a tight polyester shirt with the top buttons undone, bell-bottom slacks, and a thin gold chain around his neck. He had black hair that he wore in a perfect slicked-back style. Most people who saw him thought he was trying to look like John Travolta from *Saturday Night Fever*. Both he and Denise were twenty-two years old, and she could already tell that he was a guy who was going to be stuck in the seventies for a long time. He held a stack of records in his hands and plopped them down on his desk next to the twin turntables. He looked up and saw her.

"Ay, lookin' good," he called in his thick New Jersey accent. Denise smiled and lifted one hand off the mop handle to wave at him. She was a pretty girl with soft, slightly mousy features that made her look young. Smooth talking, well dressed guys like Freddy always seemed to be flirting with her, but she liked Freddy well enough for not getting too carried away with it.

He leaned into the microphone at the DJ booth and said, "This one goes out to the prettiest girl on the rink."

"Dancing Queen" by ABBA began pounding out of the huge wall mounted speakers. Denise laughed and shook her head at him. He was always telling her that if she bleached her hair blonde, she would look exactly like "that babe in that ABBA group." Denise knew who he was talking about, and although she didn't think she looked anything like Agnetha Faltskog, she always accepted his compliments with a smile.

She listened to the song as she skated, and felt the cool air whip at her large white button-up work shirt. She always wore it with the sleeves rolled up to her elbows, and almost totally open, with only the lowest button done. Just beneath that lowest button, she tucked it into her red, high-waisted shorts. Under all that she wore the shiny red leotard that Geno wanted her to wear. She usually only took off the button-up shirt if it was really crowded and hot, otherwise she felt too self-conscious wearing the skimpy outfit. The uniform was one of many reasons why she wanted to get out of this boring dead-end job. She had only been here nine months and already felt that she was outgrowing it. Some nights she would stand behind the snack counter waiting on teenagers and think, *One of these kids should be back here doing this, not me. I'm getting too old to be doing this shit.*

She watched the litter pile up at the head of the mop. Lollipop sticks, gum wrappers, a used Band-Aid, a crumpled receipt, a few Arcade game prize tickets, a girl's hair tie; it never failed to amaze her how much trash people left behind. She rounded the far corner of the rink and came back toward the DJ booth again. Lying in the middle of the floor ahead of her was a black rose. She pointed her toe, dragging the pink rubber toe-stop on the front of her skate against the floor, and slowed herself down. After coming to a complete stop in front of the rose, she knelt down to pick it up. She had found some weird stuff out on the floor the few times she had swept the rink--a dirty sock, a metal fork, even a whole Spider-Man comic book. A black rose though, that was a new one.

Denise delicately picked up the rose, being careful not to prick her fingers on the thorns. It felt moist, freshly cut. She held the rose up to Freddy and pointed at him as if asking *is this from you?* He leaned over the edge of the DJ booth and shrugged his shoulders. She returned the shrug and tossed the rose into the center of the rink where the litter would wind up at the end of the sweep. She felt a touch of regret at tossing away something as beautiful as a fresh black rose, but what else could she do with it?

The dusty cloud of litter in front of the mop eventually piled up with the rose in the center of the rink. Denise slowed to a stop and shook off the few dust bunnies and pieces of trash that clung to the mop. They fluttered to the floor and down on top of the black rose like snow. She returned the mop to its usual place in the back corner of the cramped rental skate storage room, behind the metal stairs that led to the roof. Then she grabbed the dust pan and brush.

Back on the rink, Denise approached the dust pile and stared at the dark rose. *Who could've left it here?* she wondered. *Some teenager who got rejected for a New Year's Eve date?* Probably not, there were usually only little kids here with their mothers during the day. And those black petals, they seemed like something more suited to bring to a funeral than to ask for a date.

*What? Are you Mrs. Columbo now? It's just a stupid rose, get on with it.*

Denise sighed, and with another pang of guilt, she swept the rose up with the rest of the trash.

## 2

She had to put all her weight into pushing the door open. There were two emergency exit doors evenly spaced along the right side of the rink, this one was the closest to the dumpster on the side of the building. As she heaved, she heard the brittle crack of a layer of ice along the outside of the door frame. She also had to push back a foot of thick, partially melted snow that had piled up against the building. It was wet slush with a top layer of icy crust an inch thick. Once she had the door pried open a foot, she examined all of this and shook her head.

"Jeez Louise," she muttered and squeezed the bulging black trash bag out the door in front of her. She was careful to leave the door open a crack so she wouldn't get locked out and have to trudge around to the main entrance at the front of the building once this chore was done. Thick plumes of steam rose from her mouth as she hauled the trash to the snow covered dumpster. She hadn't bothered to put on a jacket or take off her skates, and now she realized *that* had been a mistake.

The temperature had already dropped at least twenty degrees since she walked into the building a half hour ago. Big clumps of snow clung to the pink wheels and laces of her skates, weighing her down with each step. She reached the dumpster and hurled the trash bag over the side. Unlike the usual dull thud the dumpster made, there was only a soft *flump* as the trash bag fell down onto a cushion of snow.

Denise shivered and looked up at the gray overcast sky, pulling the open ends of her white work shirt tight together. Her bare legs had already broken out in thick goosebumps. The first few snowflakes were just starting to fall. They came down so lightly that she almost thought her eyes were playing tricks on her. *Yeah, it's coming, and it's probably gonna be a bad one*, she thought dismally as she hurried back to the building.

She almost stepped back inside, but looked down and remembered the huge clumps of snow covering her skates. Mr. Atkinson would have a cow if she tracked a bunch of snow onto the polished skate rink floor. She hurriedly kicked the concrete side of the building, and only succeeded in shaking off a thin dusty layer of snow. There were still far too many compacted chunks left clinging around the wheels.

"Damn it," she grumbled, angry at herself for not really planning this snowy excursion out at all. She knelt forward, resting her toe-stops against the ground, and began brushing the snow off the bottoms of the skates with her fingers.

Suddenly, she sensed that she wasn't alone out here. It was the creepy feeling of eyes watching her, like invisible ghost fingers lightly caressing her skin. She slowly looked up from her skates. From where she knelt, the south side of the building, she looked directly west towards the main entrance and the parking lot. A tacky, green chain-link fence divided the far end of the parking lot and the old graveyard. The new fence had been placed around what was left of the Hart Hill Cemetery during the construction of the skate rink, and it looked out of place in front of all the crumbling old headstones within.

Just looking at the cemetery, Denise could tell that it had once been elegant and beautiful, but now it had fallen into disrepair. Tufts of grass and scraggly bushes grew wild, poking out of mounds of compacted snow. Dead, knobby tree limbs hung heavy with the weight of snow and ice, looking like tortured skeletal fingers. Many of the old headstones looked crooked and neglected, leaning in toward the graves they marked. One of the arms of a tall cross had crumbled off, leaving only a jagged fragment sticking out of the side. Far back near the center of the graveyard stood a statue of the grim reaper complete with a scythe and a dark gray cloak. Its hood was pulled up over its head, keeping the face in shadows. Denise had been to a few cemeteries in the past and they always seemed so peaceful and neat. This was the only one she had ever seen that had the genuine, exaggerated spookiness you'd expect to see in a horror movie or a Halloween decoration.

Denise was about to look away from the cemetery when something caught her eye, a movement back behind the headstones. She scanned back and forth quickly, trying to figure out just what it was that caught her attention. A chunk of ice falling off a tree branch? No, a branch would be bouncing back from the change in weight, and they were all still. A bit of snow falling off one of the headstones? Maybe.

Then she saw it, the grim reaper statue. Its head had tilted just slightly, and the folds in its cloak seemed to have rearranged themselves. Was that a *person* standing back there among the dead, watching her under that dark hood?

Denise stood up slowly, her eyes locked on the reaper, trying to catch some kind of movement. Her mind raced with suspicious thoughts. *If that really is a statue, has it always been there? I don't remember seeing it before.*

*Don't be ridiculous*, she scolded herself. *Why would anyone stand out in the snow? And furthermore, why would they be out in that goofy get-up? Its New Year's Eve, not Halloween. Wrong holiday, man.*

Despite the logical arguments, that feeling of being watched seemed to focus in on the reaper and intensify now that she really looked at it. Deep down in her gut, she knew there really *was* a person under that cloak. She could almost feel a malevolent presence coming from the shadows under that dark hood. It made the hairs on the back of her neck stand up.

Suddenly, there was a muffled crunch of snow behind her and she whirled around. A dirty man with long, greasy, graying hair stood behind her, making bizarre jerky movements. Denise let out a startled scream and backed away from him, almost falling backwards as her skates rolled unexpectedly.

"Hey, man. Chill out. He'll hear you," the man said in a low, slurred and dreamy voice. Denise realized that she had seen him before. Every day on her way to work there was an old hippie who stood on random street corners along 92nd avenue. He always played air-guitar, nodding and pointing at the cars as they passed. He didn't look quite dirty enough to be homeless, but his mind was obviously fried from years of hard drug abuse. He didn't always stand in the same spot, but he did stick to the same stretch of road down near the trailer park. He wore the same dirty vest and jeans, sometimes with a battered old denim jacket on over the vest, and he was always rocking out to some song only he could hear. She realized those were the jerky movements he was making now.

Some of her coworkers knew the air-guitar man too, and they had talked about him once or twice. Denise bet that none of them had ever been this close to him before though. She wondered what he was doing this far away from his normal stretch of road. His usual stomping grounds were at least twenty blocks farther south of Rollerville.

"Wh-what do you want?" she asked breathlessly, her voice sounded more nervous than she intended. She watched him cautiously, waiting to see if he was going to try to attack.

"He'll hear you, man," the air-guitar man repeated, staring at her with drooping eyelids.

"Who'll hear me?"

"Him, man. Y'know?" The air-guitar man stepped closer to Denise. She inched back toward the wall, creeping towards the door back into the building. *Oh God, here he comes*, she thought bracing herself for his dirty hands to come lashing out. But he didn't make another move towards her. Instead he leaned a few inches closer, almost as if he wanted to whisper a secret in her ear.

"He's comin' tonight, man. It's startin.'"

"What is?"

"The Year of Blood." His voice lowered and he said it with no trace of drugged-out slur. Without another word, he turned away from Denise and walked back toward the parking lot and the road, jamming away on his air-guitar. Denise watched him go with a growing sense of relief. She held her hand up to her heart, feeling it hammering under her thin work shirt and leotard.

A gust of wind brought Denise back to reality and she realized that her hands and toes were aching from the cold. A thin layer of snowflakes had begun to pile up on top of her head. She turned to go back inside, ignoring the snow that she would track onto the floor. Just inside the doorway, she looked back at the graveyard. The person in the grim reaper costume was gone. She slammed the door, blocking out the cold and the ominous darkness that seemed to be everywhere outside. Skating across the floor she let the warmth and the pounding disco beat wash over her, bringing her back to reality. The cold in her hands and toes faded away, but the air-guitar man's words continued to echo in her mind. *It's startin.' The Year of Blood.*

## Chapter Two:

## Picked Up

**1**

The crowd of teenagers standing in the snow on the brick steps in front of DeAngelo High School let out a cheer as the old school bus lumbered around the corner toward them. The bus had been repainted white over its original yellow, and the Rollerville logo was on each side in a glossy red, outlined in blue. A ghostly trail of powdery snow blew off the bus's roof, swirling around behind it like a misty veil. With a loud hiss from the brakes, the bus came to a stop at the curb, and its door folded open. A relieved and slightly haggard looking Geno Atkinson, the manager of Rollerville, sat in the driver's seat. An unlit cigar poked out of the corner of his mouth.

"All aboard," he called in his husky smoker's voice and thick New Jersey accent.

Over sixty kids crowded around the doors of the bus and pushed their way in, ignoring their teachers' shouts for a single file line. A steady stream of tennis shoes caked with snow and slush clomped onto the bus, rubber soles squeaked loudly down the linoleum aisle. They shivered with relief, shook snowflakes out of bushy manes of hair, and trundled bulky overnight bags and backpacks onto the worn leather seats.

The last two people on the bus were the two chaperons: Coach Richards and Mrs. Bauer. Coach Richards was a tall, burly weight-lifting and typing teacher at DeAngelo High. He was in his early thirties, had a tight crew cut and a trim beard. He wore a comfortable gray Adidas track suit underneath his ski jacket. Mrs. Bauer was a tiny Sophomore English teacher. She was in her sixties and looked like a caricature of a librarian with short curly hair, pinched features, and a perpetually stressed-out expression on her face.

This odd pair had volunteered to organize and chaperone tonight's New Year's Eve Lock-In at Rollerville. Back in September, four students had died in a tragic drunk driving accident. Two of the students had been on Coach Richard's wrestling team, and one had been one of the most promising young writers Mrs. Bauer had ever seen. Despite their two completely different subjects, and a thirty year age gap, the two teachers joined forces to organize this all-night party in an attempt to prevent more students from suffering the same grisly fate.

"Gee, I'm sorry I'm late. It's these roads. They're gettin' real slick, y'know?" Geno Atkinson babbled apologetically. He was a gaunt man in his late fifties with a droopy face that had been prematurely aged by chain smoking. He had a mop of wavy graying hair that he slicked back with Brylcreem. His face was even paler than usual as he sat behind the wheel, dreading the icy drive back to Rollerville with a bus full of screaming teenagers. The snowfall had gotten much worse since he'd first left, and it didn't show any signs of slowing down.

"It's no problem at all," Coach said. "Safe driving, that's what tonight's all about. This does mean we're all gonna get in free though, right?" Coach Richards grinned widely with his perfect white teeth. Geno only laughed and turned forward to shut the bus's folding door. Considering how bad the weather looked already, he would be making more money tonight than he had any right to expect. In the wide mirror above the windshield, he saw that the kids had all taken their seats and were safely chattering amongst themselves.

"Here goes nothin,'" he muttered as he pulled back out onto the slick, snowy road.

Coach Richards took his seat next to Mrs. Bauer in the front row behind the bus driver and made awkward small talk. They really had nothing to talk about besides their students and the Lock-In they had organized. Beyond that, they were from two completely different worlds. They eventually settled into a comfortable mutual silence. Mrs. Bauer thought about the paperback she had brought along and hoped to get to during the quieter parts of the night. Coach Richards contemplated who would win in the Orange Bowl and the Rose Bowl tomorrow. He wondered if he might be watching one or two of his own students playing in one of the college bowls in a few years. He looked back over his shoulder and saw the one student who might have a chance at that future.

Three rows behind the teachers sat Paul Johnson and Sarah Whitlock, DeAngelo High's sweetheart couple. They had been a couple since the eighth grade and everyone in school knew that they would be together forever. Paul was a big guy, standing at six-four with a muscular Olympian body, he was roughly the same size as Coach Richards. Sarah was tiny, only five feet tall, and pretty in a cute, girl-next-door way. Physically, they were polar opposites, yet somehow they seemed to fit together perfectly. Their extreme difference in size charmed everyone who saw them walking down the hall holding hands. They were also easily the two friendliest people in the entire 1981 graduating class.

Both of them were extremely athletic. Paul was an all-star wide receiver for the DeAngelo Dolphins football team. Sarah was a dancer, cheerleader, ice skater, and roller skater. She had choreographed all of their roller-disco routines and taught Paul how to do all of his best moves. She had entered them into the Rollerville Disco King and Queen Competition back in September, and they won skating to Blondie's "Heart of Glass." Sarah's raw talent mixed with Paul's likable sense of humor won the crowd over, earning them a $100 grand prize and another trophy to add to their huge collection. Mrs. Bauer had set up an encore performance for tonight's Lock-In party in hopes that they could get more kids to sign up. Sarah and Paul had spent a lot of their Christmas vacation rehearsing for their encore performance as Rollerville's Disco King and Queen of 1980.

"You think it's gonna snow all night?" Sarah asked, brushing her long, straight brown hair back behind her ear.

"My dad said it was supposed to be pretty bad," Paul replied. "They're saying on TV that there's gonna be at least three feet of snow. And it's supposed to be down below zero all night."

"Really?" Sarah turned and looked out the window at the driving snow that seemed to be getting steadily worse. After a moment, she turned back to Paul and they shared a smile and an awkward laugh.

Ever since they started rehearsing their new routine, there had been an uncomfortable tension growing between them. They were both nervous, but not about the new skate number. They had practiced that over and over in Sarah's garage, and were comfortable enough performing in front of others. They were nervous about the fact that this would be the first night that they ever spent together. After all the excitement died down tonight, they planned on finding themselves a nice carpeted corner and falling asleep in each others arms, getting a sweet preview of what they both hoped their future nights would be like.

Paul leaned over and kissed her softly, reassuring both her and himself that tonight would be one to remember forever.

"Oooh!" called out two taunting male voices. Paul and Sarah abruptly broke away and glanced over their shoulders at the group of goofy, popular guys that were now laughing uproariously and teasing them from across the aisle and a few rows back. Jack Flynn and Mike Cavallo, the loudest and wildest guys in their group of popular "class-clowns," had started the cat calls. Paul smiled at them, then faced forward and amiably flipped them his middle finger disguised as an innocent scratching of his head. This only made the group laugh even harder.

Jack Flynn and Mike Cavallo were both well-dressed, good-looking guys. Jack had long dark hair that was feathered out and hung down to his shoulders, he was always brushing it back with his hands. Mike had an olive Hispanic complexion and a big Afro that girls were always playing with. They were shoe-ins for the Class Clown section of the senior superlatives for the 1981 yearbook and were well-loved in the general opinion of DeAngelo High School.

Only the nerdy kids ever saw their ugly sides. Only the geeks heard their cutting remarks, or caught the brunt end of their practical jokes. Short kids, kids with glasses, skinny kids, and ugly kids had no love for guys like Jack Flynn and Mike Cavallo. Those unfortunate kids would open the combination on their lockers only to have Jack Flynn smash them closed as he walked by, cheekily calling, "Oops!" over his shoulder. A handful of girls knew about Mike Cavallo's pushy, aggressive advances at parties. Some had even given in, and were later ignored and tossed aside as if they were some kind of desperate groupie. Despite their nasty sides, Jack and Mike put on a good show for everyone. When they made jokes, everyone laughed, maybe not with genuine laughter, but with a kind of participatory in-crowd laughter. Some of those geeks and discarded girls still gave them a kind of perfunctory laugh only because they didn't want everyone else looking at them as if they were weirdos.

    Jack reached down and unzipped his athletic duffel bag on the floor to grab himself a new pack of Juicy Fruit gum. He always chewed Juicy Fruit and had brought along two jumbo sized packs for tonight. The piece of gum that he was currently chewing had lost its flavor an hour ago, and he felt like he needed to freshen up his mouth. He found the gum he was looking for and zipped his bag closed. He popped a fresh piece of gum into his mouth, spit the old piece into the wrapper, crumpled it up, and tossed it over his shoulder.

    The wadded up piece of tin-foil sailed back four rows, over the pig-tailed heads of a group of tall freshman girls that were all on the DeAngelo High basketball team, and got caught in Jim Young's greasy dark brown hair. He felt the soft impact and quickly picked out the wrapper. He grimaced as he felt the warm gum squish inside the wrapper between his fingers. He looked toward the front of the bus in annoyance and saw the group of popular guys near the middle. Jack Flynn briefly glanced backward, confirming Jim's suspicions of who threw the gum wrapper into his hair.

"What the fuck?" Jim asked to no one in particular. He quickly threw the wrapper back toward Jack Flynn's seat and sank down so no one would know who threw it. He then brushed his heavily gelled hair back, making sure it was perfect.

Jim and his best friend Gary Nelson hated guys like Jack Flynn and Mike Cavallo. They couldn't understand why those jerks got all the love and respect from the entire school. Neither of them were tall or athletic. Jim was skinny and wore his hair gelled down in a kind of messy greaser/punk style that he had modeled after Joe Strummer from The Clash. Tonight he wore an old leather motorcycle jacket over a black Ramones T-shirt. Gary had straight, medium-length, sandy blonde hair. He wore a heavy ski coat over a polo shirt with orange and white stripes, and flared out khaki slacks. They weren't exactly geeks, but they definitely weren't popular either. They had a small group of friends that existed in a kind of mid-level popularity purgatory. They joked around and kept to themselves, hanging out in their own little corner of the upstairs hallway in DeAngelo High, a place they called "The Spot." Their sense of humor was kind of peculiar, and most of their jokes were inside jokes.

Jim and Gary were sitting sideways in their seats on opposite sides of the bus. They had been in the middle of a five-way conversation between themselves, their girlfriends (who sat near the middle aisle), and Dan Parsons. Dan was another guy from their group, he sat alone behind Jim at the back of the bus.

"What was that?" Gary asked Jim.

"Ah, one of those douche bags up front threw their gum into my hair," Jim replied.

Gary peered over the seat and saw the Flynn Cavallo group. "Ugh. What a bunch of assholes."

Jim and Gary had been doing most of the talking since they met up to wait for the bus at DeAngelo High. Their girlfriends went to Jefferson High School on the other side of town. Suzanne Banks (Jim's) was a pretty, but chunky girl with dark brown hair cut in a medium-length bob. Lindy Connel (Gary's) was a skinny redhead who wore a pair of huge glasses and had mousy features. Both girls craned their necks to look over at the popular guys that their boyfriends seemed to despise.

"I swear if either Jack or Mike comes near me at all tonight, they're gettin' tripped," Jim said, pointing towards the front of the bus.

"Oh, forget about those guys, dude. Hey," Gary reached over the seat and tapped Dan on the shoulder with the back of his hand, "at least they didn't bring Queen Bitch with them. Am I right?"

"Who?" Dan asked. He hadn't been listening, he'd been staring out the window watching the snow fly.

"You know, Mary Anne."

"Yeah, *Scary* Anne," Jim chimed in.

"Oh yeah, right. *Her.*" Dan made a gagging sound and stuck his finger down his throat, his friends laughed. Mary Anne was Dan's ex-girlfriend, and his group of friends hated her. They had begun calling her names like Queen Bitch and Scary Anne while she and Dan had still been dating.

Jim and Gary turned back to each other and began talking over their girlfriend's heads again. When they got going, it was hard to break into the conversation. Suzanne interrupted the conversation by asking Jim something about renting skates, and Lindy took the opportunity to start her own conversation with Gary. Soon the two couples were deep into their own separate conversations, and sharing brief kisses. Dan glanced over at them a few times, proud to see that they had finally gotten girlfriends of their own. For the longest time, he had been the only person in their group with a steady girlfriend, now he was the single one. He thought it was ironic how the tables had completely turned. Feeling like a fifth wheel, he slid down lower on his seat and stared out the window.

Dan hadn't seen much of his friends over the past year and a half, he had been too distracted dating Mary Anne. None of his friends liked her, they all thought she was a rich, stuck-up bitch. His family didn't like her, they thought she had too much attitude. It seemed that he had been caught in the middle between his girlfriend and just about everyone else in his life. That hadn't mattered much at first, things had been so great with her. Then, sometime around September she had changed. She had become quieter and more prone to snap at him. Soon it seemed that all they did was fight. Finally, he decided enough was enough. He broke it off with her and....

There he was doing it again, thinking about Mary Anne. He sighed and forced himself to think about other things. This morning he had woken up from some vague bad dream about being chased, he couldn't quite remember much else. It had put him in a bad mood, one depressing thought led to another and he was thinking about Mary Anne again. He decided then that his New Year's Resolution would be to put the past behind him and move on with his life.

He was one of the top skaters at DeAngelo High. He owned his own custom-made, sleek, black roller skates with bright yellow wheels and toe-stops. Lightning bolt decals flashed along the sides of the skates and wheels. Despite all the money he had spent on the skates and all the time he had spent practicing, he hadn't been skating in months. Mary Anne was always at Rollerville, now hanging around with guys like Mike Cavallo and Jack Flynn. In the halls at school she took every opportunity to make him jealous, and he didn't want anymore of that after school hours. So he had stayed away from the roller rink for the last few months. Tonight would be different though. Tonight he would stop avoiding her and just let himself have a good time. The only way to get her to move on and stop bugging him was to move on himself. He couldn't let her bring him down.

*Just like that ELO song "Don't Bring Me Down." That's my theme song today*, he thought. The song had gotten firmly stuck in his head that morning and refused to leave. To his pleasant surprise, Mary Anne hadn't showed up at DeAngelo for the bus to pick them up. According to the rules of the Lock-In, you had to ride the bus to Rollerville from the pick-up spot at the high school, you couldn't drive your own car. It looked like he wouldn't have to deal with Mary Anne at all tonight. He smiled at the thought of a Mary Anne free night, and began to sing "Don't Bring Me Down" softly under his breath again as he looked out the back window of the bus.

Outside, the snow was really starting to come down hard. Big, fat, bumblebee-sized snowflakes tumbled down from the sky, adding to the thick coat of ice and slush that already covered the roads. Looking down at those icy roads, he was glad that his old Karmann Ghia was parked safely back at school and he wasn't behind the wheel. He looked up at the driver at the front of the bus and thought, *Better you than me, buddy.* He and his friends would all be safe inside Rollerville for the night.

Dan turned back to the window and the snowfall seemed to have tripled, blowing sideways and slamming against the steamy windows of the bus. Dan wiped away the condensation on the window. Another harsh gust of wind and snow slammed against it so hard he could hear the powdery tapping of snowflakes hitting the glass like little pinpricks. In the fading daylight, Dan could barely even make out the other side of the street. He saw what looked like the vague outline of a chain-link fence a few feet back from the sidewalk.

Suddenly, he felt himself being thrown violently forward as the bus slammed on its brakes. His hands flew out to grab the seat in front of him, and then everyone on board let out screams of terror as they felt the bus slide violently out of control.

## 2

Geno Atkinson spun the wide wheel as fast as he possibly could. He pumped the brakes, stomping down over and over, his jaw clenching tightly in panic.

He had been driving along at a reasonably slow pace along Hart Hill Road. Out of nowhere, a huge tree branch fell into the street right in front of the bus. It was a gigantic old cottonwood branch that stretched out across the entire road. It was over a foot in diameter at its widest end. Geno slammed on the brakes, knowing that the knobby branch would destroy the whole front end of the bus. The rear wheels locked and they had hit a smooth patch of black ice. The back end whipped around in a counter-clockwise arc. The bus tilted up at a crazy angle, threatening to tip over on its side.

Dan and his friends clawed tightly into the leather seats in front of them. Suzanne and Lindy screamed as they clung tight to Jim and Gary. Even Jack Flynn and Mike Cavallo let out terrified screams.

The bus slid to a stop, still tilted up on only its right wheels, then crashed back to the ground. Everyone that had been chattering so loudly and excitedly only a minute ago was now dead silent.

Geno Atkinson's white-knuckled fists clung to the wheel for a moment, his jaw still clenched on the flattened cigar in his mouth. Then he came to his senses and stood up at the front of the bus.

"Is everyone okay?" he shouted. His only responses were wide-eyed looks and a few nods from pale, scared faces.

"What happened?" Coach Richards asked breathlessly.

"That giant tree branch just fell out in the middle of the road. If we'd hit that thing, we would've crashed for sure."

Dan turned and looked out his window. The bus's back end had swung around so far that Dan's window on the side of the bus was now facing forward in the direction they had been going. Sure enough, there was a huge knobby limb caked with ice and snow lying in the middle of the road.

"Jesus Christ! Look at that thing," he said to Jim and Gary. They both turned to look at it and their mouths dropped open.

"Holy shit," Jim whispered, his voice full of awe.

Coach Richards got up and spoke to everyone in a louder, more commanding voice, his wrestling coach voice.

"Are you guys all okay? Nod your heads if you're all right." Everyone gave him nervous nods, and a few of the more out-spoken people actually answered him.

"We're right around the corner, one more block and we're there," Geno Atkinson added in his own loud commanding voice. "Just gotta get out and move that thing out of the street."

"Right," said Coach Richards. He turned to

look back at the students again. "Okay, Paul, Jack, Mike, Steve. You guys come on and help us move that thing out of the way." They all got up and followed Geno out through the front door. Jack Flynn turned around and began rolling up the sleeves on his ski jacket.

"Don't worry, girls. I'll get that 'sumbitch outta the way," he joked in a macho, muscle-man voice. There was the usual laughter from almost everyone on the bus. Jim and Gary looked at each other and rolled their eyes.

Jim coughed loudly into his hand, masking the word, *"Douche!"* within his cough. Jack Flynn either didn't hear, or chose to ignore this.

One by one, the six of them stepped out into the snow on the side of the road. A blast of icy wind hit their faces almost immediately, and each of them winced as snowflakes flew into their eyes and melted.

"God *damn!*" Jack Flynn yelled, the wind ripped the words right out of his mouth.

They walked along the side of the bus to shield themselves from as much of the wind and snow as possible. A few strong gusts made them lean forward and shield their eyes with their hands from the flying snow. One of the younger freshman kids in the middle of the bus tapped on the window as they walked past. Mike Cavallo reached up and pounded on the glass, making the kid jump and the others around him giggle.

Coach Richards squinted and saw the limb lying in the road near the back of the bus. It sprawled out all the way across the road and already had a half inch of fresh snow piled up on top of its ice encrusted bark. In the last dim threads of daylight, he tried to look up at the cottonwood that had dropped it, but he could only make out a faint outline through the swirling snow.

"Must've been the weight of all the snow that brought it down," Geno Atkinson shouted loudly to the Coach. He nodded back at him.

"Look at that thing!" Steve Fields shouted, pointing at the limb.

"It's gotta be the whole top half of the tree," Jack Flynn said.

Coach Richards raised his coaching voice to its highest level over the wind. He pointed to Mike Cavallo and Steve Fields. "All right, you two go help drag that top half to the side of the road. Jack, Paul, you help me push the heavy end out of the way." Geno tossed away his crushed cigar and bent down to help the Coach, Paul, and Jack roll the heavy end of the branch out of the road.

Mike and Steve began dragging the branch off the road by a few handfuls of thin twigs. A few of the brittle branches broke off in their hands and they had to find new places to hold on. Coach and the others began to clumsily roll the heavy end of the tree away. They grunted and heaved, thick plumes of steam rose from their mouths and noses. Their feet slipped on the icy street. The thick limb weighed a ton, and an extra two inches of snow clung to the bottom side where it had fallen into the street, adding to the weight. It rolled lopsidedly and kept wanting to rest on the heavy side with all the snow. A few slushy chunks peeled off as they rolled it away, leaving bare patches on the bark.

They finally managed to move it into the small drainage ditch on the side of the road, and sighed as they brushed the snow off their numb hands. A few of the lighter branches brushed against the green chain-link fence on the other side of the ditch, knocking down the snow that had stuck against it. Paul saw the top of a gravestone on the other side of the fence and sunken divots in the snow. He instantly recognized where they were.

*That old graveyard. Are we that close to Rollerville already?* he wondered.

Paul looked back down at the tree limb again.

His eyes seemed to be drawn to it, as if something wasn't quite right, as if there was something unnatural about it.

"Okay, everybody back on the bus," Mr. Atkinson yelled over the wind. The others all ran back toward the bus, shuddering with the cold. Paul stayed where he was though, staring at the limb. Suddenly, he realized what had caught his attention. The heavy end of the limb was strangely smooth where it should have ripped away from the tree. It hadn't fallen from the weight of the snow, someone had deliberately sawed this tree branch off.

"Hey, slacker, what are you waitin' for? Let's go!" Coach Richards shouted at him from the doorway of the bus.

"Coming," Paul yelled back. As he ran back to the bus, he looked back over his shoulder at the limb and the green chain-link fence behind it. He thought about the gravestone he'd seen back behind the limb and the divots from all those other flat grave markers.

He stepped back into the warmth of the bus and smiled as he heard the round of applause everyone was giving the guys for pushing the big branch out of the way. He brushed the snow out of his short hair and off his shoulders, then sat back down next to Sarah.

"What was that all about?" she asked.

"What was what?"

"What were you looking at back there?"

"Ah, it was nothin.' Just looking at that branch." He flashed a smile at her. She shrugged and turned back to look out the window. Sarah had been with Paul since eighth grade, and by now she knew him well enough to not try to pry something out of him. Doing that only seemed to annoy him, and she didn't want to spoil their first night together by starting off with an argument.

Paul looked out the window over Sarah's

shoulder, and one last thought about the graveyard popped into his mind. At first, he had thought those divots in the snow were just low spots from other flat grave markers. Now it occurred to him that they were much too close together to be grave markers, they looked more like footprints.

*Come on, forget it,* he thought to himself. *Why would anyone have cut that limb off? Why would anyone be out in this shit in the first place?* He looked back out the window one last time as the bus started up again, wishing he could get another look at those low divots. He realized with some disappointment that even if he could go back for another look, they would probably already be filled up with snow.

**3**

"That's that old graveyard back there, isn't it?" Jim asked as they watched the guys drag the huge branch out of the way.

Dan squinted his eyes and he could make out the faint shapes of a few headstones. "Yeah, I think it is."

"Ooh, spooky," Jim said, turning to Suzanne and tickling her with eerie, wiggling fingers. She shoved him away playfully. "What would you do if we got stuck out here and had to spend the whole night in the graveyard?"

"Jim, stop," Suzanne scolded. She was a huge chicken when it came to anything even the slightest bit scary.

"You know this Rollerville place is built over part of the old graveyard, right?" Gary added in a completely serious voice.

"Oh yeah. That's right," Jim joined in. "And

tonight after midnight, all those dead people are gonna climb up out of the ground." He broke his clawed hand out from his other enclosed fist mimicking a dead hand rising up from the grave.

"Yeah, and they're gonna come pound on the front doors of the rink, just like in that movie *Dawn of the Dead*." Gary moved stiffly and groaned like one of those zombies in the horror movies.

"Quit it, you guys!" Suzanne shouted and covered her face with her hands.

"Yeah, knock it off, Gary," Lindy said, punching her boyfriend on the arm.

"Aww, come on, Suze, you know I'm just kiddin' around," Jim said. "There's nothing to be scared of from an old cemetery. See?" He turned to look out the window. "Ain't nothin' in there but a bunch of snow. Look." He continued to look out the window at the cemetery and didn't notice the hands creeping over the seat behind him. Suddenly, Dan grabbed Jim's shoulders roughly and screamed right near his ear. Jim let out his own genuine scream and jumped a foot off his seat. He turned around and Dan gave him a sweet, innocent grin. The girls burst out laughing.

"Oh, you're real funny, man," Jim said amiably enough.

"That's what you get," Suzanne laughed, giving Jim another little shove. "I like you," she said to Dan, giving him an appraising smile. Dan gave her a slick wink and point with his index finger, then turned and slapped Gary a high-five.

"Now that's the old Dan we all know and love. So glad to have you back, man," Gary said. Throughout the past year, while he'd been dating Mary Anne, Dan had been away from his group of friends. Even when they were at school, Dan hadn't been around much. Now they always seemed to make a big deal about how he was back. At first he had tried multiple times to tell them that he hadn't gone anywhere. Eventually, he just gave in and humored them.

"Glad to be back."

After a few slippery turns, Geno Atkinson managed to get the bus pointed back in the right direction and they made it the rest of the way to Rollerville without incident. Dan was smiling as they pulled into the parking lot. They came to a slow stop in the drop-off lane near the glass double doors at the front entrance. The whole brick building was painted in white and red stripes. Dan always thought it looked like the sawed-off bottom half of a giant popcorn box. He peered out at the building through his backseat window, waiting for everyone else to get off. He could see large snowdrifts piling up at the base of the building and wondered how big they would be by tomorrow morning.

Everyone thanked Geno as they walked past him, and he nodded back in acknowledgment. When Dan finally reached the front of the bus, he clapped Geno on the back and said, "You did it, man." Geno shook his head and let out a weary sigh.

Dan stepped out into the snow and looked up at the glowing neon red and blue *Rollerville* sign at the top of the building. The snowflakes falling in front of the bright letters seemed to glow red and blue like little colored fireflies. Jim walked up, put his arm around Dan's shoulders, and stared up at the building with him.

"What a fuckin' shithole, man," Jim said, and Dan immediately burst out laughing. This was one of their inside jokes that they had been quoting since freshman year. Almost every morning, as they walked into DeAngelo High, one of them would repeat *What a fuckin' shithole, man,* and they would promptly crack up.

They followed the crowd, trudging through the snow and up the concrete ramp that led to the front doors. The roof came out over the short ramp, shielding it from falling snow, but not from the gusts of wind that blew snow up from the parking lot. The sound of a powerful revving engine and the muffled pound of a disco beat thundered towards them in the parking lot. As the noise got closer, Dan recognized the song as "Get Down Tonight" by KC and the Sunshine Band. It was one of Mary Anne's favorite songs and he'd heard it a million times. He glanced over his shoulder and his heart sank.

"Oh great. Just what I needed tonight," he mumbled to himself.

The sleek bright red 1979 Corvette skidded into the nearest icy parking space. The front door opened and Dan's ex-girlfriend, Mary Anne, got out with a big grin on her face. She had dark brunette hair that she wore flipped out like Farrah Fawcett. She wore big hoop earrings and had impeccable makeup. Her fur-lined white coat hung open, revealing a thin red halter top, a wide belt, and flared-out black pants. Her platform shoes were so high that even the deep snow in the parking lot didn't reach her pant legs. Her shirt was cut low, showing off a lot of cleavage. *Dressed to impress, or to make me jealous?* Dan thought with a frown and turned away from her.

"Hey, Mike! Jack!" Mary Anne called with so much excitement in her voice that she sounded like an actress playing the part of a lonely wife being reunited with her husband after World War II. Mary Anne brushed closely past Dan and his friends without giving them the slightest glance. She threw her arms around Mike and hugged him tight, then began to lightly touch his Afro.

"Oh God," Jim muttered. Gary turned around and stuck a finger down his throat, making gagging noises. Dan tried his best to suppress a twinge of jealousy as Mary Anne animatedly hugged each and every person in Jack Flynn and Mike Cavallo's group. She even kissed a few of them on their cheeks.

*Well, there goes my fun, Mary-Anne-Free night,* Dan thought, *or at least part of it. Why didn't I just stay home?* Jim and Gary noticed the crestfallen look that Dan couldn't really keep off his face.

"Hey, Dan. Fuck her, man!" Gary said. "Just stick with us tonight. Pretend she's not even here."

Dan nodded and gave his friends an appreciative smile.

"Who's that?" Lindy whispered in Gary's ear.

"His ex-girlfriend," Gary whispered back. He gave her a very brief explanation of their breakup. Dan ignored them and continued walking into the building.

Geno Atkinson parked the bus and lit up one of his cigars. He hung back, enjoying the smoke as the large group filed into the front doors of Rollerville. Coach Richards held the door open as the students walked in, shivering and brushing snow off their heads and shoulders. Geno tossed away the last smoldering stub of the cigar and took one last look out at the parking lot to make sure there weren't any more stragglers left out there. It was all clear. He looked up at the snow that continued to dump down from the storm clouds overhead. The temperature had now dropped to three degrees Fahrenheit.

*We're in,* he thought, shaking his head at the storm and the freezing temperatures. *Thank God, we're in for the night.* Many of the students shared the same, or similar, thoughts as they walked into the warm lobby, totally unaware that many of them would never walk back out.

# 4

"Everyone wait here before going in! Do *not* go in yet!" Coach Richards shouted in his commanding Coach voice. All the kids piled up in little groups and stood around waiting for whatever Coach had in store for them. "We're going to have everyone sign in so we know you're here, okay? When you get this clipboard," he held it high in the air, "sign your name and wait where you are. Everyone got that?"

Mrs. Bauer took the clipboard from him and approached the loud group that included Mary Anne, Jack Flynn, and Mike Cavallo. Mary Anne clung to Mike's arm a little too tightly, and laughed at all their jokes a little too loudly. She didn't really contribute much to their conversation, and when she did, her responses were met with only short answers.

"Mary Anne?" Mrs. Bauer interrupted their conversation. They all turned and looked at her with mild, insolent annoyance. "What are you doing here? You didn't ride the bus in."

"I know, Mrs. Bauer, I drove my Corvette in," Mary Anne explained with a little laugh. She talked down to Mrs. Bauer as if explaining some common fact to a child. To listen to her tone, you'd think the teacher had never heard of a teenager driving a car before.

"Mary Anne, you know the rules of the Lock-In. No one drives their own car, remember?" Mrs. Bauer explained with a stern frown on her face.

"Gee, I'm sorry, Mrs. Bauer, but I had stuff to do." She continued to smile sweetly at Mrs. Bauer as if the rules were only suggestions.

"Mary Anne...." Mrs. Bauer gave her one of her

trademarked exasperated sighs. She was desperately trying to figure out what to say to handle this situation. It wasn't like they were at school and she could use her usual means of punishment. "Do I have to call your parents?"

"Why? I made it on time. What's the big deal?" The teacher didn't have a leg to stand on and Mary Anne knew it. "Do you want me to go home or something?"

Mrs. Bauer sighed again. "No, just write your name at the bottom of the attendance sheet and sign it. And next time pay attention and follow the rules, got it?"

"Sure thing, Mrs. B.," she said amiably enough. Mrs. Bauer walked away shaking her head in exasperation, and Mary Anne made an ugly face at her after she turned her back. Mary Anne casually tossed her dark hair over her shoulder, and turned back to her group of boys.

While they waited for the attendance sheet to come back, Coach Richards produced a heavy metal chain from his duffel bag. He began wrapping it around the metal handles of the glass double doors at the front of the building in a tight figure eight pattern. He had borrowed the chain from the DeAngelo High janitor who used it to lock the school up during the few weeks between the spring semester and summer school. He had also borrowed a thick metal padlock.

"Is that really necessary?" Geno asked. "I mean, I can just lock the doors, won't that be enough?"

"It's really just for show," Coach explained.

"It's kind of a ceremonial thing to officially kick off the Lock-In," Mrs. Bauer chimed in.

"Well, it's technically against the fire code," Geno said. "But I doubt any fire inspectors are gonna be out tonight. Plus, we have two emergency exits inside the rink. That's where everyone will be anyway."

"If it's a problem, we can skip it," Coach

suggested.

"No, no. It's fine. Just leave it kinda loose, because I'm gonna have to go out there a few times and plow the parking lot."

Coach nodded. "Copy that."

"You boys ready for this?" Mrs. Bauer asked. Geno shrugged.

"Ready as I'll ever be," Coach replied, tossing one last loop of chain around the handles.

Mrs. Bauer double-checked the attendance list once it was passed back to the chaperons standing at the front doors. All the signatures were filled in next to the names. She turned to Coach and Geno, who seemed to be looking distractedly out at the storm.

"All here," she said and they nodded.

Coach Richards let out an ear splitting whistle between two of his fingers and everyone quieted down. "Okay, now let's go over the ground rules. We got four major rules tonight." Several kids let out groans. "Rule Number One: No smoking in here. Rule Number Two: No booze." Even louder groans. "You guys wouldn't do anything like that, would you? You're all good kids, right?"

Two-thirds of the large group immediately shouted a resounding *"NO!"* Coach couldn't help but laugh.

"Aww, come on, guys. You're all gonna be the perfect little angels that I know you are. Okay, Rule Number Three. For all you lovebirds, I wanna see hands above the belt-line, you understand? That means above, here," he demonstrated at his own belt-line, "at all times."

"Don't touch Coach below his belt-line, people!" shouted Mike Cavallo. Everyone in the cramped front lobby cracked up.

"Yeah, you're the expert on *that*, Mike," Jack

Flynn fired back. More laughter erupted even harder at this and Mike punched him on the arm. Even Jim, Gary, and Dan couldn't help but smirk at that one. Coach ignored the comments and pushed on.

"You're gonna act like civilized adults and show these employees, who are spending their New Year's Eve with us, just how well behaved DeAngelo High students are, okay?" Jack Flynn and Mike Cavallo stood straight at attention and began saluting the Coach. Mary Anne laughed out loud in her high-pitched giggle. Dan looked over and saw Gary do a mocking, laughing impression of the popular guys and Mary Anne. He grinned at Gary and slapped him a high-five.

"Last, but not least, Rule Number Four. Once we lock this door here, everyone stays put. You guys got that? That means no going outside to smoke, no little road trips, no snowball fights in the parking lot. You're in until morning. If you go outside, you are gonna be out past curfew. Also, the weather forecast is calling for about two to three feet of snow, and the temperature is gonna be below zero. I don't want to find your frozen body outside tomorrow morning looking like Jack Nicholson at the end of *The Shining*." This actually got a genuine laugh out of everybody in the crowd. Coach leaned down to Mrs. Bauer. "Do you have anything to add?"

"No, I think you covered it quite eloquently," she replied.

Coach turned back to the padlock and held it out for everyone to see.

"You guys ready?" he shouted. Everyone cheered back with a loud *"YEAH!"* Coach clicked the padlock shut and held up his fist triumphantly. A cheer rang out and dozens of fists joined Coach's in the air. With that one almost inaudible click, their fates were sealed.

# Chapter Three:

# Locked In

## 1

The carpeted double doors burst open and the crowd of teenagers poured into the rink shouting and hollering with excitement. The three employees working in the rink all turned their heads to the sound of the stampede. Denise leaned forward from behind her snack counter and watched them rush in. The students gave cries of admiration at the look of the rink as soon as they stepped inside.

Colored streamers and balloons were strung up everywhere. The streamers blossomed out from the big disco ball in the center of the rink. All the balloons had the words *HAPPY NEW YEAR 1981* printed on them in white ink. They floated from the smooth three-foot-high cinder block walls that separated the rink from the carpeted areas. More bunches of balloons were tied to the corners of the elevated DJ booth, the tables in the dining area, the corners of the snack counter, and all the machines in the small arcade area back behind the bathrooms. They had also filled up a lot of extra balloons and just let them float to the ceiling, giving it a bubbly look. The day shift employees had spent that whole slow morning and afternoon decorating and filling up all those balloons with helium from the tank they kept behind the skate rental counter. A large two-sided banner hung from the gap between the ceiling and the low rink wall, perfectly placed so that everyone could see it. In bold colorful letters, it said *HAPPY NEW YEAR 1981!!!*

Right on cue, Freddy Atkinson, up in his DJ booth, dropped the needle down on one of the record players, and "Don't Stop 'Til You Get Enough" by Michael Jackson began to thump from the eight huge overhead speakers that circled the rink.

Some of the kids owned skates, and had already put them on in the front lobby while they waited to be released into the rink. These kids found suitable spots to dump off their overnight bags: on the tables in the dining area, near the circular carpeted seats on the left side of the rink, or in random corners. Then they quickly began to roll out onto the smooth, glossy hardwood floor.

Reggie Jackson, the skate monitor, smiled at them as he rolled around in a lazy circle and bobbed his head to the beat of the music. He was black and had a large Afro even bigger than Mike Cavallo's, it bounced with his head to the disco beat. He wore his uniform, a tight white polo shirt with the Rollerville logo embroidered on the upper left-hand corner, and bell-bottom jeans over his black skates. He tried to ignore the nagging thoughts that kept telling him that he'd much rather be downtown with his friends than up here in the 'burbs babysitting a bunch of white kids. With a resigned sigh, he reminded himself again that this job was a breeze, and made more money than his friends downtown. Those night school business classes wouldn't pay for themselves. Also, the music was good, Freddy

Atkinson's music tastes had enough jive to make Reggie feel like he wasn't a complete outsider.

He approached Freddy's DJ booth and spun around backwards, then raised his left hand high. Right on cue, Freddy reached out and slapped him five. This was an almost daily ritual between the two of them. Freddy winked at Reggie and pointed at him as he spun around forwards again and knelt down, extending his right leg out in front of him as he went around the curved corner of the rink.

Freddy smiled and looked down at his stack of records, he was also bobbing his head to the music. He had his tentative music playlist in front of him scribbled on a yellow legal pad between the two record players. Eighty percent of the night's music had already been planned out, but he left a few open spots for requests, there were *always* requests. If he got a request for something that was on the list for later that night, hey, no problem. Freddy was an easygoing guy, and he would just switch his set list around a little.

He was the only employee that actually wanted to be here. He liked the DJ gig, and hoped he could make more of a career out of it in the future. Maybe he would even move to New York City and try to break into radio. Tonight was his though, he was the star of the show. He imagined that he was hosting one of those big New Year's Eve parties they had on TV. He was in the driver's seat like Dick Clark or Casey Kasem. The disco ball was turning, the music was loud, the party was here, and everything felt just fine for Freddy Atkinson.

Behind Freddy's DJ booth, a steady stream of kids hurried to the counter in the back corner where they could pick up rental skates. Tony Tanner rushed as fast as he could behind the skate rental counter. The kids piled up on the other side without even trying to form a line. They all shoved their wet shoes at him and shouted at the same time.

"I need size nine and a half."

"I need elevens."

"These ones are too small."

"Too tight."

"They hurt my ankles."

"These ones smell funny, I don't think they got cleaned."

Tony struggled not to lose it and walk out on this shitty job. He hated working here, and it was moments like this that made him want to walk away and never ever look back. He had better things to do tonight anyway. His girlfriend, Michelle, was going to her white trash friend, Leslie's, New Year's party, and Tony was absolutely certain that some sleazebag would try to put the moves on her. And where was he? Stuck here with a bunch of stupid, spoiled brats.

The crowd seemed to intensify. More kids crowded in and thrust their dripping, slushy sneakers at him. He tried to take them one at a time, giving them the shortest possible answers. He rushed back and forth between skate shelves in the back room and the counter to exchange pairs of shoes for pairs of skates. Every time he was out of ear-shot, he muttered to himself.

"Where the fuck is Geno? I can't do this shit by myself. I'm gonna give that cheap son of a bitch a piece of my mind as soon as I can find another job and get the--" He grabbed a pair of size nine-and-a-halves and a pair of elevens and rushed back to the counter, clenching his jaw and shutting himself up. The image of his girlfriend alone with some sweaty dude materialized in his mind again, and he knew he was in for a long night.

# 2

As the skates were dispensed, the crowd near the skate rental counter began to thin out. Kids filled up the rink, skating and laughing with big grins on their faces. Some of them spun around, executing skillful roller disco moves. Others were as clumsy and prone to fall as the kindergarten kids that had been there earlier that day.

Denise watched them skating around the rink and couldn't help but smile. She remembered a time not so long ago when she was a carefree high school senior too. Looking at these kids made her feel kind of sad. Now she was twenty-two and had no idea what she was supposed to be doing in life. She longed for the good old days that these kids were currently experiencing.

A group of girls rolled by the low white cinder block wall. Denise's eyes followed them, then landed on a single lonely guy on the dining area side of the wall closer to her. He was sitting at the table in the corner, and was also watching the skaters. She couldn't see his face, but he had a mop of slightly curly brown hair. He wore a light blue polo shirt and jeans, a modest outfit for roller disco. Judging by the custom black skates that were already on his feet, she could tell that he wasn't just a wallflower. Yet somehow he seemed to stand out from the rest of this group.

Then, as if he sensed someone watching him, the boy turned and looked directly at her. He was handsome, with smooth, strong, aquiline features. With his olive complexion, she guessed that he had some Greek or maybe Italian blood in him. She met his gaze and almost turned away.

*Why should I turn away from him? I've gotta be*

*at least five years older than him. Stop being ridiculous.*

On impulse, Denise gave him a friendly, sunny smile. The boy returned the smile, and it lit up his whole face. He raised a hand in acknowledgment, then looked down at the floor. She continued to watch him, and could almost see the reluctance wash over his face at that polite break of their eye contact. Turning her own gaze away, she focused on wiping down the counter with a rag. She wanted to look back up at him again, but forced herself not to. The last thing she wanted was to seem like she was staring at him too obviously. Her chest felt like it was filled with electricity, a nervous tingle of excitement that spread to her neck and upper arms. Her arms broke out in goosebumps. She hadn't felt like this since...well, since she was these kids' age.

*Five years older....*

So what if she was five years older? He was just some cute high school guy, it wasn't like she was picking out wedding invitations. She was single, she could flirt with any cute guy she wanted to.

Denise tried to think of something to say to him and she heard her own interior voice immediately clam up. *Come on*, she scolded herself after a minute. *It can't be that hard to think of something to say. Ask him anything. Ask him about the damn weather if you're that short on conversation material.*

It actually wasn't a bad idea. They were in for one hell of a storm tonight, and if he was as lonely as he looked, maybe they could keep each other company.

She looked up in his direction again and saw him staring up at one of the TVs that were mounted up on the polished wooden beam that curved along the edge of the rink. *Dick Clark's Rockin' New Year's Eve Countdown* had just started and Dick Clark was talking about Pat Benatar and the Beach Boys who would be doing live performances on the show tonight. Denise drew in a deep breath to call out to him, planning to ask him if he thought they'd be completely snowed in by morning, then let it out when she heard another voice call out to him.

"Hey, Dan!" It was apparently one of his friends, a kid with a punk rock haircut and a black Ramones shirt. He stood with another kid and two geeky looking girls. "Come on, man. We're all skated up and ready to go."

"Coming," Dan replied and rolled away from the table on his skates. He was smooth and graceful on them, skating with a practiced finesse. He stole one more quick glance at Denise before joining up with his friends. She smiled at him again, but this time he only looked away quickly and didn't return the smile. He and the others rolled down the short wide ramp out of the dining area and disappeared into the crowd of kids. Denise sighed, feeling a hint of disappointment.

*Well, so much for that. Hey, look on the bright side though, it'll be a long night. He'll probably be back.* Inwardly, she shrugged and felt a little better about the work night ahead of her. Then, all thoughts of the cute guy named Dan disappeared from her mind as her first customer, a chubby sophomore, rolled up to the snack counter and ordered a hot dog and a Pepsi.

### 3

"Allllllright, DeAngelo High!" Freddy's voice boomed out of the big overhead speakers. He leaned forward into the microphone and held down the button at its base to make his announcement. "I'm DJ Freddy and we wanna say that we're so glad you all could come out here on this cold, snowy night and spend New Year's Eve with us here at Rollerville. I just have to remind you guys that there is no smoking, food, or drink out on the disco floor. If you do get hungry or thirsty throughout the night, head over to our snack counter and see the very beautiful and talented Denise. She's gonna keep it open all night long." Freddy pointed over to Denise and right on cue she gave him and the crowd her customary wave.

This was a speech Freddy gave on an almost nightly basis, although, tonight it had been modified to fit the all night Lock-In.

"I'll be up here all night spinning all your favorite disco records, so if you have any requests, don't be shy, stop on by. And dat's about it. So you guys ready to party?" A few of them gave him a weak, lackluster cheer, the rest ignored him. Most of the kids had tuned out Freddy's speech and were skating around or talking in big groups.

"I gotta tell ya, that was pitiful. My mutha'd be cryin' if she heard that." He got genuine laughter from most of the kids for that one. "Alright, let's do this again. *You guys ready to party?!"* A wild, enthusiastic cheer erupted from the disco floor. "That's bettah."

Freddy immediately dropped the needle onto the 45 of ELO's "All Over the World," and the pounding beat and synthesizers shook the entire place.

Dan had the song in his record collection at home, and a big grin spread across his face. He'd had ELO stuck in his head all day, and he welcomed the song. It seemed to reinforce his New Year's Resolution about getting over Mary Anne. He skated alongside his friends Gary and Jim as they held hands with their girlfriends, Suzanne and Lindy. They all bobbed their heads to the music, and Dan swayed around ahead of them in a lazy S shape. He spun around backwards, kicked one leg back and forth to the beat, and kept himself going with the other leg. He hopped, tucked his arms into his chest, and did a fast spin in mid-air, coming down forward again gracefully.

Lindy, who had switched out her huge glasses for contacts, turned to Gary and nudged him. "Now *you* do something like that. Let's see what you got." She had to yell over the blasting music.

Gary laughed out loud. "You kiddin' me? I ain't got nuthin' on Dan."

"Aww, come on. You too chicken to try some of those moves?" she teased.

"I'll show you some moves," Gary retorted.

Without missing a beat, Gary tilted his skate forward, dragging his rubber toe-stop against the floor and slowing himself down. Lindy turned her head to follow him and almost lost her balance. She faced forward and corrected herself, swinging her arms wildly. Gary put on a burst of speed and came up directly behind her. He wrapped his arms around her waist, then lifted her off the floor while still skating forward. She screamed as she felt herself lift up in Gary's unstable embrace. Several people turned to look over at them. They burst out laughing at the sight of Gary holding the girl up in the air as her legs kicked awkwardly.

"Put me down! Gary! Put me down!" she shrieked and giggled.

"How's that for moves?" She ignored his comment and went on laughing and screaming. He finally relented and let her down as gently as he could. He held on to her waist after letting her down so that she wouldn't fall, unsure either of them would be able to keep their balance. Luckily, they stayed upright after a few wobbly moments.

Jim rolled up beside Gary laughing hysterically and clapping him on the back.

"That was awesome!" he laughed.

Gary and Jim looked over at Lindy. She was falling behind them and trying her best to look mad at Gary, but a smirk refused to leave the corner of her mouth. Suzanne caught up with Lindy and scolded Gary.

"Are you crazy? Are you out of your mind?"

Gary and Jim stuck their tongues out at the girls in crazy wide-eyed expressions.

"Hey, I have an idea," Jim said. "You wanna see something hilarious?"

"Definitely!" Gary replied.

Without another word Jim sped forward.

## 4

Mike Cavallo, Jack Flynn, Mary Anne, and four other kids from their usual group of friends stood near the entrance onto the rink in a tight social circle. Jack and Mike, as usual, were doing most of the talking in an animated slapstick way. They had to practically scream at each other to hear themselves over the blasting disco music, their usual volume wasn't much lower. "All Over the World" had faded into "And the Beat Goes On" by The Whispers. Mary Anne stood farthest out onto the rink, skaters closest to the outside edge had to swerve around her. She had ditched the black pants and jacket, and now stood in her tight red short-shorts and knee-high rainbow socks. She stood so close to Mike Cavallo that their arms were touching. Jack had flipped the collar up on his pink polo shirt and was doing some kind of jive-talking angry character. All his friends were bellowing with laughter, or in Mary Anne's case, shrieking with laughter.

Behind Mary Anne, Jim Young skated past and tapped her on her right shoulder. Before she could turn around and see him, he ducked down and skated away to her left in a crouched position. Mary Anne looked around and saw no one close enough to tap her shoulder. Some of the people in her group watched her and also looked around with suspicious curiosity. Mary Anne noticed their distracted glances, so she stopped looking around and laughed even harder at Jack Flynn. Apparently, Jack had been so deep in character (or was it caricature?) that he hadn't noticed any of it. Mary Anne looked directly at Jack and laughed in all the right spots, but kept her ears tuned behind her.

A few seconds later she heard snippets of a loud conversation between two people somewhere off to her left.

"Oh my God! Did you see her turn?" a guy's voice asked.

"That was amazing!" another guy shouted and laughed.

Mary Anne recognized those voices.

"Where's Dan? God, I hope he saw that! Hey, DAN!"

Of course, it all made sense. Jim Young, Gary Nelson, and her ex, Dan. She turned and glared over her shoulder, listening as they shouted Dan's name repeatedly and skated away toward the far corner of the rink.

"Mary Anne! Mr. Cavallo! Mr. Flynn! You need to move along. You're standing in the way." Mary Anne faced forward again to see Mrs. Bauer yelling at them from the outside of the low rink wall. She made counter-clockwise twirling gestures with her finger and shouted shrilly over the music.

"Golly, Mrs. Bauer. I'm sorry, Mrs. Bauer," Jack Flynn said in a false innocent voice. He sounded like some prim and proper character from a 1950's TV show.

"Just get going, Smarty Pants," she said in an irritated voice. The group laughed even harder at that.

"Okay, I sure will. Thank you," Jack said, still hamming it up. He turned back to the group with a big grin on his face. Mrs. Bauer stayed there looking sternly at them with her hands on her hips until they merged with the rest of the skaters.

"Hey, Jack," Mike said. "Isn't it almost time we get the, uh...y'know..."

"Yeah, you guys! Go get them on!" Mary Anne said with ton of enthusiasm.

"Shut up!" Jack snapped at her. "You'll ruin it!" Mary Anne slapped him on the arm and tsk'd loudly.

"Don't tell me to shut up, asshole!" she crowed.

Jack ignored her. "Yeah, man. We might as well go get 'em on. We'll be right back, you guys."

Everyone in their little group was in on the big joke, and made little snickering comments to themselves. "This is gonna be great. They're gonna look so stupid!"

Jack and Mike turned and skated back to the exit they had just been blocking. They barged in front of two freshmen, smirking at their indignant cries of *"Hey! Watch it!"* and rolled up the ramp into the dining area.

"Hey, man, that bitch is starting to get on my nerves," Jack said to Mike.

Mike only shrugged. "Aww, don't worry. We'll get rid of her in a few weeks. She's first on my list for my New Year's Resolution."

"Oh yeah? What's that? Fuck as many chicks as possible?"

"Fuckin' A right!" As they rolled into the men's room, their booming laughter echoed off the walls.

Denise heard the whole conversation as they went past the snack counter, but she didn't look up at them. She rolled her eyes at their last few sentences.

"Oh God, gag me with a spoon," she muttered

to herself. They reminded her so much of her ex-boyfriend who thought he was Mr. Party Animal. She didn't want to think about him tonight though. It would be better to think about that cute guy. She looked up and, speak of the devil, there he was skating by. He looked over, saw her, and grinned as he waved to her.

## 5

And the girl at the counter waved back at him. Dan glanced forward a few times for safety's sake, but they were able to smile at each other as he passed the end of the rink closest to the snack bar. His heart was already beating hard from the skating, but now it seemed to ramp up even harder. There was definitely something there, a spark between the two of them. It wasn't just simple friendliness that he had suspected it might be when he had been sitting at the table waiting for his friends to get their rental skates.

As he rounded the corner and broke eye contact with her, he couldn't help the grin that spread across his face. He felt a light fluttery feeling in his chest, a nervous, elated excitement that he hadn't felt since he first started dating Mary Anne. Now that he thought about it, he hadn't felt this way in over a year. He hadn't felt it since before he and Mary Anne had taken that plunge and lost their virginity to each other on that hot August afternoon last year. That was in the past though, water under the bridge.

Now here was this new girl with light auburn hair and a cute girl-next-door face. He was curious about her. How old was she? Eighteen? Nineteen? She was probably older than him. He guessed that maybe she had gone to Jefferson High because he had never seen her in the halls at DeAngelo. Was she single? Did she have a boyfriend? By the way she smiled, it certainly didn't seem like she did. His mind raced with stupid fantasies about who she was and what she would say to him if he were to go over and talk to her.

He raised one hand and lightly tapped each of the four wall-mounted speakers as he passed underneath them. "And the Beat Goes On" faded out and "Funkytown" by Lipps Inc. took its place.

Dan rounded the curve at the far end of the rink, weaved around a few slow groups of kids that chatted and laughed together. He decided he would flirt with the girl at the snack counter as he passed by again. He took his time getting there, not wanting to make it seem like he was desperate. He passed the DJ booth and looked up at the John Travolta wannabe guy sitting up there and bobbing his head to the "Funkytown" beat. Dan swerved easily around a guy he didn't recognize who was clumsily skating with his girlfriend, looking like he was about to fall on his ass. The girl at the snack counter came into view again.

She was looking up at something, probably watching *Dick Clark's Rockin' New Year's Eve* on one of those mounted TVs. She looked down as he came into view, and he immediately spun around, skating backwards. He looked back over his shoulder and met her eye. She smiled at him again, and he grinned back at her. As he rounded the curve he was facing her again. He took one last look and spun back around facing forward again.

As he turned around, he saw Reggie, the skate monitor, skating beside him. Reggie caught Dan grinning as he thought about the girl behind the counter. Reggie had seen only a few seconds of their flirty exchange and recognized the infatuated grin on Dan's face. He glanced back at the girl at the counter, then gave Dan an encouraging point and a thumbs-up as if to say, *Go for it, brother.* Dan nodded, returned the thumbs-up, and laughed. He sped forward, half embarrassed and half bursting with that nervous excitement.

The next lap around, he spun around backwards and put his foot up on the cinder block wall around the curve, then leaned back and put his hands behind his head. The girl behind the counter laughed and rolled her eyes at him.

He circled around again and this time he ducked down near the top of the low cinder block wall. Then he poked his head up and held his hands underneath his chin, looking back and forth curiously like a gopher. She laughed hard at this and covered her mouth with her hands. God, he loved the way she laughed, it seemed to brighten up her whole face.

He came around again and coasted on his skates, then began making paddling motions with his arms as if he were rowing in a canoe. She cupped her hands over her mouth and called out to him.

"You're a DORK!"

Dan laughed and rounded the curve again. Once he made his way back around the circle for a sixth time, he started wobbling awkwardly on his skates, acting as if he couldn't keep his balance at all. She laughed a little, but looked away to help a group of younger kids that were skating up to the counter. With a twinge of disappointment, Dan stopped goofing around and skated normally.

He looked over and saw Steve Fields, one of the dumber members of the Flynn/Cavallo Group, skating bent down with his legs spread apart and his hands pulling him forward. Several girls around him were laughing hysterically. Dan couldn't help but see the similarities between this idiot's stupid attempt at humor and his own silly skating tricks. He hoped he didn't come off looking like *that* to the cute girl behind the counter.

*Don't worry about it. Steve's a burnout moron, you're not. Besides, she's got a job to do. She can't just sit there and watch you all night. If you want to get her attention that bad, why don't you just go up and talk to her like a normal human being?*

He shrugged to himself, deciding that he might just do that, at least in a little while.

"Dan! Hey, Dan! You missed it, man!" The voice came from his left. He turned in time to see Jim and Gary come skating up beside him.

"You missed it! It was awesome! I went up behind Scary Anne and tapped her on the shoulder, then ducked down like this."

"Yeah!" Gary interjected. "She started looking around like, *what the hell?*" Gary did an exaggerated impression of a confused Mary Anne looking around. Dan gave them a vindictive little laugh that he didn't really feel. He wanted to humor his friends.

"Ha! I guess you sure showed her." Gary and Jim did their own vindictive laughs and slapped each other a high-five. Lindy and Suzanne rolled up and joined their boyfriends. Dan felt a touch of disappointment as he watched the girls join their group. For a minute there, it had been just him and his friends, just like old times. Now he was the fifth wheel again. They skated together for a while, but every now and then Dan would glance back at the snack counter and think, *Well, maybe I won't have to be a fifth wheel all night. Maybe....*

# 6

Bryan Barnham slammed his fists down on the Pac-Man machine. He had fallen short of the high score yet again. He'd gone through almost ten dollars so far, but he just *had* to beat that damn high score. He wouldn't feel like the night had been a success at all unless he replaced those damned FA initials (whoever that was) with his own BB. Unknown to Bryan, FA stood for Freddy Atkinson, the guy spinning the records up on the DJ booth. Freddy often played after hours and had gotten pretty good.

The arcade was in a little secluded corner of the roller rink, back behind the bathrooms and next to the snack counter. It really only had a couple of Skee Ball lanes, a Foosball table, an old Whack-A-Mole, and the newest, coolest addition: the Pac-Man game.

Bryan began to dig in his pocket for another quarter to pump into the machine.

"Come on, man. Give someone else a chance," whined the little kid behind him. It was a DeAngelo freshman named Joe Jacobs.

"Yeah, quit hoggin' it, will ya?" the other little kid said. He was Ray Stone, Joe Jacobs' best friend, and the braver of the two of them.

"Get lost," Bryan muttered without looking up at the little kids. They were just a couple of dumb freshmen, and a couple of geeks judging by their Star Wars T-shirts. Bryan was a junior and outweighed the both of them by fifty pounds. He wasn't about to take any shit from a couple of fucking freshmen.

"Give it a rest, dude," Joe pleaded. "You've been on it for an hour."

"Beat it, ya fuckin' freshman."

"Move!" Ray said.

"Fuck off."

Joe and Ray turned to each other and shrugged. Joe hung his head, completely out of ideas. He'd had two Pepsi's within an hour, and needed to use the bathroom, but held it while he had been waiting in line for the Pac-Man machine. Now that it seemed hopeless, he simply couldn't hold it anymore. He leaned in toward Ray and quietly said, "I gotta go take a piss."

Ray rolled his eyes, he had been expecting Joe to give him a bright idea on how to deal with this big fat bully. He turned back to Bryan Barnham.

"If you don't get off that thing, I'm gonna go tell Coach Richards."

"Go ahead. I don't give a shit."

"Asshole," Joe muttered to himself. He turned and skated toward the Men's Room, it was on the left of the two white cinder block bathrooms.

"Ah-h-hem," a girl gave a slight coughing, throat-clearing noise off to his left. He turned and saw a pretty senior with dark flipped out hair standing up in the dining area directly across from the bathrooms. She was dressed in a skimpy red shirt and shorts and had high rainbow socks. She was leaning on the short brick wall that separated the dining area from the little walkway that led past the bathrooms to the arcade. She was facing away from him, looking out at the rink. For only a second, he wondered why she was just standing there all by herself, then shrugged it off. Who knew what went on in pretty girls' minds.

As Joe turned, a huge black cloaked figure with a rotting skull for a head swooped out of the bathroom. It bellowed with inhuman rage. Joe screamed and fell back onto the carpet towards the arcade as the black death thing fell over him, filling the world. It had sorrowful empty eye-sockets and gray fragments of flesh dripping off its white skull face. Horsey teeth jutted out from a black decaying gum line.

Joe scrambled back as it floated towards him. His bladder nearly let go. The pretty girl who had been standing there burst into gales of screaming, giddy laughter.

The death thing's bellow of rage turned into a high pitched giggle. It pulled its skull head up and revealed the face of Mike Cavallo. The cloak's hood fell back as he pulled off the mask. The kid remained breathless and white-faced on the floor as Mike threw his fists up in the air and cheered.

"Gotcha!" Mary Anne, the senior girl, screamed at Joe. Jack Flynn rolled out of the bathrooms and gave Mike a two-handed high-five. He wore only his skates, a pair of white athletic shorts stuffed with toilet paper, and a sash over his chest that read *1981*. Joe now also noticed a white sash on the black death costume as well, it said *1980*. They were dressed as the *Old Year Man* and *New Year Baby*.

"Oh my God!" Mary Anne screamed at Mike and Jack. "Did you see the look on that kid's face?"

"Bet your ass, I did!" Mike shouted. He suddenly gave Mary Anne a hard slap on the ass. She gave a flirtatious little yip of surprise and jumped. Mike ignored her and pulled the mask back down over his face. Jack and Mike took off hooting and hollering, skating through the dining area at top speed. Jack had a noise-maker in his mouth and blew on it in short furious blasts. Mike had a few of those plastic party poppers, and as they turned the corner and skated onto the rink he popped a few of them, spraying confetti all over the rink floor. Mike's black cloak billowed out behind him revealing his all-black long sleeve shirt and long pants beneath.

They skated around the rink laughing and

shouting at the top of their lungs. All the guys and girls in their regular circle of friends applauded them and burst out laughing. Their enthusiasm was infectious and soon almost everyone in the entire place was clapping and laughing at them. Even Coach Richards and Mrs. Bauer clapped and laughed politely. Dan, Jim, and Gary looked at each other and rolled their eyes.

Jack and Mike circled all the way around to the DJ booth, banging on its carpeted walls with their hands. Freddy smiled down at them and grabbed the microphone.

"Allriiiiight, let's give it up for Old Man '80, and Baby '81!" The applause and cheering erupted again. Jim and Gary made gagging, throwing up gestures and it was their girlfriend's turns to roll their eyes.

Jack and Mike whipped around the center of the rink and stopped in a little circle that had formed under the spinning disco ball. Only the best skaters stood here, strutting their stuff and doing a coordinated kind of line dance on skates, led by Reggie. Jack and Mike, no slouches on skates themselves, joined in the dance.

"Fantastic Voyage" by Lakeside was just ending and Freddy broke in again on the microphone.

"Alllllllright all you show-offs in the middle there, hope you aren't too young for this one."

The rhythmic start of Van McCoy's "Do The Hustle" started up. Reggie the skate monitor pointed over at Freddy as the song began to play and started in on his Hustle skate routine. The others watched him and tried to keep up.

Over near the DJ booth, Dan, Jim and Gary stood leaning on the low wall, watching the group in the middle doing The Hustle.

"You oughta' get out there dude," Jim said, nudging Dan on the shoulder.

"Yeah, man. You're a way better skater than

those assholes," Gary added. "Go show 'em how it's done."

"I don't know, you guys," he shrugged. "Mary Anne's out there." She had just joined the group on the side closest to the far wall, positioning herself next to Mike Cavallo.

"So? Who gives a fuck about her?" Jim said, waving a dismissive hand in Mary Anne's direction. Dan looked over again as his friends nudged and encouraged him. He saw an open spot on the opposite side of the group, the side closest to the snack counter. That cute girl would be able to see him from where she was. He glanced over and saw her watching the group in the middle of the rink.

He finally shrugged and skated forward. "All right, you talked me into it."

"Hell yeah! Atta boy!" Gary and Jim both shouted eagerly.

Dan rolled up to the group and spun around into place just before the hook of the song started up. They did a sliding version of The Hustle, rolling back two steps, then forward two steps, spinning around to the right, then spinning back. On the spins, Dan looked over and caught the girl at the counter smiling and watching him. The music pounded, the group danced, the others skated around them in their endless circle. Dan was so aware of that cute girl's eyes on him that, for a while, he was able to completely forget about his ex-girlfriend.

# 7

In the midst of Jack Flynn and Mike Cavallo coming out in their crazy get-ups and The Hustle, Steve Fields lit up a joint. He was a terrible skater, so he stayed away from the group in the middle. He skated in a small circle near the back of the rink, kept his joint down at hip level, and constantly looked around for the eyes of his teachers or anybody who would possibly narc on him. Whenever he took a drag, he would face the wall, inhale, then turn back holding the precious smoke in his lungs as long as he could.

He had almost finished the joint when he looked over and saw Coach Richards standing by the low wall near the DJ booth sniffing the air. Coach was onto him, he must have gotten a whiff of the skunky marijuana smell. He involuntarily gasped and choked on the smoke. He almost fell as he launched into a coughing fit.

Steve raced back behind the group doing The Hustle. He cut off two sophomore girls and slammed against the carpeted wall. They gave him indignant cries of, *"Hey!"* and *"Watch it, jerk!"* He ignored them, desperate to get rid of the smoldering joint in his hand before he got in deep shit with his teachers. He skated a few feet along the wall toward one of the emergency exit doors. He planned to open it a crack, toss out the joint, then skate off casually as if nothing had happened.

Steve pushed the crash bar in and heaved against the door, but it wouldn't budge. His skates slid out behind him and he almost toppled face-first into the door. He hauled himself back up, anchored his skates sideways, and shoved against the door with all his strength. The damn thing wouldn't move at all, it had no give. The door itself was ice cold, but as he pushed against it, he didn't even feel a slight wisp of the frigid air outside seeping in.

Unknown to Steve, the gusting winds and thick wet snow had slammed up against this wall constantly for the last hour and a half. Now a sheen of ice three inches thick had caked onto the crack of the door jamb.

If Steve had been just a casual skater, he might have said something to one of his teachers or one of the employees about being unable to open the emergency exit door. He was trying to get rid of drugs though, and wild horses wouldn't drag any information regarding the doors out of him. *What doors? Oh, those doors? Gee, I hadn't even noticed them.*

Steve turned back and saw Coach Richards skating on the other side of the dancing group, coming towards him. He still held his chin up, and his nose wiggled as he sniffed the air.

"Fuckfuckfuckfuck!" Steve whispered under his breath. He desperately looked around for another place to dispose of this stupid joint. He looked around, made sure no one was watching him, then tossed it on the floor and skated away slowly. He whistled to himself along with the theme from "Do the Hustle" and stayed as far away from that side of the rink as humanly possible.

# Chapter Four:

# Couples Only

### 1

Mike Cavallo pulled off the rubber death mask, his Afro had flattened considerably underneath it. Before he could even savor the cool fresh air, Mary Anne had spun around into his arms and started kissing him. The Hustle had just ended, and he was eager to get his stifling hot black death cloak off. Suddenly, there she was jamming her tongue into his mouth. He gave in for a few seconds, making out with her, running his tongue over hers.

Jack Flynn turned to them and said, "Oh, God. Get a room." Mike broke away from her for a second and she thrust herself toward him again.

"Mmhey! Hang on a second!" he said, the words came out muffled against her own mouth. "I gotta get this damn thing off. I'm fuckin' dying under here." Mary Anne gave a couple of quick glances over in Dan's direction while Mike pulled the cloak's sleeves back and stuffed the mask in the back pocket of his jeans. Then he immediately felt Mary Anne pulling him forward with both hands.

"Come with me, then," she said in a low seductive voice. She leaned in close and whispered in his ear. "*I'll* help you take it off." The feel of her hot breath in his ear melted his brain, and he allowed himself to be led by her. She was annoying, but what was he supposed to do, turn her down? She grabbed his hand and together they skated off the rink.

Some other disco song started up on the speakers, but Mike barely heard it. They rolled past the DJ booth and exited the rink, then Mary Anne began pulling him up the short ramp toward the tables in the dining area. Mike tugged back, stopping her at the top of the ramp. She leaned forward on the toe-stop of her skate and looked back at him.

"Whoa, whoa, whoa. Where you going?" Mike asked.

"Up here, to sit down at a table," she said in that contemptuous tone she used whenever anyone questioned her.

"Uh, are you kiddin' me? Coach Dick and Bitchy Bauer will see us and be over here in a second," he replied, matching her contempt in his own voice. He leaned in close and lowered the volume of his voice. "No, we gotta go find some place private."

"Where?"

Mike looked back and forth, not noticing the way her eyes flicked over to the rink, checking to see if Dan or anyone else was watching them. When he turned back to her, he gave her a sideways nod toward the two carpeted doors that led to the front lobby.

Now *he* was the one pulling *her* by the hand. When they reached the lobby doors, he put his hand up on the soft surface and looked carefully back and forth over his shoulder for signs of any of the chaperons.

Mary Anne also looked back and saw that everyone was still out on the rink minding their own business. Both teachers were completely out of sight, deep within the crowd somewhere. Mike gave her a light smile, one that was filled with eager lust and anticipation. Then he pushed the door open and pulled her into the front lobby.

Mike had been expecting it to be empty, but he stopped dead in his tracks when he saw the man standing at one of the long vertical windows, looking out at the storm.

"Oh, shit," Mike said startled. He felt all the lust drain away instantly, as if he'd been doused with a bucket of ice water. The man also jumped at the sound of Mike's voice and turned back to look at them. Mike instantly recognized him as that old guy who drove them here on that beat up old bus.

Geno Atkinson stood there in his coat, with snow melting on his head and shoulders. He stared at them with wide eyes, then looked around the room as if he had forgotten where he was. Mary Anne had stopped pawing at Mike and also stared at Geno.

"I was just, uh...I was just warming up from plowing the parking lot," Geno stuttered. He turned away from the window and walked past them, back toward the entrance doors leading into the rink.

Mike and Mary Anne gave each other a curious glance. Geno stopped before he was all the way out the door. He turned back as if he had almost forgotten to tell them something.

"You kids might wanna find some place else," Geno said, eyeing them suspiciously. "Your teachers have been checking in here every once in a while. Don't wanna get caught, uh...doing something you shouldn't."

"Okay, we just wanted to take a look at the storm too. We won't be long," Mike explained, trying to sound friendly and innocent. He wondered if he could trust the old guy. He had told him an obvious lie, and he could tell by the look in the old bastard's eyes that he didn't believe it at all. "But hey, thanks for the heads up anyway, man."

Geno gave them a long look, as if he were deciding whether or not to invoke his adult authority and tell them to get their asses back out on the rink. Then he took one last glance over his shoulder, looking out at the raging blizzard again, and left the room.

"What the fuck is that guy's deal?" Mike asked once Geno was out of sight.

"I don't know," Mary Anne said in a flat voice.

Mike shrugged and skated over to a corner near the front doors. He pulled both the black cloak and the black long-sleeved shirt he'd worn underneath it, up over his head and tossed them down in a heap on the floor. Now back in his white t-shirt and thin suspenders, he held his arms out, tilted his head back, closed his eyes, and gave a great sigh.

"Ahhh, that feels so much better," he said. "I was bakin' under that stupid thing. He pulled the crumpled up death mask out of his back pocket and tossed it on top of the cloak.

"Now where were we?" he asked. He beckoned to her with two fingers. She looked back at the doors nervously.

"What if that guy comes back?" she asked.

"He won't."

Mary Anne reluctantly came toward him as he knelt down on the floor. "It's cold over here."

"I'll warm you up." He leaned forward, softly grasping her by the wrists and pulled her down on top of him. He leaned back against the brick wall, let go of her wrists, and held her light body by the waist. With a little gasp, she put her hands down on the floor in front of her to hold herself up, and her right hand came down on top of the rubber death mask.

She yielded to him as he kissed her hard, jamming his tongue into her mouth. She seemed to have lost some of her aggression, but Mike figured that was probably because she was nervous. He knew how to fix that though. He started lightly tracing his fingertips up and down her arms and began kissing her neck, lightly sucking it. Her breath sped up. He felt her body tensing with excitement.

With one hand, he continued lightly caressing her arm, while his other hand crept up underneath her red halter top. He cupped his hand over one soft breast and began to squeeze. She gasped sharply and grabbed his forearm.

"Don't fight it, baby," he whispered in her ear. *She was all over me back on the rink in front of everyone. Now we're alone and she decides to play hard to get.* He didn't have much time to mess around. Anyone could come in at any minute, and he knew he had to speed this up.

His other hand left her arm and slid to her waistline, creeping down underneath the elastic of her red short shorts. His fingers lightly felt their way down her soft lower belly. She tried to pull his hand away and lost her balance. Her hand fell on the death mask again.

Suddenly, she jerked upward and fell back into an awkward kneeling position in front of him. She didn't look horny now, she looked furious. Mike was genuinely taken aback.

"What?" he asked incredulously. She only glared at him. "Seriously, what's the problem?"

"Do you have to be so *fucking pushy?"* she spat the question at him.

"What? Don't act like you don't want it. A few minutes ago you were all over me out there. Now all of a sudden you change your mind?" She only narrowed her eyes, glaring at him. "Oh, I get it. You're just trying to make your ex-boyfriend jealous. Is that it?"

"Oh, shut up!" She stood up and turned her back on him, staring out the window. Without even realizing it, she now stood where Geno Atkinson had been only a few minutes ago. Outside in the parking lot, she saw a white mound of snow and remembered that her Corvette was buried under it. Through the huge, heavy snowflakes gusting around out there, she could barely make out that green chain-link fence around the old graveyard across the parking lot. The snowdrift against the building had already reached the bottom of the long window. She focused on these things, not wanting to deal with Mike anymore.

Behind her, she listened as Mike stood up and brushed himself off. He rearranged his pants and underwear so that no one would see the slowly shrinking bulge at his crotch.

"You're pathetic, you fuckin' tease." Without another word, he pushed the door open and went back into the rink. Mary Anne didn't turn to look at him, she didn't want him to see the look on her face, didn't want him to know that she was getting ready to cry. She pretended to stare out as the snow gusted against the windows, continuing to bury her Corvette deeper and deeper, but bitter tears blurred her vision.

## 2

"Allriiiiight! For this next one we're gonna do Couples Only," Freddy's voice boomed out over the speakers. "So all you swingin' singles out there, clear the floor. And all you lovebirds out there, take that special guy or gal by the hand and take it slow, 'cuz this one's for you." Freddy dropped the needle down on the turntable and the soothing disco tones of Michael Jackson's "Rock With You" flowed out over the rink.

Dan lazily turned his left skate sideways and let it drag behind him, slowing himself down. He stood at the opening in the low white wall, and waited for three couples to take their first tentative steps out onto the hardwood. He recognized the couple with the guy who didn't know how to skate very well, then Jim and Suzanne came up hand in hand.

"Hey, couples only," Jim teased Dan in a macho voice. He imitated the DJ by doing a very passable thick New Jersey accent. "Get off the floor ya swingin' single." Dan pretended to be mad at him, holding up his fists, gritting his teeth, and shaking his head. He mumbled incoherent cartoon swear words at Jim and they both laughed. He clapped Jim on the back and let them roll out onto the floor.

Dan exited the rink and leaned down against the low white wall. He watched the couples skating with their arms around each other. There were Gary and Lindy, she rested her head lovingly on his shoulder. There were Paul and Sarah, the champion Disco King and Queen of 1980. Paul was skating backwards and holding her by the waist. He had to kind of hunch over to reach her because he was so much taller. She had her hands up on his shoulders and they gazed into each other's eyes. Everyone out there looked happy with each other, and Dan honestly felt happy for them. Things may not have worked out in his own love life, but he was confident that he wouldn't be lonely forever. Like that old saying went, there were plenty of fish in the sea.

The thought suddenly reminded him of the girl at the snack counter. He looked over at the counter and there she was, leaning forward with her cheek resting on her knuckles. She had no customers at all. Now was the perfect time to make his move.

Denise sensed him coming toward her, but kept her head lowered, wanting to remain aloof. He rolled up to the counter and stopped himself with his hands. At first, she looked up only with her eyes, smiling out of the corner of her mouth. One strand of auburn hair hung down, framing the left side of her face. Dan thought she looked amazing.

"What can I get ya?" she asked.

"Can I get a Pepsi, please?"

"Sure thing." She reached down to the cup dispenser beneath the counter. "Small or large?"

"Ummm, how bout small?" He knew that a smaller cup meant more refills, more chances to come back and talk to her. She scooped some ice out of the ice box, pulled up the Wunder Bar soda dispenser, poured the Pepsi, and handed it to him. As he stared at her, he felt fizz from the Pepsi lightly misting the top of his hand.

"That'll be a quarter," she said.

"Oh, right." He had been so focused on her and the thought of what to say to her that paying for the drink had totally slipped his mind. His cheeks began to burn as he dug in his pocket for some change. *Oh great, I look like a huge geek already.* He finally fished a quarter out and handed it to her. She smiled and turned to the cash register, punched in .25 and TOTAL, and deposited the quarter inside.

"Looks kinda lonely over here tonight," Dan said and took a drink of his Pepsi.

Denise shrugged. "It's not so bad. I wouldn't be doing anything else tonight anyway. It's either be lonely here or be lonely at home. At least here I'm getting paid."

"Yeah, I hear ya. It was either this or play board games with my little sister all night. And she cheats."

She laughed. "And where did she learn *that* from, huh?"

Dan held up his hands defensively. "Hey, I have never once cheated in my life. Now if she gets her Monopoly money stolen while she's not looking, then she's just not paying enough attention."

"Yeah, right. Uh huh, sure."

"I mean it. Why do you think I'm up here talking to you right now? I'm just trying to distract you so I can steal all the quarters out of that cash register over there. Free Pepsi's all night."

"Oh gee, thanks. Way to make a girl feel wanted."

"Well...that's not the only reason why I'm up here."

"Oh yeah? And why else would you be up here?"

He glanced back at the rink. "Well, it's Couples Only right now, and my buddies are out with their girlfriends. I don't have a girlfriend right now. But, hey, that's okay, I'm just...I don't know, enjoying my loneliness. So when I saw you up here all by yourself, too, I thought, hey, maybe we could be lonely together."

*This is it*, he thought. *This will either make or break it. Either this is the part where she tells me she's got a boyfriend or....*

She gave him a genuine smile that lit up her whole face. He even thought he noticed her cheeks flush just the tiniest bit.

"Well, I think that's really sweet of you. I'm Denise." She pointed to the name tag pinned to her work shirt.

"I'm Dan." He held out his hand and they shook softly and briefly. "Nice to meet you." He instantly regretted saying that once the words came out of his mouth. It seemed like such a lame and prissy thing to say. She didn't seem to notice though. "So, let me ask you a question, Denise. It's probably none of my business, and you don't have to answer it. But how does a girl as pretty as you wind up with nothing better to do than spend New Year's Eve with a bunch of us DeAngelo Dorks?"

She burst out laughing and covered her mouth with her hand.

"That's seriously what they call us at other schools. DeAngelo Dorks, DeAngelo Dumbasses, DeAngelo Douche Bags...."

Denise laughed even harder, and Dan couldn't help but laugh along with her. She had a sweet infectious laugh, and right then he wanted to do nothing else but make her laugh the whole night. She finally got a chance to catch her breath, but she didn't answer his question right away.

"How old are you, Dan?"

"Fourteen," he replied in a fake, squeaky, puberty voice.

"No, really."

"How old do you think I am?"

"Ummm...I don't know. Maybe seventeen?"

"Actually, I just turned eighteen last month. How old are *you*?"

"Guess." She gave him a saucy, conspiratorial look that he found sexy as hell. He actually guessed twenty, but he shaved a year off that. Hadn't he heard somewhere that girls never liked to be told that they looked older than they actually were?

"I don't know. I'm gonna say...umm...nineteen?"

"Nope."

"Twenty?"

"Keep going."

"Really? Jeez, I don't know. Twenty-one? Twenty-two?"

"You got it."

"Twenty-two? Really? Wow. I could've sworn you were around my age."

"Well, thank you. We all kind of look young in my family. Good genes I guess."

"*I'll* say." It flew out of his mouth without warning, and he instantly wondered if he had gone too far, been too forward. *Whoa, rein it in, man. Don't blow this.*

Denise only seemed to blush a little more. "To answer your question, I moved here from Massachusetts and I don't really know anyone out here."

"Are you going to college or something?"

"No. I've thought about it, but I just can't afford it right now."

"Why move *here* then? I mean, no offense, but if I were you, I'd have moved somewhere where it's warm and never snows. Somewhere near the ocean."

"I moved here to be with my boyfriend."

"Oh." Half of Dan's smile seemed to instantly melt off his face. Now it was Denise's turn to regret something she said. She didn't want to drive him away. She quickly held up a hand and continued on.

"*Ex*-boyfriend now. We broke up a few months ago." His smile brightened up again. She wondered if he looked just a little bit elated under his attentive, smiling poker face. "He's...well, he's a fucking idiot."

Dan snorted with surprised laughter. He had not been expecting bad language to come out of her mouth. In his opinion, girls who cussed were either batshit crazy or totally cool. At this point, it was way too soon to tell if Denise was crazy or not, so he had to hope that she was cool.

"It's funny that you mention moving somewhere near the ocean though," she continued. "I was just thinking about that myself earlier today. I was taking out the trash here, and looking out at that old graveyard all covered in snow. It just looked so depressing. It made me think of how nice it would be to never see snow again."

Dan sighed dreamily. "That would be amazing, wouldn't it? I've actually been looking at colleges out in San Diego and Florida. There's even one in San Antonio that might be okay."

"That'd be great! I hope you get into one of those."

"Thanks! Who knows, maybe we could both go." Dan shrugged and she shrugged back. He thought about adding, *maybe we could stay warm together*, or something cheesy like that. Thankfully though, he kept that one to himself. He was temporarily at a loss for words, trying to decide which way to take the conversation next. He really didn't want it to veer off into a discussion about college. God knew he got enough of that from his folks at home. Frankly, the idea of going off to college somewhere just didn't really excite him at all. To him, it was just another four more years of school, big deal.

Denise picked up the slack in the conversation for him. "Now let me ask you the same question. What's a cute guy like you doing over here talking to me? Shouldn't you be out with some high school girl doing Couples Only skate right now?" Dan felt his own cheeks flush hard now and laughed. He rubbed the back of his neck, it was a habit he always had when he was nervous.

"Well, to be honest with you, I'm kind of a fifth wheel tonight. My buddies have their dates here and I'm really happy for them. But, y'know, I want them to be able to enjoy tonight without having to worry about me. Also, I *had* a girlfriend, but we broke up back in October."

"Awww, I'm sorry. What happened?"

"It's no big deal really. I'm over it. It's just...she was fucking crazy."

"I know the feeling. I--"

"Ah-h-hem!" It was that familiar coughing, throat-clearing noise that Dan knew so well. For an instant, he felt deeply guilty, and some of the color drained out of his face. He turned around and there stood Mary Anne with her arms crossed over her chest.

"I hate to break up this *great* conversation but I'll have a water." Dan stood aside and Mary Anne rolled up to the counter, intentionally ignoring him as if he were unworthy of her attention.

"Umm, sorry about that. What size?" Denise asked innocently.

"Small." Every word out of Mary Anne's mouth dripped with bitter sarcasm. Denise poured out a small cup of water and handed it to Mary Anne. She snatched it out of Denise's hand without a word and stalked off.

*Oh great, just what I needed. Thanks for the bucket of cold water, Mary Anne.*

Dan and Denise watched her roll off toward the rink in silence for a moment, waiting until she was out of earshot. He slid back in to his place at the counter again.

"Speak of the devil," Dan finally said.

"That was her?!" Denise asked.

"Yeah." Dan let out a huge sigh of relief.

"Yikes. I see what you mean. What'd you do to her?"

"*Me?* I didn't do anything. She's the one--"

"Relax, I'm only kidding."

Dan let go of his defensive posture and smiled at her. "Sorry about that. That's just the way she is."

"Don't even mention it. I've known plenty of girls that are just as bad, if not worse."

"Oh the stories I could tell you. Like... Well, I

won't go into it. See, I made this New Year's Resolution to not let her bring me down anymore. To just live my life and move forward. Just forget about the past. You know?"

"Sounds like a pretty good resolution to me."

"What's your New Year's Resolution?" he asked.

Denise honestly considered the question for a moment. "I have absolutely no idea."

"Oh, come on. You've gotta have something."

"Well, yours sounds pretty good. You mind sharing it with me?"

"Not at all. It's yours." He stuck out his hand to shake on it.

"Ours," she corrected. She grasped his hand and they gave each other one firm shake. Her hand felt so soft and warm, Dan hated to let it go.

## 3

Back behind the skate rental counter, Tony Tanner couldn't let go of the strong, paranoid visions his imagination kept conjuring up about what was happening to his girlfriend, Michelle, at that damned party. In his mind, he saw some greasy scumbag continuously supplying her with drinks and shots, then putting his sweaty hands all over her after she was too drunk to do anything about it.

Looking out at the crowd of sweaty, horny teenagers was not helping at all. Minutes ago, he had been forced to watch the kid wearing the stupid 1981 Baby outfit aggressively making out with some ditsy high school girl. They sat on one of those circular benches directly across from Tony at the skate rental counter. The idiot in the baby costume was practically laying on top of the young girl and had his hands all over her. *Just like what might be happening to Michelle right now,* part of his mind stubbornly insisted. Finally, the little old lady chaperone came by, broke them up, and sent them back out onto the skate floor.

Tony watched them go and tried to shake off the thoughts of Michelle and the party, but it was no use. *How drunk is she? Who is she with? Who's touching her? Who's got their hands on her? All over her? All over MY girlfriend?!*

"That does it!" he said out loud. He spun around and hurried into the back room. There was an old wall-mounted rotary phone back in the corner to the left of the door. What had once been yellow plastic was now faded, black dirt and old grease filled up old dents and scratches. He dialed Michelle's friend, Leslie's house, the location of the hateful party, and put the phone to his ear. Tapping his foot impatiently, he listened and waited for the burring tone of a ringing phone on the other end. There was only silence. He jiggled the phone cradle and listened for a dial tone. Still he got silence. He listened carefully to make sure the line wasn't busy. He even blocked out the pounding disco music in his free ear with one palm, and still he heard only silence.

"What the fuck?" he muttered under his breath. *The stupid phones must be out*, he figured. *Maybe the phone lines got damaged somehow in the storm.* All week he had been hearing two things about New Year's Eve: how bad the blizzard was going to be, and how crazy Leslie's party was going to be. When someone tried to talk with him about either of these two topics, his response had been a doubtful, cynical *"It won't be that bad."* Now he found himself eating those words.

Tony slammed the phone down on the cradle. There was no way to get a hold of Michelle. No way to make sure that she wasn't being assaulted or raped by

75

some drunk asshole. No way to make sure she wasn't letting it happen, maybe even liking it....

He'd had an idea earlier, and now it came back to him. *Why not just leave work right now?* He could make up an excuse to Geno, tell him he was feeling sick to his stomach or something. He had to play it just right though. *Maybe I could tell Geno that I'm feeling sick and might have to go home in a little while, plant the seed in his mind. Then I'll wait for an hour, and finally kiss this place goodbye. Hey, maybe I'll even get lucky and Geno will just tell me to go home right away. You never know. Also someone should tell Geno that the phones are out.*

That pretty much decided it for him. Tony planted his hands on the counter and swung his legs over. Geno's office was way over on the other side of the rink in the corner near the front lobby doors. He walked quickly along the far side wall, running his hand over the empty coat hooks and swerving around few groups of talking kids. He punched a few low hanging New Years' balloons out of his way as he neared Geno's closed office door.

High up on the door was a drippy black stenciled word: MANAGER. Tony knocked directly on the black letters, then leaned in and listened for a response on the other side. Sometimes Geno just yelled, "Come on in," without opening the door, and if you didn't hear him over the pounding disco, he would get really irritated. Tony knocked twice and got no response.

"Geno?" He turned the knob and peeked into the office. It was pitch black dark inside, Geno obviously wasn't in there. *He's probably out plowing snow in the parking lot.*

Tony walked over to the front lobby doors and poked his head in. The chain around the doors was firmly padlocked in place. Geno couldn't be out plowing, he had to be inside somewhere.

*Well, where the hell is he? Maybe in the men's room?* Tony hadn't seen him all day. When he had arrived at work, Geno had already left to pick up these brats. Freddy would know where he was though.

Tony turned and walked over to the elevated DJ booth. On the way, he kept an eye out for Geno. Maybe he was out on the rink bullshitting with the chaperons, or over at the snack counter talking to Denise. No such luck, only lovey-dovey high school couples were on the rink, and Denise was flirting with some kid at the snack counter.

He walked past two more couples who were either making out or working their way up to it. It was that damn Couples Only Skate that Freddy liked to do, and it was driving Tony crazy. *Freddy couldn't have picked a worse time to do this*, he thought. *I should be out somewhere with Michelle. Not sitting around in this dump with my thumb up my ass, while some guy or guys are probably trying to make time with my probably drunk girlfriend.*

He hopped over the low white wall and walked up the steps into the DJ booth.

"S'happ'nin, Tone?" Freddy asked after glancing at Tony. He was busy reviewing the playlist on his notepad and searching through a stack of records. He bobbed his head to the last chorus of "Rock With You."

"The phones are out," Tony said flatly.

"It figures."

Tony narrowed his eyes at Freddy. "What do you mean, *it figures?* What if someone has to make a call?"

Freddy shrugged. "It's a fuckin' blizzard out there. What d'ya expect?"

"Fuck!" Tony scanned the rink for Geno again.

"Did you tell Geno?" Freddy asked.

"No, I can't find him. Did he take off somewhere?"

"I don't think so."

"Well, have you seen him anywhere?"

"Uh...I saw him a little while ago. He brought me a Pepsi." As if that reminded him of his drink, Freddy leaned over and took a few slurps of melted ice through his straw.

"When was that?"

"Oh, I don't know. A couple hours ago, I guess."

"Well, he's not in his office. And I think I'm comin' down with something. I think I might need to go home." Tony knew it sounded lame, but it was the best line he could come up with.

"Oh bullshit!" Freddy laughed. "You just wanna go home and flake out on us, you turkey."

"I mean it, man. My stomach is killing me. I think I might throw up."

"Get real! You're full of shit, man. Don't walk out on us. We're short-handed as it is."

"I'm *not* lying!" Tony shouted defensively, he hated the fact that he sounded like one of those whiny kids out on the rink. "Where's Geno?"

"What am I? His babysitter? I told ya, I don't know where he is. I'm tryin' to work up here." Freddy turned away from Tony and pulled the microphone close to his face. "Allllright, thanks to all you lovebirds out there. Now we're gonna get back to the regular all skate, so everybody get those wheels back out on the rink!"

Tony turned away from Freddy just as he said his stupid *Allllright* catchphrase, he seemed to use it before every single announcement he ever made. He jogged back to the skate rental counter as everyone piled back onto the roller rink. In a rush, he hopped over the counter, went into the back room, and kicked a deep, angry dent in the metal trash can in the back corner.

## 4

    While Gary and Lindy were having a great time snuggling on the skate rink during the Couples Only skate, Jim and Suzanne were really starting to get on each other's nerves. They had been unable to keep up with Gary and Lindy all night because of Suzanne's skates. No matter how many pairs she tried on, they never fit her feet comfortably. They were too tight, or too loose, or too long. They had strange things poking into her ankles, or they squished her toes. The laces kept untying.

    After trying on three pairs of skates at the beginning of the night, she had settled on the pair that was too loose. She felt her feet slipping inside them as she skated. She had fallen painfully on her butt once, and had three other close calls. After that, Jim insisted that she change her skates. Since then, she had exchanged them again while Jim skated with Gary, and taken those off for a half hour to sit by herself on one of the circular benches beside the rink and rub her aching feet. Sitting by herself like that felt so humiliating she wanted to cry. She was already constantly self-conscious about her weight, and sitting alone made her feel like even more of an ugly loser. Jim didn't seem to care about her skates or her aching ankles at all, and she knew she was making him mad. She put the skates on again, determined to tough it out.

    Jim and Suzanne skated side by side during the Couples Only skate. In Jim's opinion, they were going at a ridiculously slow pace. Suzanne *still* fell behind. Jim looked back and saw the pained expression in her scrunched up eyebrows.

"What's wrong with you now?" he asked, his jaw kept wanting to clench in frustration.

"It's nothing. These skates are still just hurting my feet," she whined. Jim let his jaw clench and rolled his eyes. It never crossed Jim's mind that Mrs. Bauer had made this exact same expression at him in class, he had imitated it behind her back dozens of times.

"How many times do I have to tell you to go get another pair?"

"I've already switched them out twice. I just need my own skates, that's all."

"Well, it's a little late for that now. Do I have to just go sit down with you all night?" Jim asked in a condescending tone. She only gave him a miserable, irritated expression and continued skating just to spite him. Jim turned away from her and muttered an exasperated, "fuck," under his breath.

They rounded the far corner and went straight along the low white wall. As they passed the DJ booth, Suzanne felt something clunk under her skates, and the floor seemed to drop an inch. She let out a weak scream, wobbled wildly, then fell forward onto the hardwood floor.

Several of the other couples let out hurt, sympathetic cries as they watched Suzanne's hard fall. Jim glanced back and saw her on the ground, then leaned his toe-stop forward to slow down.

"Oh, for fuck's sake!" he growled.

The first couple who came racing over to help Suzanne out was Paul and Sarah, DeAngelo High's cutest couple. They both saw Suzanne's fall and broke apart from their tender embrace to help her out. They stopped and got down on their knees next to her.

"Hey, you okay?" Paul asked.

"Sweetie, are you all right?" Sarah asked.

"I'm okay," Suzanne hissed in pain. "I think I tripped over something on the floor."

Reggie raced over too and skidded to a stop in front of them. He knelt down on one knee. "You okay? Does anything feel broken?" he asked.

"No, no, no. I'm okay, really." Suzanne was grateful for their concern, but she was also totally embarrassed.

Paul looked around behind Suzanne's legs for whatever it was on the floor that had tripped her. He only saw the smooth, shiny surface marred by a couple of rubber skid marks.

Jim finally came over. "Y'Okay, Suze?" he asked dully.

"Fine," she said icily to him.

"Here, we'll help you up," Reggie said. Both Paul and Reggie grabbed her arms and gently lifted her to her feet despite her protests. She smoothed out her dark hair, aware of all the eyes on her as people skated by and gawked.

"It's okay," Jim told them. "Thanks guys, I got her."

"You need anything? Water?" Sarah asked Suzanne.

"I'm fine. I just need to sit down for a while." Paul and Sarah finally took the hint and left her with Jim. With her arm over his shoulder, she slowly limped off the rink in tiny, painful baby steps.

"What the hell happened?" he asked sounding honestly interested, but still unconcerned.

"There was something on the floor and it made me trip."

Jim looked back and also saw nothing in front of the DJ booth. "What was it? A piece of trash or something? I don't see anything there now."

"I don't know. It felt like one of the floorboards

81

lifted up and tripped me."

"Babe, those fuckin' things are nailed down tight. That floor's solid."

"I know that!" she snapped. "I'm just telling you what it felt like. I don't know what the hell it was, okay?"

"Okay, sorry," Jim snapped back defensively. He helped her to a circular bench and sat her down without saying anything. Both of them had just about had it with each other for the night. Jim sure as hell didn't want to sit here in awkward silence with her until morning, especially while all his friends and classmates around him were having fun.

"So what are we gonna do for the rest of the night?" he asked.

"I don't know," she sighed miserably. "I just--"

Suddenly, the needle dropped on a new record, a New Wave song that Jim was very familiar with started up. Jim cut her off in mid-sentence with an excited scream. "OOOOOHHH!" The song was "Whip It" by Devo. He and Gary had been quoting the song all semester in Coach Richards' Weight Lifting class. Anytime Coach would say anything like *Get into shape,* or *Move ahead* (meaning to switch stations in the weight room) they would immediately launch into the chorus of the song. Coach would always call them slackers, tell them to get lifting, and they would laugh like hyenas.

"I'll be right back. I gotta find Gary and Coach."

Jim rushed off onto the rink. He met Gary who was also screaming his name. Gary had also ditched Lindy in *his* excitement.

"I don't believe it! They're actually playing it!"

"COACH!" they both screamed at the same time. Coach Richards was across the rink, and clearly heard them shrieking his name. They rushed over to him and started quoting the song. He looked at them with a puzzled smile and shook his head. He laughed at their goofy enthusiasm.

"This is that song?" he asked.

"Yeah! This is it!" They quoted along with it.

"You slackers need to get a life!" he laughed at them.

They followed him around for the rest of the song, quoting it and laughing their heads off at their own inside joke.

Across the rink, Suzanne stood up and limped over to the low wall. She leaned over the edge next to the DJ booth, and peered down at the floor. There was nothing there, just like Paul and Jim had said, but she thought she saw an uneven line between some of the boards. It was almost as if they didn't quite match up. At first, she thought they were warped right at the ends, but the longer she looked at the boards, it didn't look like they were warped at all. That faint line almost seemed like it was covering up something under the floor. She stared at it a while longer, then "What I Like About You" by The Romantics started to play. The upbeat rock song seemed to draw everyone out onto the rink, and the crowd grew too thick for her to see that uneven spot in the floor. She sat back down and nursed her sore knees and elbows, wondering if anyone else had tripped over that spot tonight.

# Chapter Five:

# Disco King and Queen

## 1

At roughly ten-thirty, Freddy let the music stop and directed everyone to gather around in a big circle in the middle of the rink. It took a few minutes, but with the help of Coach Richards they managed to get everyone to line up in two clusters; one in front of the DJ booth, and another along the opposite wall between the two emergency exit doors. Gary and Lindy had been skating right next to the DJ booth when Freddy made his announcement, so they stayed where they were. They stood close to the spot where Suzanne had taken her fall earlier, and waited for Jim and Suzanne to come join them.

Gary happened to look down at the hardwood floor and saw what he thought was a dead leaf. He almost ignored it, then looked closer and saw that it was a black rose.

"Hey," he said with mild, pleasant surprise. He bent down and carefully picked it up, avoiding the thorns. He held it out for Lindy to see. "Look, it was just sitting on the ground there."

"That's weird," Lindy replied. "Who do you think it belongs to?"

Gary shrugged. He held it out to her as if presenting her with flowers on Valentine's Day. "For you. Sorry, I looked for a red rose, but this was all I could find on short notice."

Lindy placed her hands dramatically over her chest like a Southern Belle. "Oh, why thank you! It's lovely." She took the rose from him and they both laughed.

A minute later, Gary spotted Jim and Suzanne standing near the edge of the crowd. He called their names and waved them over. Jim heard the call and they slowly worked their way through the crowd to join up with their friends. Almost everyone was on the rink so Freddy began his introduction.

"Allriiiiight. Well, for those of you that don't know, we had a little contest here at Rollerville back in September to see if we could crown the Disco King and Queen of 1980."

Dan came straggling into the crowd and joined his friends.

"Hey, where the hell have you been all night?" Gary asked, keeping his voice low so he wouldn't interrupt the DJ. Jim also gave Dan an inquisitive look.

"Oh, just talking with that girl over at the snack counter," Dan replied, he couldn't help the big grin that spread across his face. Gary and Jim both looked over at Denise, then turned back to Dan with identical impressed expressions that said: *Damn, what a babe!' Good job, m'man!* Dan grinned even wider and gave them a little shrug.

"What are you guys talking about?" Lindy asked suspiciously.

"Hmm? What? I wasn't talking," Gary quickly replied, then wrapped his arms around her and faced the DJ. Lindy narrowed her eyes at Gary, and after a moment, he noticed her suspicious gaze. "What?" he asked innocently. She smiled and shook her head at him, then they both turned their attention back to the DJ.

"The competition was pretty tough, but when these two came out, I think we all knew exactly who was gonna get the crown," Freddy continued on dramatically. "Tonight they're back!" The crowd began to cheer, most of them already knew who Freddy was talking about. "Ladies and Gentlemen, your Disco King and Queen of 1980: Paul Johnson and Sarah Whitlock!"

Freddy flipped a switch on his lighting controls and held out a hand over the heads of the students standing near the DJ booth. They all spun around to see Paul and Sarah standing hand in hand under a spotlight in the middle of the rink. They erupted in wild cheers and applause for their fellow classmates. Paul and Sarah beamed at them and gave small waves and nods of acknowledgment to a few of the people who were screaming and whistling loudly. As always, Paul towered over Sarah, their odd mismatched sizes somehow made them the perfect ying and yang. They had decided to stay down to Earth and not wear any coordinated disco outfits. Paul wore the DeAngelo Dolphins football T-shirt and jeans he'd had on all night, and Sarah was still in her purple leotard and high athletic socks. Paul did a goofy little John Travolta finger-pointing disco move with his free hand. As he did it, he pouted out his lips and scrunched his eyebrows together in a mock arrogant way. Sarah caught the tail end of this and nudged him playfully with her elbow. The crowd went wild with laughter.

Freddy broke in again. "Alright. Now when we found out they were coming tonight, we asked if they could prepare a routine for us, and I gotta tell ya, you guys are in for a treat. Can these two skate or what?!" More wild applause from the students. Jack Flynn and Mike Cavallo's group erupted in shouts of *"Paulie!!!"* and *"Owww!"* and *"Get Down!!!"* Suzanne held her hands to her mouth and cheered enthusiastically for them, remembering how nice they'd been for helping her up after she'd taken that fall a little while ago.

"So Paul, Sarah...you know what to do." Freddy immediately dropped the needle down on the song they had picked, "Gimme, Gimme, Gimme" by ABBA, and the King and Queen began to skate.

They started out slow at first, letting the music build before they did anything too fancy. Then as the synthy flute noise and the beat kicked in, they really started to move. It was almost more of a coordinated disco dance more than skating at first. Then they got into more technical skating moves once the first chorus kicked in. They spun, they skated backwards in tight circles, their legs crossing over each other. They were flawless, executing each move with perfect grace and precision, making everything look easy. Their faces held expressions of youthful exhilaration and disco cockiness. They worked the crowd like rockstars. They looked as if this song were written just for them, the rink built just for them, the night was theirs.

Dan smiled and clapped politely as he watched them, but inside his head, he was deep in the past. The last time he had set foot inside Rollerville had been the night of the Disco King and Queen competition in September. He and Mary Anne had been one of the pairs of contestants. They had been skating out in the middle of the crowd with all eyes on them, just like Paul and Sarah were now. They had been skating to ABBA also, only they had chosen the song "Dancing Queen." Well, Mary Anne had chosen the song for them, it was her absolute favorite. She had chosen everything; the song, the tight sparkly Disco outfits that had embarrassed the hell out of him, and the dance moves which she had choreographed all herself. Ever since she heard about the contest, she'd had this strange hunger, this insatiable need for everything to be perfect. She had sucked all of the fun out of it. Paul and Sarah were having fun out there now, and they'd had fun that night too. The smiles on Paul and Sarah's faces were genuine, Dan's and Mary Anne's hadn't been. She had worn a big Pageant Girl Grin on her face, but practically everyone could see that competitive hunger hiding under the surface.

Paul and Sarah raced around the circle of kids backwards, slapping a few of them high-fives. Then they separated in the middle of the circle, skating to opposite ends. Right on a beat, they rushed at each other, looking like they were going to collide. Dan knew they wouldn't though, because he and Mary Anne had done this same move in September. Mary Anne had rushed into Dan's arms, and he lifted her up into the air, her long, flawless legs straight out behind her.

Paul lifted Sarah and started to spin.

Except Dan hadn't held Mary Anne up. Maybe it was the crowd, the pressure of all those eyes on them, but somehow she had seemed heavier, the move ten times harder. On the first spin he'd felt his arms giving out at the elbows.

Dan had dropped her right there.

Paul held onto Sarah though. His muscular arms locked solidly in place, not shaking, not buckling under Sarah's weight like Dan's had under Mary Anne's. Dan watched them with tensed shoulders, as if waiting for the inevitable drop, but it never came. Paul spun away, and Dan saw past them, saw Mary Anne's eyes glaring at him from across the rink.

Dan was startled at the sight of her out here, in

real life, at the scene of their relationship's destruction. It was the first time he had really looked at her since they broke up. She was the only person standing in the crowd with a scowl on her face. She was the only person, besides Dan, who now had their eyes on anyone other than the Disco King and Queen. By the look on her face, Dan knew exactly what she was thinking. *This is your fault. All your fault. We should be out there right now. I'm supposed to be the Disco Queen and you robbed me of that. I hate you!*

Dan knew her voice, heard it perfectly clear in his head. He hadn't spent the last year and a half of his life as her boyfriend without getting to know how she talked. The smile faded from his face as he stared back at Mary Anne. He broke eye contact with her for only a few uncomfortable seconds, but still felt her angry glare burning into him. He looked back, expecting her to have turned to Mike Cavallo or one of those guys, but she still hadn't looked away. She still had that ugly scowl, her lips twisted down in that sneer. All that petty bitterness directed at him, over what? A stupid Roller Disco competition? The whole situation was completely absurd.

Now Dan started to feel his own anger stirring. *Just let it go, man,* he reasoned with himself. *Don't let her bring you down, remember? Just let her--*

*No, fuck this!* Sometimes the voice of reason just isn't enough.

*"What?!"* Dan muttered harshly to her. He knew she couldn't hear him over the pounding music, but she wouldn't have to read his lips to see what he was saying. He held up his hands in a challenging gesture. Mary Anne narrowed her eyes, squinting at him like a mean cat. Dan felt another surge of anger at her. He flipped her off, knowing it was a childish gesture, but he couldn't deny that it felt good. He just hoped no one else

on that other side of the rink thought he was flipping *them* off.

Mary Anne turned and slipped through the crowd, heading towards the front of the rink. Dan felt himself relax a little now that she had broken her death stare with him. *Good, now she's going away. Just let it alone. Let that be the end of it.* But would that be the end of it? Dan seriously doubted it. It had been almost three months and she was still glaring at him, still acting like a spoiled brat.

Dan watched her uncertainly. He felt his heart ramp up and his fists clench as she left the rink. She seemed to be heading towards the snack counter. *Oh great, now look what you started. Where is she going? Is she going to fight Denise? You can't let her do that, you can't allow it.* He waited for her to make a move towards Denise, getting ready to run over there and stop her.

Mary Anne didn't go near the snack counter though. She headed towards the front doors, the ones that lead into the lobby. She silently shoved open the exit doors and disappeared.

*You know what? You had better go settle this right now. Stop this before things get too heavy. Go put an end to it once and for all before she starts trouble and ruins the whole night.* Dan started moving through the crowd. His friends gave him strange questioning looks, then turned back to the spectacle that was Paul and Sarah: Disco King and Queen of 1980.

**2**

As Dan hurried toward the front doors, he glanced over at Denise. She gave him a wide-eyed look

90

of concern. He gave her a slight smile to show that everything was okay, then he focused his gaze on the front doors. He pushed through the exit doors and burst into the front lobby. The first thing that hit him was the surprising difference in temperature in here, it was freezing, at least twenty-five degrees colder. Mary Anne stood in front of the window with her back to him, staring out at the snow. Her red halter top and short-shorts were outlined in more red from the neon light that framed the window. Her fists were tight with white knuckles, and her shoulders were tensed. She didn't turn around, although Dan knew she heard him enter the lobby.

"Hey!" Dan said loudly to her.

"What do *you* want?" she asked icily.

"Turn around and look at me. We've gotta talk."

"What if I won't?"

Dan crossed his arms over his chest and waited. They had played this game many times. If she decided to pull The-Silent-Treatment or Contradict-Everything-Dan-Says, he simply crossed his arms over his chest and gave her his most condescending frown. It was the kind of look he would use on a toddler throwing a fit. That look always infuriated her and usually made the fights worse, but it was also effective in getting her to stop playing those stupid games, stop stalling and just get on with it.

Now Mary Anne saw his expression in the reflection in the window and grimaced. Dan caught a glimpse of her tight grimace. She slowly turned around and they faced each other for a moment in silence. She continue to glare, Dan gave her a pitying look.

"What the fuck is your problem?" he finally asked.

Her eyes narrowed at him, but she kept her mouth shut.

"You got something to say to me? Why don't you just come right out and say it? To my face."

She remained silent. This was both the Silent Treatment and the Contradictory Game.

"Okay, well *I've* got something to say to *you*. Grow up. Quit acting like a fucking baby, and leave me alone. You brought this all on yourself."

The door behind Dan opened as he said that last word. He turned around and saw Mrs. Bauer standing there looking sternly at him.

"Mr. Parsons," she said stiffly. "Is there a problem in here?"

"No, Mrs. Bauer," he replied calmly. "I just had to tell Mary Anne a few things."

Mrs. Bauer stood there staring at them.

"Could you give us a minute? We're just about done here."

Mrs. Bauer contemplated this for a second. She took an extra long look at Mary Anne, as if trying to figure out if the girl was being threatened in any way. Mary Anne looked mad enough to defend herself though. Mrs. Bauer decided to remain standing outside the door, listening for sounds of a struggle just in case.

"One minute." Mrs. Bauer held up one finger to emphasize. "Then I want you both back out there. And don't let me catch you in here again."

"Yes, Mrs. Bauer. Thanks."

Mrs. Bauer finally turned and left the lobby, letting the door shut softly behind her. They were alone again.

"Well?" Dan asked. "You got anything to say to me? This is the last chance I'm gonna give you. After this we're done. For good."

Mary Anne stayed silent and still as a statue.

"All right then. Get bent."

Dan turned to leave and Mary Anne finally

spoke.

*"Fuck you, Dan!"* The words came out in a harsh, whispery growl, full of bitterness. Dan looked over his shoulder at her with disdain. She read his thoughts just as he had read hers back out on the rink. *Is that it? Is that the best you've got?* He smirked at her and shook his head, then turned and skated out of the room.

As he rolled back into the rink he heard applause. The Disco King and Queen had apparently just finished their performance. Dan liked the sound of it though. A small part of him imagined that the applause was for him, like they were all cheering him on for standing up to Mary Anne and her childish games once and for all.

As far as Dan was concerned, he was finally fully leaving her in the past. Leaving her back in 1980, where all his bad feelings would eventually be forgotten. He hoped that only the good memories, what little he had left of her, would remain.

Mrs. Bauer pushed open the door and saw Mary Anne still standing there scowling, staring at the floor. "Let's go, Mary Anne." Mary Anne looked up at her teacher with a sour glare, then obediently skated back out into the rink. Mrs. Bauer walked closely behind her making sure she went back out to the rink, and not right back into the lobby where she wasn't supposed to be.

As Mrs. Bauer escorted her back into the rink, Mary Anne felt eyes staring at her on her left side. Geno Atkinson stood leaning in the doorway to his office watching her, twirling a set of keys lazily on his index finger. He gave her a shrug that said, *Told ya so. Didn't I say you'd get busted by your teachers for going in there?* Mary Anne gave him an angry squint and turned away as she neared the rink.

As soon as Mary Anne and Mrs. Bauer lost

themselves in the crowd, Geno left his office, letting the door shut behind him. It was time for him to plow the snow in the parking lot again. He walked back into the lobby, still twirling the small key ring on his finger.

## Chapter Six:

## The Countdown

### 1

In the last half hour before midnight, everyone inside Rollerville seemed to take on a lighter, reflective mood. They forgot about petty squabbles and minor irritations with their peers, and instead, looked back on all the fun and great times they'd had in 1980. Almost everyone stood or sat around in small groups talking and laughing. Very few of them continued to skate, Reggie and the teachers let them stand in their groups on the rink without giving them any hassle to keep skating.

Freddy was largely responsible for the lift in everyone's spirits. He had planted a seed in their minds as he made one of his periodic time announcements, counting down the hours and minutes until midnight. At 11:30 he had suggested that they all spend the next half hour with friends. He told them to look back on all the good things that happened to them in 1980. Freddy had expected them all to ignore him like they did ninety percent of the time, but he was pleasantly surprised to find that this time they all took his advice to heart. In order to let them talk, Freddy played ballads and more mellow songs, he even turned the volume down a bit.

With the help of Coach Richards, the two freshmen, Ray Stone and Joe Jacobs, had successfully gotten that jerk Bryan Barnham to get off the Pac-Man machine. They had taken a few turns on it, but quickly got bored and went back to the rink. Now they stood in a corner reliving moments from their two favorite movies of the year: *The Empire Strikes Back* and *Airplane!* Seeing those movies had been some of the highlights of their year.

Earlier that evening, a group of tall freshman girls in skimpy athletic shorts had approached Reggie. This had been after he had led the group in the middle of the skate rink doing The Hustle. They had twirled their sporty pigtails with their index fingers and made small talk, a few of them lightly touched his huge Afro. One of them finally asked him to teach them how to do some of those disco skate moves. They were flirty and giggly and they cracked up at all of Reggie's jokes. He knew they were way too young for him and he wouldn't mess with them, but he had to admit they were cute, especially the one on his left with the dark hair and bright blue eyes. Reggie imagined this is what football players must feel like a lot of the time as the girls laughed and gushed over how well he skated.

Jack Flynn, Mike Cavallo, Steve Fields, and the rest of their usual meat-head group stood on the rink next to the DJ booth. Jack still stood shirtless in his goofy New Year's Baby costume with the 1981 sash draped over his shoulder. Mike still wore the black pants and the 1980 sash over his T-shirt and suspenders, but he hadn't bothered to go grab the black cloak or mask from the front lobby or change back into his athletic shorts. They stood in a circle, passing around a large cup from the snack counter that was filled with half Pepsi, half Jack Daniels. Earlier that day, Jack had swiped a half-empty whiskey bottle from his dad's liquor cabinet and brought it to the rink in his athletic duffel bag. They talked loudly, made jokes, and recalled crazy late nights cruising around town and getting drunk throughout the past year. While one person drank, the next person in the circle kept a lookout, and the rest simply acted casual. All of them were getting a pretty decent buzz, slurring their words and giggling just a little too much. None of them noticed the distinct aroma of liquor they were giving off.

Coach Richards sat down on one of the circular benches and gave his aching legs and feet a rest. Luckily for the Flynn/Cavallo group, they were on the opposite side of the DJ booth from him. Even though he couldn't see them, he could hear them, and he had a sinking suspicion that they had been drinking and probably smoking grass too. Richards was about fifteen years older than them, and not long ago, he had been known to be quite a party animal too. As long as they didn't get too carried away with it, he would let a few drinks and a few joints slide. Besides, they were safely locked in here. It wasn't like anyone was going anywhere, especially in the middle of this blizzard.

Mrs. Bauer finished reading a chapter in her romance paperback at one of the tables. It was based in nineteenth century France and she wished she were there right now, instead of sitting in this dank skating rink surrounded by irritating teenagers. Still though, this was the first time she'd gotten a chance to sit down since the bus ride over, and she was glad to put down some pages in the book. She checked her watch, gave one of her trademark sighs, and put the book down. It was time to get up and get ready for the big New Year's celebration out on the rink.

Jim came off the rink and sat down next to Suzanne on her circular bench near the skate rental counter. She looked at him cautiously and he smiled at her.

"Can I sit here?" he asked.

"Knock yourself out," she replied dully.

He watched her for a moment, trying to think of something clever to say.

"You mad at me?"

"What do you think?"

"Well, I don't see how you could stay mad at me with a face like this." He held his hand under his chin, grinned, and batted his eyelashes at her. Suzanne only snorted a sarcastic laugh and turned away. Jim wrapped his arms around her. "Hey, come on now. I'm really sorry."

Suzanne ignored him. After a second, he let go of her and leaned down to untie his skates.

"What are you doing?" she asked.

"Taking these things off so I can be with you. Ahh. Man, it feels good to get those fuckin' things off my feet."

"You don't have to sit here with me. Just go."

"Nope," Jim replied stubbornly. "Not going anywhere. You're stuck with me." He picked up one of her sore feet and started massaging it. She couldn't help but smile at him.

"I'm still mad at you...Jerk," she said with a smile on her face. Lindy joined them a minute later so they could all be together for the start of the New Year.

## 2

Across the rink, Dan was skating toward the

snack counter to go talk to Denise again, but he was stopped by someone calling his name.

"Hey, Dan!" Dan turned and saw Gary rolling up to meet him.

"Hey, Gare," he said casually.

"Hey. You gonna hang out with us at all tonight? Seems like we've barely seen you."

Dan shrugged. "Well, you guys were with your girlfriends. I didn't want to get in your way."

"Shit, man, we don't care about that. Come hang out with us. We're all ringing in the New Year over in the back corner."

"Ah, you guys have fun with your girls at midnight. You know how New Year's Eve goes, it's Make-Out Time at midnight." He finished the sentence in a sleazy, frat brother voice. "If I'm lucky, I might get some Midnight Make-Out Time myself." Dan nudged him with his elbow and Gary laughed in the same dumb, frat brother laugh.

"Okay," Gary conceded, returning to his normal voice. "I see your point. Just...don't forget about us again, okay?"

Dan was taken aback. It seemed like such a heartfelt statement coming out of Gary's mouth. Dan rarely saw Gary or Jim with serious expressions, he almost never heard them say serious things. He came close to blurting out, *What are you talking about, man? I never forgot about you guys*. But he knew in his heart that that would be a lie. The truth was, he *had* forgotten all about those guys during his time with Mary Anne. He had missed out on all of junior year and the first half of senior year spending all his time with her. The weight of everything he had missed suddenly came crashing down on him. All of the Friday and Saturday nights that he had missed, all the movies at the Westview Mall Theater, laughing and throwing popcorn at the screen, all the hot summer days at the Countryside pool, and golfing with Gary. All that precious time he could've spent with his friends, but he had just...forgotten about them.

And here he was doing it all over again, but with that Denise girl this time.

"I won't forget about you guys. I promise." He said it with as much seriousness and heart that Gary had shown him just a second ago. Gary smiled as Dan reached out and they both shook hands tightly, like brothers. "I'll see ya in a little bit."

"See ya next year. Huh huh huh!" Gary replied, adding a stupid laugh at the end.

"Oh yeah," Dan laughed. He added his own goofy laugh. "See ya next year. Catch ya on the flip side."

They turned away from each other, Dan heading up toward the snack counter, Gary heading back toward his girl over by the skate rental counter.

Up in the DJ booth, Freddy dropped the needle on the last song to be played in the final minutes of 1980. Appropriately enough, it was ABBA's "Happy New Year."

Dan rolled up to the snack counter and Denise's face instantly lit up with a smile.

"Hey, it's my Resolution Buddy," she said.

"Hey! I like that. Resolution Buddy, that's not bad."

"Well, it's pretty slow back here tonight. I had a lot of time to think it up."

"I know, I'm sorry. I haven't been keeping you company like I said I was going to. I'm a terrible Resolution Buddy."

"I know, I've been up here all alone and abandoned." She let out a fake sniffle as if she were about to cry.

"Apparently, I do that to people a lot."

Denise started laughing, but quickly heard the change in Dan's tone and saw his mood darken as he looked back toward the rink.

"What do you mean?" she asked.

"Oh, I don't know. I was just talking to my friend out there and he told me not to forget about him. You know something? I think this is the first night this whole entire year that I've actually spent hanging out with my friends instead of well, you know..." Dan opened his eyes and mouth wide in a whacked out Bride of Frankenstein face to indicate that he was talking about his ex-girlfriend Mary Anne.

Denise gave Dan a mock horrified look at the mention of Mary Anne. "Sounds like a rough year. Almost sounds as bad as my year."

"What was wrong with *your* year?" Dan asked, honestly interested.

"Let's see, uh, I moved out here," she began, listing things and counting them off with her fingers. "My boyfriend turned into a giant asshole and we broke up, I had to use up all my savings to go get my own place, my car broke down three times. Oh, and both my grandma and my cat back home died."

"Ouch. Sorry about all that," Dan replied sympathetically. "1980 really did bite the big one."

"Yeah, well, at least it's just about over now," Denise sighed.

"And hopefully 1981 will be better," Dan added. Denise nodded in agreement. They fell into an uncomfortable silence for a moment, both of them disappointed that they had steered their conversation into such dismal territory. They both tried to think of something more upbeat to say, and Denise beat Dan to the punch.

"Well, maybe you should go hang out with your friends," she suggested nonchalantly, not wanting to make herself sound like she desperately needed him to stick around. Although, she really did hope he wouldn't go back to his friends. It really was lonely back here, and it was nice to have the attention of a cute guy.

"I could, but..." he said, and glanced back at the rink again. "I think I'm right where I want to spend my New Year's Eve."

"Oh yeah? And why would you want to spend your New Year's Eve over here?"

"Isn't it obvious?"

"No, tell me."

"Allriiiiiight, this is it boys and girls," Freddy's voice interrupted them. "It's the final countdown, sixty seconds until 1981! Everybody head out on the rink now for the big countdown!" They both looked back and saw all the stragglers shuffling out onto the middle of the rink. They clustered in front of the DJ booth, and all turned their attention to the huge clock on the wall across the rink.

Dan and Denise looked up at one of the TVs mounted over the tables and saw the camera cut away from Dick Clark, Pat Benatar, and a few other celebrities to show the huge lighted ball in Times Square slowly making its way down the pole towards the building. A little clock in the corner of the screen showed that it was 11:59 PM.

"Almost midnight," Dan said, turning back to Denise. She had leaned in closer to him on the counter, pretending that she was trying to get a better view of the rink and the TV.

"Better hurry up and answer my question before it's the New Year."

"Why would I want to spend New Year's Eve over here? Well, this might sound stupid, but I think you're really beautiful." She couldn't help but smile and blush at that. "And...I don't know, talking to you, I get the feeling that you're just like me. Kinda lonely and...not sure where to go next, you know?"

"Allright, here we go. 10!" Freddy shouted into the microphone. The entire crowd out on the rink joined in with him.

"Also we're Resolution Buddies, so that's gotta count for something."

"9!" Reggie and the freshman girls shouted, he and the tall girl with the dark hair glanced at each other and smiled.

Denise leaned even closer toward Dan. "I don't think that sounds stupid at all."

"8!" Coach Richards and Mrs. Bauer shouted out the numbers, keeping their eyes on the clock.

"And I don't think that's the *only* reason why you're up here."

"7!" Paul Johnson and Sarah Whitlock, the Disco King and Queen of 1980, held their arms around each other, shouting out numbers.

"Why not?" Dan asked.

"6!" Joe Jacobs and Ray Stone pounded their fists in the air along with each number.

"Because I think..."

"5!" Freddy put his hand on the record player to drop the needle on the scratchy record of "Auld Lang Syne" as soon as the clock struck twelve.

"...you're up here..." Their eyes locked as they drew closer, mesmerized.

"4!" Jack Flynn and Mike Cavallo stood in front of the DJ booth screaming out numbers and holding their Pepsi cup low, getting ready to take a long swig of the heavily spiked Pepsi right at midnight.

"...just so you can get..." Closer, their faces only inches apart.

"*3!*" Jim and Suzanne held each other tight, all was forgiven between them at this moment. Gary and

Lindy also clung to each other, watching the clock, waiting, their hearts thudding.

"...a New Year's kiss."

"*2!!*"

Dan and Denise's eyelids began to drop as they leaned in even closer for the kiss. They were so close that they could feel the heat radiating off each other's faces. Electricity seemed to crackle and rage between them. Denise didn't even realize she was standing on her tip-toes to lean as close to Dan as she could.

"*1!!!*"

The lights went out. The entire roller rink was thrown into pitch black darkness.

Dan and Denise immediately broke apart from each other, looking around guiltily and nervously in the dark. Anticlimactic sighs blew out of deflating lungs. There was nervous laughter and confused muttering. There was a loud wooden *BANG*. A few seconds later, everyone inside Rollerville rang in the New Year with screams.

**Part Two:**

**The Year of Blood**

**January 1, 1981**

## Chapter Seven:

## The Death of Disco

### 1

    Jack Flynn let out the first scream a few seconds after the lights went out, a high girly scream meant only for laughs. A few people gave him short nervous laughter, but that was the best he got. He felt a rush of cold air on his bare legs and calves, then heard the wooden bang and felt the vibration of it through the floor. Someone was moving around in the dark behind him, he could hear the *whish* of cloth between himself and the DJ booth. Jack looked over his shoulder and strained his eyes to try to see who it was, but couldn't make out anything.

    Skate wheels stomped down on the floor behind Jack with two hard clunks.

    Suddenly on his right, Mike Cavallo let out a gagging *OOF* noise. Then he started making a kind of chuffing, choking noise like something was stuck in his throat. Jack and a few others in their group began to laugh, thinking it was all just another joke. They didn't know that he actually did have something stuck in his throat, a long curving blade.

Then Jack felt something rip into his exposed belly, tearing him open just above his bellybutton from one side to the other. Jack jerked up straight for a second on impulse, his piece of Juicy Fruit gum flew out of his mouth and landed on the floor. Then he stumbled backward as he felt his own insides begin to pour out of his abdomen. With clumsy hands, he tried to catch all the slimy warm stuff as it slipped through his fingers. He involuntarily began to make weird retching noises, *"ACHH AGH!"* His skates slid in the wet, warm blood that was dumping out of him, and he fell backward against two guys and a girl from his group.

*"Hey! Watch it!"* they yelled. They felt warm liquid from Jack Flynn's hands wipe against their arms and legs as he fell into them. A wave of the putrid stench of Jack's blood and intestines suddenly washed over them. They began to cough and choke.

*"Ugh! What's that smell?"*

A sharp piece of metal tore into Steve Fields' cheek and ripped a long deep gash all the way down to his rib cage. As another member of the Flynn/Cavallo group tried to wipe Jack's blood off his pants, he felt sharp metal slash across the backs of his thighs. Both he and Steve began to scream almost instantaneously.

*"OWW! Shit!"*
*"What the fuck?!"*

Heads were turning in all directions, trying to see what was going on near the DJ booth. People were beginning to scream. Over at the snack counter, Dan recognized the voices of Jack and Mike's friends screaming in the crowd. He heard Mary Anne's piercing, overly dramatic scream ring out a few times too. *Oh boy, she's at it again. What a fucking drama queen. What a faker,* he thought.

Jack Flynn dragged himself backward on his hands, and grabbed the first person he bumped into. It was one of the freshman girls from the basketball team that had been learning roller disco moves from Reggie only a few minutes earlier. She whipped around as sticky, clutching hands wiped streaks of blood down her bare legs.

"Eww. What--"

*"El...Elp meee...!"* Jack gagged out the words through bubbles of blood. The girl began to shriek.

Loud murmuring intensified. "What's going on?"

"Somebody turn the lights back on."

Mike Cavallo stumbled around weakly clutching his throat, and bumped into his killer. The killer stabbed him in the chest with the long curved blade and shoved him backwards. Mike let out a gurgling cry and crumpled to the hard floor with a series of thuds.

The killer rolled forward and slashed out again. The edge of the blade parted the skin and meat of someone's else arm. They began to hiss in pain and scream. A second slash tore through their left butt cheek and they fell forward.

*"Whatever's going on, I want it to stop right now! Somebody get those lights on!"* Coach Richards screamed into the chaotic darkness. He sensed the growing panic and knew that this wasn't a prank, something was terribly wrong.

In the corner near the skate rental counter, Suzanne clung tightly to Jim's arm.

"Relax," Jim said dismissively. "Those jackoffs are just pulling another dumb prank."

Another person began to shriek out in the darkness as the killer ripped into them.

"Are you sure?" Suzanne asked. "It doesn't sound like a prank to me." Jim had no answer for her.

Several of the other freshman girls from the basketball team came forward to see what their friend was screaming about. Jack Flynn's blood-soaked hands shot out of the dark, scrabbling at their arms and legs. They all began to shriek along with their friend and awkwardly back away in their skates.

Coach Richards stood in the middle of a crowd of screaming teenagers, his head darting back and forth, trying to figure out how to handle this situation. He was afraid that if these kids didn't calm down, they would stampede and people might get trampled.

*"Somebody get those goddamn lights on right fucking now!"* he screamed in his loudest Coach voice.

Two more cawing shrieks of pain rang out as another two people went down. Another girl felt a razor sharp blade stab sideways into her gut, piercing organs and popping them like grapes. It poked out through the skin on her other side. She grunted and gagged, doubled over and knocked her head against someone else's on the way down.

Freddy sat there frozen in the dark, refusing to believe that this was anything but some sort of elaborate prank. *Why doesn't Uncle Geno hit that emergency light switch in his office?* he wondered. He waited for the lights to come on, but nothing happened, and the screams were getting worse. The smell of people's insides, a coppery smell mixed with shit and something out of one of his high school biology dissection classes, finally wafted over him and he grimaced.

*Where the fuck are you Uncle Geno?*

Once the Coach chaperone started to scream, he sprang into action. Someone had to go into Uncle Geno's office and hit that switch. He shot up out of his seat in the DJ booth. His legs felt stiff and began to tingle, but he ignored this as much as he could. As he hurried down the carpeted steps out of the DJ booth, he walked right into a thick piece of wood. Its hard pointy edges jammed into his shins, sending spikes of pain all the way up his legs.

*"Ah! Shit! Sonuva...."*

The wood thing, whatever it was, fell forward and slammed back down on the rink floor with a clattering thud. Freddy fell back onto the steps, clutching his aching shins. More fresh screams rang out and fresh panic distracted him from the pain. He stood up, launched himself over the side of the DJ booth and sprinted for his uncle's office.

Something lashed out at a girl, tearing the back of her shirt open. She suddenly thought it was some guy trying to take advantage of the darkness and chaos to rape her. Screaming and flailing her hands wildly behind her to fend off any potential rapists, she pushed forward into the crowd of kids. She pushed the person in front of her, who pushed into the person in front of them, and a tidal wave rocked the crowd forward.

Coach Richards and Mrs. Bauer, both on opposite ends of the crowd, felt a tidal wave of kids crushing against them. Their worst fears were beginning to come true.

*"Hey! Don't panic! Everyone don't panic! Stop shoving!"* they both yelled out. The teachers cries went ignored, drowned out against all the other screams. Another tidal wave shoved them all forward. Almost everyone was helpless on wheels, totally unable to push back against the surge of kids.

Coach Richards tried to work his way through the crowd toward the DJ booth and the front side of the rink.

*"Somebody get those fucking lights on! You hear me?!"*

The crowd began to thin out and he felt himself gain some breathing room as he neared the DJ booth. He pushed forward on his skates with extra speed, but bumped into a kid writhing around on the floor. He fell to his knees, his shins coming down hard on a bloody abdomen. The kid coughed up a jet of blood into Coach Richards' face.

As he coughed and squinted his eyes against the sting of the blood, he felt cloth flap in front of his face. The killer spun around in front of the coach, and the long curved blade jammed into his back. He barked out a scream of pain and fury. The blade stuck in Richards back between two of his ribs, and the killer tugged at it three times. Richards barked out a scream with each tug.

The killer then kicked one skate clad foot into Richard's upturned face, the hard rubber wheels jamming into the coach's eyes and mouth. His neck bent back with a crack and a lightning bolt of pain, then he blacked out. The killer used the leverage to yank the blade out of Richard's back and the Coach's body fell forward. With the weapon free again, the killer rushed forward toward more fresh prey.

"What the fuck is going on out there?" Denise whispered. She clung tightly to Dan's hand, feeling both of their pulses pounding wildly in terror.

"I-I-- I don't know," Dan stammered. All thoughts of jokes and pranks were gone. Something awful was happening in here. He tried to swallow but his mouth had gone completely dry.

Denise heard someone running in their direction and she jumped. Then she recognized Freddy's frantic cries and and allowed herself to relax a little.

*"Uncle Geno! Somebody! Hit the emergency lights!"* he screamed out.

Freddy barked his aching shins on one of the circular benches in the dark. He bounced off the bench and cried out, almost losing his balance. In pure terror and a rush of adrenaline, he raced onward. A moment later, he slammed into the painted cinder block wall in the front corner of the rink. He silently thanked God he'd had his arms out in front of him to break his momentum, otherwise he might have broken his nose. He groped along the wall for the door to the office.

After what felt like much too long, he finally found the middle hinges of the office door and pawed for the handle. He found it and yanked the door open. The office was also pitch black dark, but Freddy knew the emergency breaker box was on the wall directly to the right of the door. He fumbled for the breaker switch on the side of the box, feeling its sharp metal corners dig into his hands.

"Come on come on come on come on," he muttered.

Freddy's hands tapped the breaker switch, recognized it, and grasped it tightly. He heaved it upward and the rink suddenly filled with red light from a dozen bright red emergency lights that had been placed throughout the entire rink. In the hellish red light, Freddy saw something out on the rink amid the raging sea of panicky bodies that made his blood run cold. *God forgive me,* he thought, and slammed the door shut.

## 2

Denise's mouth dropped open as her eyes adjusted to the harsh red emergency lights and she finally got a good look at the chaos out on the rink. Dark splashes of blood were everywhere, but it was hard to tell how much of it there really was in all the red light. More than half of the crowd out there was already down on the floor, either lying still or writhing around in agony. A lot of them were piled on top of one another, making the skate rink look like some sort of bloody battlefield. The other half of the crowd had split into two groups and were piling up against both emergency exit doors. They shoved each other frantically and slipped around on their skates; falling, stumbling, roughly shoving each other.

When she saw the killer, her stomach dropped. It was the same guy, the one who had been staring at her from the graveyard earlier that day. It *had* to be him. A black cloak swept out behind the killer, its hood covering a masked head. When the killer turned, she could see it was that same ugly rotting skull mask that had been part of the Old Man 1980 costume a few hours earlier. Black gloved hands wielded a long deadly scythe and swung it around wildly, stabbing kids and slashing across their backs, legs, throats, any body part within reach. The killer was lightning fast, and tore through the crowd like a hurricane, filled with some kind of insane rage-strength.

She and Dan watched as the killer in the death cloak spun around and slashed a deep cut right down the middle of some kid's back. Blood spurted out from the rip down the middle of the kid's football jersey. He howled and arched backward, his knees buckling underneath him. The killer spun, whipped the scythe around to the right, and slashed upwards, ripping open the kid's throat from beneath his Adam's apple all the way to his upper lip. His howl of pain was choked off abruptly and he fell backwards, his head clonking hard against the wood floor.

"Oh my God!" Denise gasped.

Bryan Barnham, the eleventh grade bully, tripped in his mad dash toward the emergency exit doors. He had been one of the closest people there, but he was terrible on skates. The wheels had slipped out from under him and he fell forward on his hands and knees. As he struggled to get up, the others stampeded past him.

Four or five of them ran over his fingers in their skates, and he yelped each time he felt the brittle pops of his breaking bones. After the worst of the stampede had passed him, he shakily got to his feet. His eyes teared up from the ripping pain in his fingers. He turned and thought he recognized Mike Cavallo skating toward him. Bryan had laughed at Mike earlier as he wore that same creepy death costume and scared the shit out of that little freshman. Now, through tear-blurred eyes, he saw Mike skating full speed at him, rearing back with a bloody scythe. He held his gruesome crooked fingers up to shield himself.

*"Mike, wait! Wait! WAIT!"* Bryan pleaded. He knew Mike in passing, and had never thought that he would snap like this. Unknown to Bryan, the killer was definitely not Mike Cavallo, and he was shown no mercy. Bryan tried to turn as the scythe swung hard into his abdomen, just below the ribs. His spinal column finally stopped its progress. The force of the blow flung Bryan into the wall, then he crumpled to the floor. His bullying days were over.

Kids slammed up against the emergency exit doors, piling into one another. A small sophomore girl stood directly against the door, hammering the crash bar as hard as she could. The door refused to budge. It was covered with a thick sheen of ice, frigid winds had hammered snow and sleet up against it for the last eight hours. Other kids piled up tighter as the killer slashed towards them, and the girl was crushed against the door, screaming out weakly.

*"Get off! Get off!"* she grunted. No one heard her, or would've cared if they did.

Those caught in the middle of the pile-up could only squirm and struggle against the weight of all the other bodies forcing them forward. The stragglers at the end of the pile shrieked out in terror as the black death thing came rushing at them.

The two freshmen kids Joe Jacobs and Ray Stone were on the outskirts of the crowd at the nearest emergency exit door. At the sight of the killer rolling fast towards them, Joe got an idea and grabbed Ray by the shoulder.

*"Come on!"* he shouted. He pulled Ray's arm and ran back towards the arcade corner, keeping as close to the wall as they possibly could. Joe got away, Ray wasn't so lucky. He got caught in the peripheral vision of Death. With one smooth movement, the killer extended the scythe out to the right and viciously sliced forward, cutting into the tender spot just below the freshman's knee caps. Ray flipped forward and landed face first on the hardwood floor, breaking his nose and knocking himself out.

Two of the girls from Reggie's group stood at the back of the crowd near the exit doors. They screamed and tried to push their way deeper into the crowd. The thing dressed in black, the thing with the rotting skull face and black empty eye sockets, the thing with the dirty, bloody scythe was rushing straight at them. One girl turned to meet the killer and held her hands up to shield herself. The blade sliced down diagonally, cutting straight through one of her wrists, amputating her left hand. The skin on her right forearm was sliced off like deli meat. The girl next to her ducked and got a deep slash across the cheek. She fell to the floor and the heaving crowd trampled her face, neck, and abdomen with their skates.

The scythe blade slashed through backs, necks, and legs. Their skates made them unsteady on their feet and most of them tripped and fell before they could run away. Nine people were stabbed nineteen times in the space of ten seconds.

One kid, writhing on the floor with deep cuts in

his calves and blood in his feathered hair, looked up and saw the killer hacking away at the crowd. The blood-soaked folds of the cloak were right in front of him on the wood floor. Without thinking, he reached up to yank the killer back by the long cloak, trying to put some kind of stop to all this insanity. The killer tipped backwards for only a second, then stomped a skate backwards for balance. The other skate then shot backwards, and hard wheels kicked the kid in the throat. He slammed backward against the floor, clawing at his smashed windpipe and wheezing for air.

The crowd dispersed, those still unscathed scrambled toward the other emergency exit door. The killer chased after them, easily matching their speed. Some tried to turn around in the opposite direction and run the other way. Under the still disco ball, the killer held the scythe tight and spun around in a complete circle, cutting through five people in one rage-filled swipe. They twirled to the ground, screaming and clutching at gaping wounds. The end of the deadly swipe curved upward, slicing up through one kid's throat. The gout of blood shot up, splattering the shiny mirrors on the bottom of the disco ball.

Jim, Suzanne, Gary, and Lindy all began backing away from the rink as they watched the mayhem. Suzanne clutched at Jim's arms.

"Don't leave me, Jim! Don't leave me!" she cried. Jim looked around frantically for a way to escape. Off to his left, he saw Tony Tanner behind the counter, backing slowly toward the door into the skate rental storage room. Jim jerked forward, ripping his arms out of Suzanne's death grip.

*"WAIT!"* he screamed at the top of his lungs.

Tony heard Jim, and bolted for the skate rental room. Jim launched himself forward and the others followed. He rolled over the counter, swinging his legs down to the other side and collided with the door as Tony tried to slam it shut with both hands. Jim fell back to the floor, and the door bounced back, rattling in its frame. Gary was already up over the side, forcing his way through the door. He shoved Tony back hard.

*"Come on!"* he shouted back to the girls who were struggling to climb up over the counter in their skates. Jim got to his feet and helped the girls over. He yanked Suzanne by the arms and practically dragged her into the storage room. The two of them rushed in, and Gary slammed the door shut behind them.

Paul and Sarah, the Disco King and Queen, stood holding each other on the edge of the crowd at the far emergency exit doors, watching as the killer slashed toward them. Gouts of blood spurted through the air. Paul looked back and forth from Sarah, the love of his life, to the oncoming death in front of him.

*No, this can't be it! This can't be the end for us. Someone has to stop this! No, I have to stop this!*

Paul gave Sarah a longing look, her eyes were fixed on the killer though.

*"Sarah, look at me!"* he shouted. She gave him only a brief glance with wide terrified eyes. *"I love you!"*

Before she could even respond, Paul flung her back into the safety of the crowd, and sped toward the killer as fast as he could. Sarah crashed against three other kids but didn't fall down. She felt herself being shoved around like a rag doll, somehow being pushed deeper into the crowd. She watched Paul speed skate forward with his arms held wide. With dawning horror, she realized he meant to tackle the killer like a linebacker.

*"NO!"* she screamed.

With a hard grimace, full of rage, Paul cried out as he closed in on the psycho in the death mask. The killer saw him coming right at the last second, and yanked the scythe out of a girl's bubbling neck. With an agile step to the side, the killer dodged out of the way of Paul's grasping arms. The cloak billowed out as the killer swept a leg back and spun around behind Paul's back. The scythe blade slammed down into Paul's shoulder blade and in between two ribs. Paul grunted and fell forward with the force of it.

*"PAUL!"* Sarah shrieked.

The killer dragged the blade out of Paul's back and raked it across the floor, leaving a long deep scratch in the wood. With a splintery squeak, the blade came up again, and Death rushed toward the crowd at the door.

*"NO!"* Dan cried from over at the snack counter. He jumped forward meaning to go out there and take the killer down just like Paul had tried to do. Dan had watched in hypnotized horror until Paul was struck down. Paul had been a damned good friend of his. Gary and Jim were out there somewhere. Even Mary Anne was out there too, as bitchy as she was, she didn't deserve this.

Two strong hands shot out from behind Dan, yanking him back by the shoulders.

*"What are you doing?"* Denise yelled. *"Are you fuckin' crazy? Get back here!"* Dan whirled around to face her, but she was still tugging him back. He came down awkwardly on his side on top of the snack counter. Denise still pulled him back by one of his arms, and he slid forward, gracelessly rolling over onto the other side of the snack counter. Denise refused to let go, and he stumbled to his feet on the linoleum behind the counter.

On the back wall, there was a door leading into the pantry. Denise opened the door and they both flew inside the dark room. Dan whirled and caught one last glimpse as the killer tore into the last small group of his classmates at the far emergency exit door. Then Denise slammed the door shut and locked it.

## 3

The heavy chain rattled against the glass doors in the front lobby as kids slammed into them. In the middle of all the chaos out on the rink, five boys and three girls had managed to slip past the bloody, swinging scythe. These few had been clear-headed enough to realize that the emergency exit doors were a dead end, so they had sprinted the other way for the front lobby, desperately hoping they could sneak out somehow. Unfortunately for them, the doors were once again chained and padlocked shut.

Among them was Reggie, the skate monitor, he was the first to enter the lobby, dimly lit with two more of those red emergency lights. As he sprinted for the doors, he saw that the padlock and chain hung loose, maybe they would be able to slip through. He shoved against the doors but they opened an inch, letting in a blast of frigid air and a swirl of powdery snowflakes. The doorway was blocked by a heavy two-foot-high mound of snow. Three more guys plowed into the door, shoving it open a few more inches.

*"Hurry! Open the doors!"* the girls behind them screamed.

*"Help me, you guys! Push!"* Reggie screamed. Veins stuck out in his neck as he pushed against the huge, heavy pile of snow. All five of them strained and struggled against the door, digging their sideways skate wheels and toe stops into the thin carpet like linebackers. The girls glanced nervously over their shoulders, expecting the black-cloaked Death figure to come charging in any second. They could faintly hear the

screams dwindling out there. There was no telling how much time they had before Death came for them.

A perfect pie wedge shape opened up in the snow as they forced the door forward. Then with a clink, the chain pulled tight. Reggie desperately tried to force himself through the tight opening in the doors. He stuck his face and one arm out into the cold. He could see the mound of snow in the parking lot that had buried his old car. It was so close, yet impossible to reach. He squinted against a blast of wind filled with tiny ice chips that melted in his eyes and stuck in his huge Afro. With his free arm, he clawed at the door handle, trying to force his way through. It was no use, there just wasn't enough slack in the chain for the doors to open wide enough.

Reggie slipped back inside and tugged on the padlock uselessly.

*"Fuck!"* he screamed in frustration as he gave the chain a hard yank.

*"The keys! Coach has the keys!"* one of the guys screamed.

"We're all gonna die," one of the girls whimpered in horrified realization.

Reggie lifted his skate up and slammed it against the door as hard as he could. The skate bounced back off the glass harmlessly. He kicked the door again, and two of the other guys copied him. The thick Plexiglass in the door vibrated, but remained strong. *"Fuck!"*

Reggie looked back and forth, scanning every inch of the room for a solution. At the other end of the lobby he saw the window into the dark office where the ticket-takers sat, and an idea popped into his head.

"The ticket window. Maybe Geno put a set of keys in there!"

Without a moment's hesitation, one guy and one of the girls rushed toward the ticket room, speed-skating across the carpet.

Just before they reached the ticket window, the carpeted double doors burst open. The killer plowed into the guy and the girl. They fell back shrieking to the carpet. The killer stumbled for only a second, then slashed down at them with the scythe blade, ripping open both of their throats in one swipe.

The rest of them jammed up against the front doors. They kicked desperately at the doors with their skates, slammed their bodies into them. Reggie forced his face back through the opening again and the others tried to help push him through.

*"HELP! SOMEBODY HELP!!!"* he shrieked out into the snow. His cries went unheard, swept up in the storm.

Two of the guys turned and tried to tackle the killer, but with two swinging slashes of the scythe, they fell bleeding to the ground. Death hacked through the rest of them easily enough. Reggie ducked away from the blade, feeling the wind from it whistling past him as it cut down the others. In less than thirty seconds, he was the last one left standing.

Reggie pulled his head back inside, his body still crammed between the double doors. The killer stopped for a moment and they stared at each other, both of them breathing hard. Reggie knew insane eyes were watching him from behind those black empty sockets on the rubber skull mask. He could almost feel the burning rage emanating from behind the mask.

In one quick movement, Reggie put his free arm up on the door frame and yanked his body back inside from between the doors with all his force. The killer reacted instantly. One black, blood-soaked glove shot out, grasped the chain just above the padlock, and yanked it backwards. Reggie's arm slipped through as the door slammed shut, but he wasn't fast enough. All four of his fingers caught in between two sharp metal edges between the doors and were sliced off.

Reggie screamed. He grabbed his now fingerless hand with the other and pulled it close to his chest. It felt like sheets of fire were flaring up his whole arm. He caught one last glimpse of Death through teary eyes just before the scythe finished him off.

## 4

From their hiding spots, the remaining survivors listened to the dwindling sounds of screams coming from all over the rink.

Joe Jacobs was curled up hiding under the pinball machine in the arcade area. One dim red emergency light lit up the arcade area, and Joe's hiding spot was like a dark little cave. First, he heard the crowd at the emergency exit door being stabbed and hacked to death. Joe cringed and covered his ears, blocking out the sound of each scream and thunder of limbs collapsing limply on the wooden floor. Then there was silence. Joe took his hands off his ears to listen for signs of the killer. After a moment, the muffled screams from the front lobby started up, he could hear them through the cinder block wall directly behind him.

Joe knew the killer would be coming for him soon. It was only a matter of time. He waited for the moment when the killer would make his way over here, forcing himself to breathe only in shuddering, raspy little breaths.

*Everyone's dead out there. Everyone except me. And I'm next.*

Joe listened carefully and could hear some of the others that were still alive out there. Maybe they had only been stabbed or slashed once, and now they lay bleeding and suffering out there on the wood floor. Some of them were crying and hissing in pain, others muttered soft prayers to themselves.

"Oh God, please," the choked voice of a girl close to the dining area said. She repeated the same thing over and over between weird gulping breaths. "Don't let me die here. Don't let me die. Please God, don't let me die."

Joe plugged up his ears with his index fingers and squinted his eyes shut to block out the noise.

A few minutes later, there was another wooden bang just like the one he had heard just after midnight when the lights had gone out. Joe jumped and took his fingers out of his ears. He listened for the whirr of the killer's skates to come rolling over, but he heard no new sounds after that flat bang. There were no new sounds for so long that Joe wondered if the killer had gone, running off into the night in search of more victims at other New Year's Eve parties. Only the whimpers of the bleeding, dying people out on the floor remained. He considered getting up and trying to find the payphone and calling the police.

Suddenly the lights came back on throughout the rink. The red emergency lights went out and the regular white, red, blue, and purple lights came back on. The glittering disco ball reflections swept over the carnage like white leopard spots, or red leopard spots from the bottom where it had been splattered with blood.

Joe gasped as the lights came on. All the extra white florescent light flooding the arcade area made him feel exposed. He inched back farther under the pinball machine and covered his mouth with his hands.

Inside the skate rental storage room, the florescent lights suddenly flickered to life again. Suzanne cried out softly and tightened her clutching arms around Jim. All of them looked around frantically, experiencing a feeling of being caught in their hiding spot.

In the pantry behind the snack counter, Dan and Denise also looked up as the lights came back on. They had their arms wrapped tightly around each other. Both of them looked white as a sheet.

"Don't make a sound," Denise whispered urgently to him.

In Geno's office, Freddy hid under a desk. The lights had been turned off in here, so he didn't notice when they came back on. As he listened, something broke the silence outside. It was the pop of the speakers turning back on, then the scratch of a record needle dropping into place. That murdering psycho was messing with his sound system.

Up on the DJ booth, a bloody black gloved hand had reached over the record player. Two drops of blood dripped onto the small forty-five record as it started to spin. The hand placed the needle down on the record that Freddy had been all set to play as soon as the new year began. The dusty sound of pops and scratches hissed out of the large speakers.

Freddy held his aching, bruised shins, and listened to the warbling old 1940's big band sound of Guy Lombardo and his Royal Canadians performing the old New Year's Eve standby, "Auld Lang Syne." The sound echoed through the walls into the office. When he had picked out that record earlier in the week from his dad's collection, he thought it sounded classy and old fashioned. "Give those kids some friggin' high class culture," he had joked to his dad, a man who frequently told Freddy that his beloved disco music was garbage. Now those crooning saxophones just sounded eerie seeping in through the walls and the crack under the door.

Someone let out an agonized wail out on the rink, cutting into the music. The wailing became a bubbling gurgle, then stopped, Guy Lombardo played on. A few seconds later, there was another one. Freddy winced at the sound of all that death mixed with the old fashioned music, it hurt his heart.

Under the pinball machine, Joe Jacobs heard what was happening much more clearly than anyone else. The killer was going after all the wounded, finishing them off one by one. Joe plugged up his ears with his fingers again and tried his best to ignore the sounds of suffering and death.

Mrs. Bauer, who had been crushed in the stampede by the exit doors and fallen among the bodies, came to. She heard the old record playing and wondered where she was. For a moment, she thought she was back in the early fifties with her first husband. Then she looked up and saw the white skull face of Death standing over her. It seemed to examine her, watching her with rapt attention.

"M--Mr. C-C-Cavallo...M-Michael...please. Stop this..." she pleaded. It wasn't Mike Cavallo under that ugly white death-skull mask. Mike was dead, his body was over by the DJ booth, draining out all of his blood from the gaping wound in his throat. The killer lifted one skate and stomped the wheels down on Mrs. Bauer's head. She let out a bird-like caw of a scream.

"That was Mrs. Bauer," Gary whispered from inside the skate rental storage room. He sounded sick to his stomach. "Oh my God. That was her, I know it."

"Shut up!" Tony hissed. "He'll hear you."

"Just don't listen to it, man," Jim said, turning away from the door. Suzanne buried her face in Jim's chest and tried to ignore the terrible wails from outside.

Dan, with his arms wrapped around Denise in the pantry, winced as he listened to the screams.

The killer went around the rink in a large sweeping circle, finishing the night's business. Anyone left moving either received a swift kick to the head with the killer's skate, or a scythe blade through the throat. The killer approached the DJ booth as the song neared its end and just about everyone out on the floor was dead. The rotting skull mask turned back and forth, examining all the bodies. Not all of them were here, there were still a few missing, but they would join the crowd soon enough.

The killer looked down at the clear spot in the floor in front of the DJ booth, the place where the massacre began. One hand reached into the black folds of the cloak, produced another black rose, and gently lay it down where it wouldn't be touching any of the blood or the bodies. As far as the killer was concerned, none of the bodies piled up on the floor deserved to be mourned.

"Auld Lang Syne" was finishing up its last few bars. Death rolled out to the middle of the skating rink floor, rocking the hooded, masked head back and forth to the old trumpets and saxophones. The killer's skate wheels rolled through thick puddles of blood, tracking it into the center of the rink. There was a clearing in the dead center of the rink with no bodies in the way. Only a few droplets of blood had dripped down off the disco ball directly beneath it. From this clearing, the killer surveyed the night's work, looking back and forth over the piles of bodies. Black sleeves dangled down over spread arms, swaying with the final swell of the song. Death spun around on bloody skates in a few lazy circles and came to a full stop under the shining disco ball as the last note of the song played.

The year of blood had officially begun.

# Chapter Eight:

# Playing Dead

## 1

They weren't all dead out on the rink, some of them were unconscious, and a few were only pretending.

Sarah Whitlock, the Disco Queen of 1980, hadn't even been touched by the sharp edge of the scythe at all. Before putting on the "Auld Lang Syne" record, and before murdering Reggie and the others in the front lobby, the killer had hacked down the crowd at the far emergency exit door. Sarah had been part of that crowd, but had collapsed under everyone as they fell. She laid perfectly still and uninjured near the bottom of the pile. Somehow, she had remained untouched throughout all the madness and murder. The scythe blade had stabbed through someone to her left, someone to her right, someone on top of her, but never into her. She had kept her eyes closed, not wanting to open them, not wanting to see the blood or the gaping wounds. Blood trickled down all around her, some of it dripped down on her forehead and she squinted her eyes shut to keep it out.

She felt her classmates writhing all around her, some of them jerked and convulsed as they were stabbed.

Then the stabbing stopped, and above all the tortured, dying screams, she heard labored panting behind that rubber skull mask. Not everyone was dead yet, but they soon would be. Less than half of them were moving, weakly struggling, dying.

Death had loomed above the pile, watching them and waiting in that black, blood-soaked cloak. The dripping scythe hung there in the killer's hands, daring anyone to try to escape or lash out in self-defense. Any sudden movements would trigger another attack.

Sarah lay crushed underneath a chubby guy who had fallen back on top of her. The last thing she remembered before falling and squeezing her eyes shut against all the pain and brutality, was seeing kids stepping on her old English teacher Mrs. Bauer in their skates while she screamed for them to help her up. After that, she had lain still and waited for the end, tuning it all out, only thinking about Paul. Two images replayed over and over again in her mind while everyone in the pile around her squirmed and suffered. The first image was Paul grabbing her by the shoulders, looking deep into her eyes, and saying *I love you*, then rushing off. The second was the blade driving deep into Paul's precious back. If she were to die, she wanted to die thinking of Paul, the love of her life.

The writhing movements were tapering off, bodies falling still. Sarah felt herself losing air under the dead weight of all the kids on top of her. Every breath she inhaled seemed smaller and smaller, as if her rib cage wasn't strong enough to push itself up against them. Her lungs cried out for air, cried out for her to push this big lump of dead meat off of her before she suffocated.

*No! Don't you move! He won't get you if he thinks you're already dead.*

Dead like Paul.

She watched him go down again and again in her mind. He had hit the floor and the killer raked the blade across his back before turning back to the crowd at the exit door. Then the stampede had blocked out her vision as the killer rushed towards them, skate wheels whirring and clomping down against the wood.

That was when the killer rushed off to the front lobby to deal with Reggie and the others that had escaped the rink in the middle of all the chaos. At first Sarah thought she was imagining the sound of the killer's skates, but she quickly realized she was hearing them in real life. They weren't coming towards the pile of bodies though, this time they were rushing away. She waited until the killer was completely gone, the sound of rumbling skate wheels muffled against the carpet, then she allowed herself to finally open her eyes again.

The blood was still dripping down on her forehead. She turned her head so it wouldn't flow into her eyes. Looking up past the chunky kid's body, she saw a tangle of legs and arms. With a grunt of effort, Sarah heaved the chunky kid off of her, he rolled away limply to Sarah's left side, freeing her top half. She sat up and scanned the front side of the rink for the killer again, and saw no one standing. She inhaled huge gulps of fresh air. Now that she could breathe again, she had to think of a way to escape.

*And what about Paul? Is he still alive?* she wondered. She looked over at Paul lying face down on the floor twenty feet away.

Sarah pulled her legs out from under a dead girl and shakily got to her feet. As she stood up, she looked down at herself and grimaced, she was almost totally covered in blood. For a second, she mourned her ruined bloody clothes. The cute little white jacket that she'd loved so much was now a reddish brown. Her purple leotard, skirt, and high athletic socks were also a stained, discolored mess.

*Forget about the stupid clothes, there's no time for that right now.*

She took a wide step over two sprawled out bodies. The wheels of her skates came down in a slippery puddle of blood. She wobbled, almost doing the splits and falling backward into the pile of bodies that she had just crawled out of. She over-corrected her balance and half-fell, half-leaned forward, then she awkwardly dropped on all fours beyond the blood puddle.

As she stood back up, the first of the screams from the front lobby rang out. Sarah jumped and glanced around, feeling like an animal caught in a predator's gaze. She quickly realized that the screams were coming from the front lobby. That maniac was occupied and she was safe, at least for the moment. She tuned out the awful sounds of tortured screams and skated over to Paul.

He was lying in a slowly spreading pool of his own blood. His head was turned awkwardly down and to the left, pointed toward the direction of the crowd at the exit door. It was as if he had died trying to look back at her.

Sarah knelt down, her bare knees resting in his blood, and gently shook his shoulder.

"Paul?" she whispered. He didn't respond, so she shook him harder. "Paul, wake up!" She felt the tears welling up in her eyes. Her lip began to shake uncontrollably, she felt her own face pulling into a grimace. "Paul! Wake up, wake up, wake up. Come on. Don't do this to me! You can't leave me like this!"

Paul suddenly gasped in a bubbly, choking breath. His eyes fluttered open. Sarah jumped, then felt the tears of relief streak down her cheeks.

"Paul! Thank God!" She leaned down and covered his left cheek with kisses, being careful to avoid the blood spatters.

"H-h-hiii..." he gurgled.

"Hi, baby! I thought I lost you," she replied and kissed him again. Paul's face contorted and he tried to flinch away from her kiss as if he were annoyed.

*"H-hide!"* he growled at her.

All the relief she felt suddenly flew out the window. He wasn't saying *Hi*, he was trying to tell her to *Hide*, to run away, to get the hell out of here before that psycho in the death mask came back.

The last screams from the front lobby were beginning to die down, and Sarah was exposed out on the rink. She was the last girl standing among all of the fallen kids. She had to get out of here, had to find somewhere to hide, had to obey Paul's last word for her own survival.

She looked down at him one last time. "I love you, too." Those four whispered words made her heart ache.

Without another second's hesitation, she got up and ran for the bathrooms. She took long strides, rolling across the floor more than running. With every loud thump of her skates on the hardwood, she prayed that the killer wouldn't hear her. On the other side of the rink, her skates slid in another slippery pool of blood, and she stumbled violently. Her free foot stomped down inches from some freshman boy's head. He seemed to bounce beneath her as her foot came down. The kid was Ray Stone, but Sarah didn't know him.

Sarah rolled off the rink onto the carpet, grateful that it muffled the rolling rumble of her skate wheels. She sprinted for the bathrooms and tore into the Men's on the left, only because it was the closer of the two. The tile and brick floor of the bathroom made every little

131

noise echo loudly, so she covered her gasping, panting mouth with one hand. She held her other hand out in front of her, groping blindly through the darkness for a stall to hide in. After a few panicky seconds, she touched the stall door on the far left side of the cramped bathroom, and went inside.

Once inside, she turned around, closed the stall door, and turned the lock. With her hands still covering her frantic breath, she sat on the toilet and prayed that the killer wouldn't follow her in here.

*Just make it till morning, gotta make it till morning, make it till morning.* She kept repeating that phrase in her head. Outside the bathrooms, the killer stepped back in from the front lobby, black cloak dripping with Reggie's fresh blood. A minute later, Sarah flinched at the sound of that wooden bang again. Less than twenty feet away, Joe Jacobs, hiding under the pinball machine, flinched at the exact same time.

Harsh whitish-green florescent light instantly flickered to life and flooded the bathrooms. Despite the sudden brightness, Sarah's eyes bulged in shock. Had the killer heard her? Had she been seen darting into the bathroom? Was she caught? She didn't know. It had been so hard to see under those dim red emergency lights. She listened for the rumble of rolling skate wheels or the swish of a black cloak and heard nothing. She lifted her legs up onto the toilet seat, hoping they would be out of sight.

She tried to peer out through the cracks between the stall door and the white chipped paint of the cinder block side of the stall. Was someone in here with her? It didn't sound like it, but maybe the killer was trying to be quiet.

That was when she heard the crooning saxophones of Guy Lombardo's "Auld Lang Syne" echo into the bathroom, sounding like a chorus of wailing ghosts. The sound of that scratchy old record filled Sarah with fresh new terror. The first new scream echoed out not long after that, and Sarah jumped. With horror, she covered her ears as the dying wails accompanied the music. She had hid in the bathroom during the end of the midnight massacre, hoping she wouldn't hear Paul's last scream.

## 2

Ray Stone also pretended he was dead as he felt the low thrum of the killer's skates approaching him where he lay. Ever since the scythe had slashed out at his knees and he'd fallen flat on his face, he had slipped in and out of consciousness. He would wake up to the sound of people's terrified screams all around him, the sounds drilling into his aching head. Everything around him looked bloody and red under the emergency lights. Then the pain in his nose and knees would ache harder and deeper, blotting out all other senses, and he would pass out again. When Sarah Whitlock stumbled in a puddle of blood right near his head, the impact of her skates had bounced his head against the wood floor and he woke up for one painful second, then dropped down into the blackness again.

Then an echoing scream had woken Ray back up, he thought that it was a sound from out of some nightmare. His eyes flew open and he felt vibration in the floor under his head, someone was coming towards him. There were other colors in the rink again, not just the bloody red emergency lights. Someone had turned the regular lights back on. He thought he was hearing the blessed sound of ambulance sirens, and for a moment he believed he was saved. Then he realized it was just some weird old record playing over the speakers. It didn't take him long to recognize it as *That New Year's Song* (he did not know the name "Auld Lang Syne.") He also realized that the low thrumming coming towards him wasn't an emergency worker either, it was that masked psycho. Summoning all his will power, he fought back against the hard throbbing in his broken nose, it seemed to pound through his entire head. He shut his eyes, held his breath, and kept as still as possible as the killer approached him.

The skates stopped only a few inches away from Ray's still arm. He felt a rush of air in the killer's wake, then the cold, blood-soaked folds of the black cloak brushed against his arm. From behind the dark black eye sockets of the skull mask and the shadows under the cloak's hood, the killer watched him, holding the scythe blade ready, waiting to finish the freshman off. Lying in the large pools of blood under his smashed nose and slashed kneecaps, he looked dead enough.

After a few seconds, the killer turned away from Ray, moving on to finish off other victims. He felt the skates rumble away through the floor for a few moments, then opened his eyes again. Another one of those awful screams burst out somewhere behind Ray.

*No,* he thought. *This is a bad dream. This can't be happening. I can't really be here. It can't be....*

Ray felt his eyes and head becoming heavy again and drifted off into darkness.

Now he came to again, feeling as if only a minute had passed. He had no idea how much time had actually gone by, but the midnight massacre seemed to be over. The "Auld Lang Syne" record wasn't playing anymore and the place was silent. Ray listened for the thrum of the killer's skates through the floor, but heard nothing. He dared to lift his head up and look back over his shoulder, wanting to see if the killer was still out here somewhere on the rink. There was no sign of the masked maniac anywhere.

*I might just be the last person alive in here*, he thought. *But not for long if I don't get my knees and my nose bandaged up.* He knew he had already lost a lot of blood because he felt so weak and lethargic. He struggled to get his sluggish mind to think. The killer had gotten him as he and Joe ran toward the arcade during the massacre. He had fallen and passed out. Then he had woken up after just about everyone was dead and the killer came up to him to see if he was dead too.

Another memory bubbled up to the surface. He remembered a loud STOMP next to his face, it had woken him up. That stomp had made his head bounce, sent daggers of pain into his nose, and made him pass out again.

*Did that just happen? Did it even happen at all, or did I just dream it? No, it was real. And it was before the killer came back and looked down at me with that old record playing in the background. Someone ran past me, not the killer, someone else. They tripped, then they ran forward.*

Ray ran the incident over in his mind and something else occurred to him, it had been a girl. He remembered hearing her heavy, panicked gasp as she stumbled. Then he had fallen unconscious again.

Now he looked forward, in the direction that the girl had gone. There were bloody tracks left by her skate wheels. They led off the rink, toward the bathrooms and the arcade.

Ray put his hands down and pushed himself up in an attempt to get back on his feet. As soon as he put pressure on his knees, he felt something stretch on his slashed knee caps. The fresh tender skin in the wounds stung like acid as it pressed against the floor. He collapsed back down, thankfully keeping his aching nose turned away from the hard wood. He lay there grimacing at the pain until it faded to a dull throb, half expecting to pass out again, but this time he stayed awake. Just to be safe, he took one last look around, tilted his knees off to one side, and began dragging himself forward with his arms.

## 3

Something was crawling slowly across the floor toward him. Joe Jacobs had been gazing blankly ahead, letting his mind drift as he waited for morning, when the movement caught the corner of his eye. He gave a startled little jerk and turned to face the slow crawling thing. From his hiding spot crouched under the pinball machine, Joe couldn't see the rink at all. He could only see halfway down the little carpeted alley leading past the bathrooms and out onto the rink. As he watched, a shaky blood-splattered arm pulled itself into view. Another arm reached forward even farther, nails digging into the carpet. Behind the arms, there came a messy ruin of a head matted with blood.

The sight of the crawling, mangled body made Joe remember a horror movie he had seen on TV, *Night of the Living Dead*. The crawling thing looked like one of those slow moving zombies from that movie.

*My God, it's one of those dead people. It came back to life. It's coming! Coming for me!* The crawling thing turned its head forward, facing Joe, and he immediately recognized it as Ray Stone. Of course it would be Ray, the guy who had been his best friend for years, the guy who had died out on the rink less than thirty minutes ago. Wasn't this how it always happened in the horror movies and the horror comics? The dead came back for revenge against the living. Ray was dead and Joe had lived, and now Ray would be coming to drag Joe down into the grave with him. That's how it always worked.

Ray dragged himself forward again, his bloody fingers scratching into the carpet. It was just like the carpet back at DeAngelo High, too thin for him to get a good grip. So his fingers curled into little fists against the tight fibers, making skittering, scratching sounds. Drying blood covered the right side of his face, and had streamed down over his nose and mouth. His nose looked mashed and flat, coming down at an ugly diagonal angle. Even his eyes looked dazed and half dead.

Ray stopped moving and let himself rest. He turned his head and lowered it to the carpet again. He breathed low through his mouth in clotted gasps.

*He's not dead*, Joe thought. *Stop being stupid. Dead people don't come back to life.*

Joe lowered his hands away from his mouth, planning to whisper to Ray and call him over. He stopped himself right at the last second.

*Wait! Don't get his attention. Don't let him come over here. He'll give you away to that psycho guy in the mask.*

As if Ray read Joe's thoughts, his head slowly turned back toward the pinball machine. Joe froze. Ray seemed to be looking directly at him.

*Oh God, does he see me? Please don't let him see me.*

Ray's bloody red hand pulled itself forward again and his fingers dug into the carpet with that scratching sound. He hauled his weak body forward, and this time Joe noticed the wet dragging sound his jeans made against the carpet. Joe wanted to shrink back even closer to the wall so Ray wouldn't see him, but he was tight up against the cinder block and the side of the Skee Ball machine. There was no more room for him to back up. Again, Ray's bloody hand slapped down on the floor and clawed at the carpet. With great effort and a tiny grunt of agony he slid another six inches closer to Joe.

*No!* Joe screamed silently inside his head. *Don't come over here! Get out of here, Ray! You're as good as dead. Don't drag me down with you. Do you want me to die too? He's gonna come back for you! It's me or you.* Part of his mind insisted that these were terrible thoughts to have about your best friend, but under the circumstances, he was too afraid to let himself feel guilty.

Ray dragged himself forward another few inches, then stopped again. He was looking down at the floor. Joe wondered if he was finally running out of energy, finally ready to collapse on the floor and die. Ray's head seemed to turn to his left. Joe couldn't see the trail of blood on the carpet he was following. Ray's left hand shot out sideways and he began following the blood trail into the bathrooms.

Joe watched him go, inwardly sighing with relief. He kept his wide eyes locked on Ray's body until his bloody skates and torn legs had disappeared from sight.

4

Sarah heard a light slap against the brick bathroom floor, followed by a thin scratching sound. Her head instantly snapped to the left in the direction of the sound. *This is it*, she thought, *he finally came looking for me*. She covered her mouth with her hands to mask the sound of her panicked breathing. She listened to the approaching sound of wet cloth dragging against the floor, it reminded her of wet jeans rubbing against each other when she pulled them out of the washing machine and tossed them in the dryer. Through the crack between the stall door and the cinder block wall, she waited to see that black death cloak to come gliding in.

There was another smack, a light scratching, then a damp slide.

*What the hell is he doing?* she wondered. *Is he trying to get me to come out? Toying with me somehow? And what the hell are those sounds he's making?* The wet slap, scratch, and slide noises came again. Whatever it was, it was working its way slowly down the hallway, coming into the bathrooms, coming closer.

Surely the killer would try to be a lot quieter than that. If this was the bait to draw her out into a trap, wouldn't a killer try to lure her out with something that wasn't so...creepy?

*Maybe it isn't the killer at all. Maybe it's someone who's hurt. Someone who saw me run in here. But the only person who saw me was--*

"Paul," she mouthed the word. Instinctively, she reached for the lock on the stall door and began to turn it. Then she stopped herself. *But what if it is the killer though? What if this is just some trick? What if the killer is using Paul to get to me?* She drew her hand back away from the lock.

*Slap, scratch, drag. Slap, scratch, drag.* It inched its way closer and closer. Sarah peered through the crack, leaning forward and trying to see whatever it was. A hand caked with drying blood came into view from beyond the white cinder block wall that blocked the bathroom from sight outside. The moist, clammy palm slapped down on the brick floor, then clawed into it, blood-clotted nails made those skittering sounds against the brick. It pressed down, then pulled the body forward just far enough that Sarah could see the top of a ratty, matted head of hair.

Sarah moved her head back and forth trying to get a better angle on the person dragging themselves into the bathroom. It didn't look like Paul, the matted hair on this person's head looked much longer than Paul's short close-cropped hair. She desperately wished she could see more. The person dragged themselves a little farther forward, and now she could make out his head and shoulders through the tiny crack. It was a boy, but he definitely wasn't Paul, much too small to be Paul. Also his skin was too light, Paul was tan even in the winter.

Sarah wondered if she should go out and help the kid. He stopped halfway into the bathroom and coughed up a few bloody gobs of phlegm onto the brick floor. His coughs seemed to bark and echo against the bathroom's thick walls. Sarah winced at the noise, it seemed deafening in the still silence.

*Shut up, kid. Shut up shut up shut up. He'll hear you,* she thought with a touch of guilt.

The kid stopped coughing and caught his breath for a moment. Then his hand shot forward and slapped down on the brick again. He was back on the move, and dragging himself toward her at a slow methodical pace.

*Oh no, don't come over here. Don't come over here, please,* Sarah silently prayed.

The boy's body was fully into the bathroom now. A long smear of blood trailed behind him, dark maroon against the brick floor. Her eyes followed his trajectory to a couple of thin red streaks of blood that led under the stall door and stopped directly beneath her skates.

*No. I led him in here after me. How could I be so stupid? I led him right here. And he'll lead the killer--*

"H-h-hello?" the boy uttered in a gravelly whisper, interrupting her thoughts. "I-is somebody there? Please, I need help." Sarah squinted her eyes shut. She couldn't let him in, the killer would hear them, maybe already had. The boy coughed again and smacked his hand down. His nails dug into the bricks with that skittering sound that grated against her nerves like nails on a chalkboard, it intensified her panic.

*Smack!* The hand came into view just outside her stall door. Sarah shrank back on top of the toilet seat. In plain view, it looked like a dead hand. Why hadn't he just stayed put and left her alone? Why hadn't he just played dead and waited for help to come?

*Why didn't YOU just play dead?* part of Sarah's mind argued. *You might have made it out just fine if you had. Now you're caught.* Sarah cursed herself, raised her fist, and slowly banged it against her own head in frustration.

Now the boy's head was visible underneath the stall door. He rolled it painfully from side to side as if he couldn't figure out which way to turn it without causing himself more pain. Finally, he rolled his head to the right, and Sarah's mouth dropped open at the sight of his smashed face. The boy looked like he had been hit by a car. One side of his face was caked with drying splatters of blood, the other side was weirdly clean. His hair was still damp with blood, but it was clotting and drying to an ugly dark brown. His flattened nose pointed in a weird diagonal angle that hurt to even look at.

Peeking out behind her fingers, she gazed down at him with wide eyes. His own dull, listless eyes met hers. He coughed again and raised one weak hand toward her.

"Please help me," he whispered. He reminded her of an old picture she had once seen in one of her Bible study classes. It had been picture of a bloody, mangled person reaching out to Jesus to be healed. The picture had given her nightmares when she was only a little girl. Now the picture had come to life, here it was right in front of her. Except she wasn't Jesus, she could do nothing for him.

"P-please. It hurrrrtsss," he hissed. His hand reached up and grasped the toes of her skate, a smear of blood wiped across the clean white leather. She tugged her skate back away from him and his hand fell to the dirty bathroom floor.

Sarah thought of the poor girl that she had helped up earlier tonight with Paul. She had been all too eager to do whatever she could to help that girl, Paul had too. But Paul was always like that, he'd give you the shirt off his back, even in the middle of the blizzard like the one that was still raging outside right that moment. Paul was dead though. And that was then, back in 1980. It was a new year now, the year of blood.

Sarah lowered her skates off the toilet seat and leaned down. She put her hands on the boy's shoulders, he looked almost grateful.

"I'm so sorry," she whispered to him in a tiny, barely audible voice. She gave the boy a push away from her bathroom stall.

"No, please," the boy's voice became louder, and he began to cough violently again.

"Quiet! You'll lead him in here!" She lowered her butt to the cold brick floor, pushed her legs out, and rested her skates on the boy's shoulders. With her back pressed against the lip of the toilet, she pushed the kid back even farther out in the middle of the bathroom floor. He continued to cough and blood dribbled out of his mouth. She pushed him as far away as she could without getting out of the stall and exposing herself, then got back up and squatted on the toilet seat again. In a few seconds the boy's coughing fit subsided and he began to cry softly with his head against the floor. Listening to him sob like that, knowing he would probably die, Sarah felt damned.

*Oh God, what have I done?* She lowered her head and shut her eyes in shame.

The boy suddenly let out a pained animal snarl of a scream. Sarah's eyes flew open, she looked out through the crack. A black thing stood in the doorway, sucking up the light. The boy was suddenly dragged backwards toward it. His nails raked against the brick, even against the ear-piercing echoes of his screams she could hear that. Standing in the doorway, the killer had stabbed the scythe blade deep into one of the boy's legs and used it to drag his body backwards.

Sarah looked around frantically for a weapon. There had to be something, anything she could use against that masked psychopath. As she glanced back over her shoulder, she spotted the heavy porcelain lid on top of the toilet tank. An idea suddenly popped into her mind.

In one quick movement, the killer ripped the blade out of Ray's calf and swept it back down again like a golf club, sliding the blade in under Ray's throat. The boy screamed and tried to crawl forward again. Before he got out of the range of the blade, the killer twisted it back and to the right, neatly slicing the boy's throat open from ear to ear. He gurgled and began to flop around on the floor like a fish.

Tears streamed down Sarah's face as she listened to these grisly sounds. She turned and pulled the heavy lid off the toilet tank as quietly as she could.

The killer saw the trail of blood leading under the stall and stepped forward over the flopping figure of Ray Stone. Black skate wheels rolled over the bricks making a low *thunkthunkthunkthunkthunk* sound.

With the lid of the toilet tank in her hands, Sarah

crouched and looked over her shoulder at the crack. A black empty eye socket stared straight through the crack at her. She could see a tiny sliver of whitish-gray skull, black gums, and grinning teeth between the door and the wall. She held her breath and waited as the killer stared at the stall door. Joe's gurgling noises had almost completely died down, and she could hear calm, even breathing under the rubber mask. She wondered how that psycho could even see through those black empty eye sockets.

The killer turned away from the crack and stepped back. Sarah had time to feel an instant of triumph before the heavy skate-clad foot slammed against the door. She let out a scream as the door splintered, barely staying connected to the wall. The killer rolled backward from the force of the kick and Sarah had time to change her strategy. She reached out and unlocked the door with one hard twist.

The killer lashed out again, and Sarah yanked open the door at the same time. The black skate plunged forward, missing Sarah by inches, and splashed into the toilet bowl.

Caught off balance, the killer wobbled. Sarah charged forward screaming. She slammed the heavy porcelain lid down onto one cloaked shoulder. The force of the blow knocked the killer down to the floor in a hard heap. The scythe blade went flying back, clattering in the hallway leading into the bathroom.

Sarah reared back with an animal cry of rage, and swung the tank lid down again. The killer saw it coming and dodged, rolling out of the way in the nick of time. The lid came down hard on the brick floor and shattered into dozens of sharp tiny pieces.

The shock of the toilet lid's impact reverberated up Sarah's arms, and she dropped the last two shards of porcelain she still held in her hands. The wheels of her skates slipped out from under her, and she struggled to catch her balance again. The killer stood upright again in a flash.

Two strong gloved hands suddenly grabbed Sarah by the hair and clamped down under one of her arms. She felt the heat and intense rage-strength under that crushing grip. With one hard yank, she was flung through the air, crashing down onto the bathroom counter. Her skates slammed into the farthest mirror and shattered it. Several shards of glass tumbled down over her legs and fell into the sink. Two of the sink faucets jammed painfully into her back as she landed against the counter. The flashes of pain were so intense that her eyes bulged, and the scream in her throat suddenly turned into a deep gasp. Her dropped mouth opened in an O, and her eyes squinted shut as she arched her back away from the unyielding metal faucets.

She rolled sideways, threatening to topple off the counter onto the hard brick floor. The killer reached out and pressed her back down as she reeled in pain. She felt the leather glove slide down the length of her body as the killer rolled over to the shattered mirror above the far sink. Sarah looked up and saw the other black glove pluck out a nice long shard of glass that was jutting forward out of the spider-web of cracks in the mirror.

The killer rolled back up toward Sarah's head, skates making that *thunkthunkthunkthunk* sound again. She looked up as the killer held the long shard in front of the skull mask, then lowered it close in front of her face. She winced and tried to roll away, but the killer's other hand held her down. The long glass shard traced a line down from the top of her forehead down over her nose, lips and chin. The tip of the shard rested in the delicate hollow of Sarah's throat. She squinted her eyes shut again, anything so that she wouldn't have to look at that awful morbid death mask anymore. She thought of Paul, wondering if he would've tried to help the kid that had come into the bathroom. Dismally, she figured he probably would have no matter what.

Using both hands, the killer suddenly jammed the long mirror shard down hard into her throat. She let out a garbled scream as the killer yanked the shard out and stabbed down again and again. The last things she saw were flashes of red light reflected off the bloody broken glass shining in her eyes.

Outside the bathrooms, Joe Jacobs could see the tip of the scythe blade poking out from the bathroom's doorway. He briefly considered grabbing it before the killer came back out, and even began crawling forward toward the front of the pinball machine. Then the gurgly struggling sounds echoed out of the bathroom, and Joe drew back into the shadows again. He covered his ears with his hands and squeezed his eyes shut against the noise. Sometimes it was better to pretend that you didn't exist at all, sometimes it was better to just play dead.

# Chapter Nine:

# Whispers in the Pantry

### 1

Dan sat with his head resting on one of the pantry's wooden shelves next to an open box of silvery Three Musketeers candy bars and a heavy metal flashlight. His longish dark brown hair hung in sweaty matted clumps, and his skin was waxy and pale. He sat with his eyes glazed open, a dazed, blank expression on his face. Denise sat next to him tearing a napkin into tiny, obsessive pieces. She also looked pale, and had dark circles underneath her eyes. A few wayward strands of her auburn hair hung down, out of place from her flipped out Farrah Fawcett hairstyle. Her collared Rollerville work shirt looked wrinkled and hung down loosely off one shoulder. It was only one in the morning, but they both looked as if they'd been up all week.

"They're dead," he said in a low voice, being careful to stay quiet. Despite the low volume of his voice—it was barely above a whisper—Denise jumped a little as he broke the silence. It had been nearly half an hour since they had heard anything outside the pantry. The echoing screams from the bathrooms had chilled them, made them cling tightly to each other again. Silence had spun out afterwards, and that was somehow worse. They couldn't see or hear what was going on out there. For all they knew, the killer could have run off into the night, or could be standing right outside the door, waiting for them to carelessly reveal their hiding spot.

"All my friends. Dead. Gone," Dan mumbled slowly. His voice sounded like he was both exhausted and trying to not be sick to his stomach. A series of images and memories flashed through his brain as he mentally inventoried all his dead friends. "Paul and Sarah, they were gonna get married someday. Everyone knew it. They were the nicest people in the whole school. No one could ever say anything bad about them. If anyone ever did, everyone else would just call them an asshole.

"Jim. He's been one of my best friends since seventh grade. Gary. *He's* been one of my best friends since *first* grade. Coach used to call us all slackers in the weight room at school. He's gone too. And Mrs. Bauer. She used to get so mad at us for screwing around in her class. Even Mar--" he stopped in mid-sentence, not wanting to even say her name. He held his breath for a second, then slowly let it out. "Mary Anne."

Denise glanced at the door before looking at Dan. She half expected the killer to come pounding against it, but there was only silence outside.

Mary Anne kept returning to Dan's mind, not because he would miss her, but because he felt terribly guilty and conflicted about *not* missing her. They had ended everything on a sour note, and Dan had told her off earlier tonight. Then she had been murdered, and that was a fact he would have to live with for the rest of his life. Dan felt bad about the others, but somehow Mary

Anne's death made him feel worse. He sat there with his head against the shelf, wanting to say all of this to Denise, to get it off his chest. He thought about where to begin, and remembered how they had ended their last conversation earlier that night.

"You know what the last thing I said to her was? I told her to get bent. Those were the last words I ever said to her. *Get bent.* God, I shouldn't have said that." He looked sick with guilt.

"You didn't know this was gonna happen," Denise finally spoke up. "When I broke up with my ex, I said some terrible things to him too. Things that I didn't really mean, but... Sometimes things just don't work out, you know?" She knew this wasn't really the best advice in the world. Her ex-boyfriend was still alive, all she had to do was call him up and apologize if she felt that bad about saying some stupid things to him. Dan's ex was gone though, apology was no longer an option.

He fell into a sullen silence for a minute. Instead of trying to give him more useless words of wisdom, Denise reached out a sympathetic hand and rubbed his back lightly. It seemed to bring him back from inside his mind.

"I dropped her out there. Back a few months ago, during that stupid Disco King and Queen competition. I wasn't paying attention, and my arms gave out, and...." He held up his hands in the same positions they had been, re-enacting the moment. "She was so mad, you could tell by the look on her face. That stupid disco thing meant so much to her, and I just didn't give a shit about it. But that's where all the trouble started. I mean, sure, we got in fights before, but after that it was different. We couldn't go one day without fighting. I just thought it was all so stupid. I just stopped caring, about her, about the whole relationship. I didn't even try to work it out with her. And finally I just got sick of all the fights and the drama. Just got sick of her in general. So I gave up. I wrote her a dumb note, telling her I didn't want to be with her anymore, we'd be better off as friends, you know, stuff like that."

Dan clearly remembered that Friday afternoon in late October, dropping her off after school at her huge house in the high class part of town. It had been a silent brooding drive from DeAngelo High back to her house, and he had made up some dumb excuse that his mom wanted him home to do some chores and study for the S.A.T. He remembered handing her the folded sheet of notebook paper right as she got out of his car, pretending he had just remembered to give it to her. It had actually been on his mind the whole way home and most of the afternoon. He could barely make eye contact with her while he handed it over, instead he looked at those four pretentious white pillars that curved around her front door. He had seen the suspicious look in her eyes, but drove off quickly, not even waiting for her to walk to the front door.

He had made it a point to leave his house that night, not wanting to spend all night fighting with her on the phone. After he told his mom what happened, she had been relieved and happy. She'd had a case of Dislike-At-First-Sight with Mary Anne. Dan asked his mom to tell Mary Anne that he wasn't home if she called. He had gone over to Gary's house to hang out with his friends, but Mary Anne had called him there. Later, he figured that she had probably called all of his friend's houses, and maybe even gone driving around looking for him in that sporty red Corvette of hers. She had begged him to come over to her house, had even gone so far as to make up some lame excuse that she was sick and her parents were gone and she needed someone to be there with her. He had coldly rejected her, telling her he was busy with his friends and there was nothing else to talk about. Then he had quietly hung up on her as she pleaded for him to stay on the phone. The whole rest of the night, he hadn't really enjoyed himself, he could only think of her. He kept imagining her in her princessy bedroom near the top of that curved grand staircase, laying on her canopy bed under the posters of John Travolta and the Bee Gees, listening to some break-up song by ABBA, maybe "Knowing Me, Knowing You," or "S.O.S." She was so obsessed with ABBA.

All these memories and bad feelings flashed through Dan's mind in a matter of seconds, adding weight to the fact that the girl he had caused so much pain was now lying dead out on that rink somewhere.

"She tried to starve herself to death or something," he continued out loud. "I heard she ended up going to the hospital for a few days. I never really got the full details."

"Jesus," Denise said.

"But that's how she was. She was always such a drama queen, even from the very beginning. That's why I didn't believe her when I heard her screaming out there tonight. All I thought at first was, *She's at it again. What a fucking drama queen. What a faker."* Dan's whispered voice took on a bitter, mocking tone. He ended the impression of his inner monologue and shook his head in shame. "I actually heard her die tonight. Do you get that? I heard them all *die!"* The tears began to well up in his eyes and Denise could see he was on the verge of going into hysterics. She dropped her shredded napkin, reached over, and gave him a hard shake by the shoulders.

"Knock it off!" she whispered harshly at him, and glanced up at the door. "And keep your fucking voice down." With her hands still on his shoulders, she looked into his eyes, reverting back to a calmer tone. "Mellow out and listen to me. None of this is your fault.

Something happened here tonight. It's still happening. I think I know who's doing this."

Dan looked up at her with wide eyes. "What are you talking about?"

Now she had his attention, and she began to tell him what she knew.

## 2

"Have you ever heard of a guy named Charlie Hart?" she asked.

Dan shook his head.

"He's the guy who works at that old graveyard next door, Hart Hill Cemetery." Now a flicker of recognition dawned in Dan's pale face, he had heard vague things about Charlie Hart somewhere, but he couldn't quite remember where. *Did my parents say something about him? Or was it maybe my grandparents? Or somewhere else?*

"I saw him today," Denise continued. "It was earlier this afternoon, right after I first got here. Supposedly no one around town has seen him in months, they say he never leaves the graveyard. Some of the people who work here have told me stories about him. They say he's crazy. This girl, Diane, she works at the snack counter too, she said she was walking out to her car one night and heard him out there in the dark crying and moaning. She thought it was a ghost in the graveyard or something stupid like that. So she got in her car, turned on her headlights, and saw him standing out there in the dark all by himself. She said he looked creepier than any ghost could ever be. I've heard all kinds of stuff about him, but I never *saw* him until today."

"What was he doing?" Dan asked.

"I was taking out the trash and it started snowing," Denise began. "I was watching the snowflakes coming down. Then I looked over, and there he was in the graveyard. I thought he was a statue at first, then he moved just enough for me to see him. He had that same costume on and he was just standing there, looking right at me."

"But *Mike* brought that costume in. It...it was Mike Cavallo, from my school," Dan said uncertainly.

"Do you really believe that Mike guy is the one who killed all your friends?"

Dan honestly considered the question. "I guess not. I mean, Mike's a dickhead, but he's not...you know, crazy. At least I don't *think* he's crazy."

"It wasn't him. I know the kid you're talking about, I saw when he and that other kid first put those costumes on. They jumped out of the bathrooms and scared this little freshman kid. Then later, right before you walked up to talk to me again, I watched him and his friends out on the rink passing around a Pepsi cup, I think they spiked it with something. He wasn't wearing that costume at all, didn't even have it near him."

Dan shrugged. Guys standing around drinking before midnight, that sounded like Mike Cavallo's gang all right. Mike getting drunk: that was totally believable. Mike murdering people though?

"Also, he looked pretty drunk," Denise continued. "Do you think you could get around on skates that smooth if you were drunk?"

"I guess not." Dan looked down, his mind racing. "But if it wasn't Mike, then--"

"I'm telling you, it's that guy, Charlie Hart. He must have just snapped."

Dan had never seen Charlie Hart before in his life. He imagined a graying, haggard-looking Charlie

Hart bursting in through the front doors, finding Mike's costume somewhere, putting it on, and....

"Wait a minute. How'd he get in the building?" Dan said aloud. "We're all locked in, remember? Chains and padlock on the front door and everything." Now it was Denise's turn to look down doubtfully, trying to puzzle her way through the question. "And all the emergency exits are locked or frozen shut or something. You saw them all out on the rink pushing up against those doors. They wouldn't budge."

"Maybe he got in here earlier and was hiding out this whole time."

"Where, though? This place is full of people. We're probably in one of the only hiding spots in the whole building. Is there any other way in and out of here besides the front doors and those two emergency exits?"

Denise thought about it for a second, mentally going over every entrance and exit. "There's the roof access back in the skate rental room. But that's locked from the inside." She shook her head, dismissing her own suggestion.

"Then how did he get in?" Dan repeated.

"How the hell should *I* know?"

They both glanced guiltily at the door, they had both been letting their voices get louder and louder. Denise mouthed the word *sorry*. They sat in silence for a minute before Dan finally whispered again.

"We *have* to get outta here. And we have to call for help. Some people might still be alive out there."

Denise thought about it. There was a phone in Geno's office, another phone in the skate rental storage room, and a payphone out in the front lobby. Every escape scenario she imagined involved finding a set of keys somewhere. Her own car keys were back with her jacket in the employee coat closet near Geno's office. She had no idea where the keys for the padlocked front doors were. They couldn't do anything without venturing out there, into the killer's territory.

"There's gotta be some way we can get out of here," Dan said with a hopeful, desperate look on his face.

"Not without leaving this room," she replied dismally. "And he might still be out there waiting for us."

Dan's pleading desperate look turned into one of frustrated anger for a second, but he winced, clenched his jaw and fists, and willed the anger away.

"Fuck!" he whispered. "Then we're trapped in here."

Denise only responded by giving him a haunted, tense look. Dan lowered his head back down on the shelf with the candy bars. They both sat back for a few minutes, the conversation running dry.

Then Denise's hand crept into his, their cool fingers lacing together tightly. Dan looked down at their linked hands, then up at Denise. Even with her pale, waxy skin, dark circles under her eyes, and disheveled hair, Dan couldn't take his eyes off her. All the swirling thoughts and memories, all those terrible voices going off in his head, Denise seemed to drown them all out. She had a kind of pleading look on her face, a look that said: *Hold me, I need someone to hold me right now.* It wasn't a sexual look, more of a desperate need for comfort.

His heart began pounding again as he sat up straight and scooted closer to her. She inched a little closer to him also. He turned his body around so that they would both be facing the door. While he rearranged his position, he didn't let go of her hand. He remembered how they had first shaken hands earlier that night, and how he had loved the feel of her soft hands against his. They had made some kind of deal, what had it been? He couldn't remember. It was so hard to think while staring into her eyes and holding her hand like that.

Dan swept his free left arm up over her head and lowered it around Denise's shoulders. As he brought his arm down, she scooted even closer, snuggling up to him. She had meant to rest her head on his shoulder and just stare off into space, yet somehow she couldn't tear her eyes away from him either. If either one of them had turned their head at that moment, the other would have also turned away. But they didn't turn, couldn't. Instead, they began to slowly lean in to each other.

*Is this really happening?* Denise asked herself. *What am I doing? This is no time for this. This is... is...*

Dan felt he was going too far. He couldn't kiss this girl, he barely knew her. And after everything that happened, what a terrible way to have a first kiss. Still, it felt so good, so right. He gave in, let his body lean where it wanted to lean, let his lips kiss who they wanted to kiss. Denise. The hot girl at the snack counter. Beautiful Denise.

Their lips came together and it was so sweet, like a red rose standing defiantly in the middle of a bleak snow-covered graveyard. They kissed and parted, kissed and parted again, enjoying each other, savoring each other's warmth and comfort.

Finally, they pulled their faces back a few inches and just stared at each other, smiling and lost in each other's eyes. Neither knew what to say, what to think. After a moment, Denise broke the silence.

"This is crazy," she whispered.

"Yeah, I know," Dan replied with an excited breath of a laugh. "What are we gonna do?"

"I don't know. Just wait, I guess."

"For how long?"

"Until he comes looking for us," Denise said morbidly.

"Don't say that."

Without a moment's hesitation, Denise drew forward and they began to kiss again. For a second, they both ran her last sentence back in their minds. Dan didn't want to believe her, but he knew that what she had said was true. Death would come looking for them...eventually. At least the wait would be sweet.

# Chapter Ten:

# The Ceiling

## 1

As soon as "Auld Lang Syne" started up, Freddy Atkinson had crawled out from under the desk in his Uncle Geno's office. If the stereo was up and running, surely the power would be working again too. Sitting in the dark listening to that ghostly music and those screams was just too much for Freddy. He reached for the small desk lamp, flicked the switch, and a dim warm light illuminated the desktop. The lamp wasn't much brighter than a child's night-light, and it cast shadows across the rest of the room.

Freddy began desperately searching the desktop for a weapon. Anything would do; a gun, a baseball bat, a knife, scissors, a letter opener. Hell, he'd even settle for a lousy screwdriver. No luck. There were only stacks of unorganized bills and invoices, accounting notebooks, and blueprints of the building, he tossed a few of these useless items to the floor. He ran his finger over the sharp tip of a pointed metal ring in one of the notebooks, and considered ripping it out to use it as a weapon.

*What the hell are you gonna do with that? Poke that crazy fucker to death?*

"Fuck!" he exhaled and bent the notebook in his clenched fists.

He searched through the stacks of papers, looking around and under them. Papers led to papers, which led to more papers, and finally dead-ended at the solid scratched surface of the desk.

"Shit! Come on, Uncle Geno!" he whispered out loud. "What the hell kind of office is this? Give me something I can use."

Panic had set in, holding Freddy in its tight grip. This was a full-fledged emergency, and Uncle Geno was nowhere to be found. He had to try to think of something, had to figure out how to stop whatever was going on in the rink, but his brain refused to cooperate and give him any answers. He snatched up the phone off the corner of the desk again, held it to his ear, and jiggled the cradle with his index finger. He had first tried the phone right after he slammed the door shut and locked it. It was still dead. He remembered Tony Tanner telling him the phones were down, and how he had calmly responded, *It's a fuckin' blizzard out there. What d'ya expect?*

*Why didn't I listen to that guy? Why didn't I fuckin' listen?*

Again he pressed the phone hard into his ear, hoping to hear a dial tone.

"Goddammit! Don't do this to me."

As Freddy gritted his teeth and jiggled the phone cradle hard, "Auld Lang Syne" ended, leaving the rink in desolate silence. He looked up, his face sweaty, his normally perfect black hair hanging down in uneven sweaty clumps. The phone slid out of his sweaty hand and he bobbled it. Luckily, he caught it mere inches before it clattered against the wood desk below. He carefully set the phone down on the cradle, trying to make as little noise as humanly possible. With no working phone and no weapons, he was out of options. The killer might come searching for him at any moment.

In slow creeping steps, he worked his way back to the corner under the desk. He crawled underneath again, trying not to let the thick heels of his platform shoes clunk against the floor. Once he was fully underneath, he carefully unbuckled the shoes and set them off to the side. It would be far better to leave them here if he had to be sneaking around, or if, God forbid, he had to run. He pulled his knees up to his chest and waited. In his hands he held the little gold medallion that hung on the gold chain around his neck. He clung to it like a man holding a cross to ward off a vampire. His eyes stared straight ahead, focused on nothing. He only listened carefully for any noise outside the door, and tried to think of how the hell he could get out of here.

## 2

As Freddy sat alone in the office, his thoughts drifted back to Uncle Geno. Just where the hell had he disappeared to? Freddy hadn't seem him in hours, and Tony Tanner had said the same thing.

*That fuckin' maniac got him. He's dead.*

No, he refused to believe it. He wouldn't allow himself to start thinking like that. Those kinds of thoughts weren't going to help the situation at all. He didn't know anything for sure yet. For all he knew, Uncle Geno had split as soon as the screams started. He could be out driving through the snow to the police station for help right now. Freddy concentrated on that, imagining Uncle Geno out in the truck with the snow plow, the windshield wipers brushing thick blankets of snowflakes off his windshield as fast as they could. The bald tires would spin and slide around in the snow all the way there, but Uncle Geno would finally make it. He would burst through the doors and scream, *There's a murderer at the rink! You've gotta come quick!* And the cavalry would storm through the blizzard and rescue all the survivors, that is, if there were any left besides him. There had to be more survivors though. That foxy Denise was away from the rink when the lights went out, she probably ran into the back pantry or something.

Freddy spent a long time with this fantasy, trying to forget the image of that psycho in the horrible skull mask and death cloak slashing through people with that scythe under all those blazing red lights, like some demon risen from hell. He tried to convince himself that this fantasy of Uncle Geno's trek to the police station wasn't just wishful thinking like the rational part of his mind kept insisting.

As his ass and legs began to ache, he came back to reality. He had to sit up, had to stretch his legs out before they fell asleep. He leaned out from under the desk, setting his hand down on one of the papers that had fluttered to the floor during his mad search for a weapon. The paper crackled loudly under his hand, and he pulled it back with a wince and a little hiss of fear.

In the dim light, he saw something on the piece of paper that caught his eye. He bent forward, peering down at some kind of map with scribbly handwriting on it. It was clearly a map of the northeast corner of town. The paper looked yellowed and old, as if it had been made sometime in the fifties. Near the top in permanent marker, someone had scrawled the words: LAND ACQUISITION & POSSIBLE FUTURE DEVELOPMENTS.

*Why would Uncle Geno have this out on his desk tonight?* he wondered. As he looked closer, he recognized the thin bisecting lines that were 120th Avenue going east and west, and Hart Street going north and south. The large rectangle northeast of the intersection was shaded light green, and the original mapmaker had labeled it: *HART HILL CEMETERY.*

*Jeez, I didn't know it was* that *big,* Freddy thought. The cemetery did indeed stretch farther north and east into what he had originally thought was just open space. He figured that at one point, the cemetery must have stretched all the way out to where the highway is now.

Near the lower middle of the Hart Hill Cemetery rectangle was another solid black rectangle, hand-drawn in pen. Based on how close it was to 120th Avenue, Freddy figured it must have represented the property lines for Rollerville. A big oval was drawn just north of Rollerville, it stretched out over most of the north end of the cemetery. Penciled in the middle of the oval was the word: *CONDOS??*

So they were developing all this land that once belonged to the Hart Hill Cemetery and the old Hart family, who had founded the town and mostly all relocated to bigger cities.

*Surely, they didn't actually use all that land for graves though, right? I mean, this town hasn't been here that long, has it? What if some time in the past they spread out from that southwest corner where the graves were so thick? If they had, then that would mean that Rollerville is....*

"....built over graves," he whispered aloud. The idea of skating over peoples graves gave Freddy a chill. How many nights had he been here past midnight? He had always wondered why he seemed to get the creeps for no apparent reason. He would get that cold tickle on the back of his neck, a feeling that went away when there were dozens of people rolling around on skates, laughing and having a good time. That feeling that evaporated with a pounding disco song blaring in your ears. Hell, he might even be kneeling over someone's grave right now, a long dead body lying underneath the floor.

Freddy moved backward instinctively, bumping into the desk.

"Stop it, just stop. You hear me?" he whispered to himself.

*There are no bodies buried underneath the floor here. And even if there are, so what? It's not like they're gonna crawl up out of the floor like some dumb horror movie. They're dead. Only the living can hurt the living, like that psycho in the death....*

The truth suddenly came crashing down on him as the pieces came together.

"It was *him*. That son of a bitch!"

Charlie Hart, that crazy drunk who took care of the Hart Hill Cemetery. That had to be him under the mask and the death costume. Sometimes Freddy would drive down the street toward Rollerville's parking lot and see him out there tending the grounds in the graveyard. He was a thin guy with a stubbly gaunt face and medium-length, gray, scraggly hair that he slicked back on the sides with Butch Wax. Every now and then, he would be out mowing or trimming the tree limbs, and would stop and glare at Freddy's car as he passed.

Freddy remembered a day back in April, the only time he had ever encountered Charlie Hart face to face. That afternoon, he parked his car in one of the farthest spaces in the back of the parking lot, one that lined up along the green chain-link fence separating the parking lot and the old graveyard. Uncle Geno asked all the employees to park in the back, and Freddy could've easily ignored him, but he wanted to show all the other employees that he didn't get special treatment just because his uncle ran the place.

He had just gotten out of his car, and a beer bottle came flying over the fence to shatter at his feet. Freddy had whipped around to see Charlie Hart standing there behind the fence, wobbling drunkenly on his feet, giving him a red-eyed, baleful glare. He held a shovel tightly in his hands, and his jaw was clenched.

Charlie Hart had said, "You tell those fuggin' kids to keep their goddamn trash outta here. Y'understand me, boy?"

"What?" Freddy had replied.

"This is 'allowed ground, ya got that? Hhhallowed ground." He had forgotten to pronounce the first H sound, then tried to make up for it by drawing out the second. "Keep your fuggin' trash off'n it. Let these poor people rest in peace. How'd you like it if fuggin' kids threw shit all over your grave, *huh?*"

"Look, Mister, I'm sorry, I have no control over what kids do out here."

Charlie Hart lashed out with the shovel, slamming it into the chain link fence at head level. Freddy ducked instinctively.

"You back-sassin' me, boy?"

"No, I'm not. Jesus Christ!"

Charlie Hart glared at him, looking like he wanted to rip Freddy's guts out. Then his hands and jaw unclenched, and he dismissively turned away, mumbling to himself.

"Gowan, get the fuggoutta here, kid." He turned back with one eye cocked at Freddy, and pointed a bony, dirty finger at him. "But next time I see more trash over here, I'll come over there an' teach you all a lesson you ain't never gonna *forget!*" Charlie Hart dropped the shovel, ran up to the fence, and started to rattle it violently. He began to rave and his words became garbled, spittle sprayed the fence.

    Without another word Freddy turned around and got back in his car. That was the last time he ever parked in the back of the parking lot near the graveyard fence. He parked near the entrance from then on, even though he knew Uncle Geno didn't like it. Freddy remembered walking up to the building and taking one last look over his shoulder at Charlie Hart. The man had a sad look on his drawn, haggard face, and his head hung low. He seemed to have gone from belligerently angry, to mournful in about two minutes. With one raised eyebrow, Freddy turned and walked into the building thinking, *What a fuckin' creep.*

    Now Charlie Hart had lost it. Somehow he had gotten into the building tonight and murdered almost everyone inside. Uncle Geno had had his fair share of confrontations with the man as well. He must have suspected something might happen tonight, why else would he be looking at these papers? That still left the question of just where the hell Uncle Geno was. Had he been out there somewhere in the crowd? No, he couldn't have been, otherwise Freddy would have heard him yelling in the chaotic darkness along with everyone else. Was he out in the plow truck? Maybe, but he had told Freddy he wouldn't be out there all night, he'd said he'd maybe only go out once tonight, and once early in the morning. Apparently, no one had seen him for hours. Tony Tanner had said so, and Freddy had also regretfully shrugged that off as no big deal.

    *The maniac got him, he's dead*, his mind repeated. Again, he went back to that fantasy of Uncle Geno driving through the snow, but this time he realized how ridiculous it was. He desperately wished that someone, *anyone*, was out driving through the snowstorm going to get help.

    *I'd even do it if I wasn't stuck in this stuffy*

*office.* The simple idea fell into his mind like a puzzle piece. Why hadn't he thought of that before? If Uncle Geno wasn't the one driving out through the storm for help, it would have to be Freddy. It would be up to him to go get help, to save them all.

But how the hell could he get out of the building? The front door was chained shut. Both the emergency exit doors were out of the question. He had no idea how it had happened, but he guessed that the emergency exits had been blocked by huge piles of snow or frozen shut or something. The only other way in and out of the building was the roof exit, but that was all the way across the rink in the skate rental storage room. And Freddy wouldn't leave this office unless he was absolutely certain that the killer had actually left the building.

*The roof, the roof. How can I get to the fucking roof?* he thought to himself. *God, my brain just ain't workin' right tonight.* He stared up at the ceiling, trying hard to think, and a third idea hit him.

The ceiling was the answer. He could push away those flimsy white ceiling tiles, climb up into the ceiling, and crawl along the grid work to the skate rental room without the killer being able to reach him.

A wave of doubt rolled over Freddy. *I can't do this. What if that psycho hears me up there? The ceiling isn't so high off the ground that that long ass blade couldn't reach me. Also it's pitch black dark up there, and there's probably spiders.*

*There are a lot worse things than spiders down here waiting to find you, probably looking for you this very minute.* He imagined himself free from the building, driving away for help, breathing in the cold clean air and feeling the snowflakes melting in his hair. That decided it. It had to be him, there was no other way.

There was a five foot tall bookshelf in the corner made of a sturdy metal frame and particle board shelves. It was an ugly utilitarian thing, meant only for backroom offices and storage spaces. It would give him enough height to reach the ceiling and pull himself up.

"Here goes nothin,'" he whispered. He walked over to the bookshelf, let out a deep sigh, and began to climb.

## 3

A thin puff of dust blew into Freddy's face when he lifted up the first ceiling tile in the corner of the office. He squinted, turned his head away, and tried to blink the dust out of his eyes. The bookshelf wobbled precariously under his feet, making him jerk with a little startled surprise. He stopped moving, steadied himself, then slid the ceiling tile out of the way. A wave of cold, musty air wafted down from the dark hole above his head.

*I can do this, I can do this.*

He placed both hands on the metal beams of the ceiling grid, bracing himself. He hopped up off the top of the bookshelf, then held himself up by his hands. The bookshelf thumped against the wall a few inches below his feet. With his knees bent, he tried to curl his legs and pull them up into the ceiling with the rest of his body. He rocked back and forth a few times, gaining momentum, then swung his feet up into the darkness. They came down just behind his hands on the ceiling grid, his socks sliding unsteadily on the smooth metal. He came dangerously close to sliding off the grid and breaking out the ceiling tiles on either side. He gritted his teeth as his body folded unnaturally. His tight bell-bottom pants dug painfully into his hips, and his lower back scraped against the bottom of the roof overhead. It felt like he was playing some deadly game of Twister with his body impossibly scrunched together like this. With a grunt of effort, he scooted his hands forward along the grid.

Now that he was in a more comfortable position, he had time to wince at the bounces in the ceiling grid and the noises he had made. He hoped to God that the killer hadn't been near enough to hear any of that. The bookshelf and ceiling grid had both settled now. He leaned back and twisted his top half around so that he could slide the dusty ceiling tile back into place. It whispered against the grid, then settled back into place with a light clatter. Except for the occasional pencil-thin beam of light shining up through holes or gaps between the tiles and the grid, Freddy was now in total darkness.

*Okay, just take it slow. Nice and easy.*

He began his slow crawl back toward the skate rental storage room in the far corner of the rink. He moved alongside the main wall in a crouched position. If he were to have removed any one of the ceiling tiles, he would see the coat racks mounted on the wall and those carpeted circular benches down below. The ceiling tiles were two feet wide by four feet long, so he squatted over one row with his hands and feet braced two feet apart on the ceiling grid. He slid his hands forward, then slid his legs forward. The roof was only inches away from the top of his head. After the first fifteen feet, he noticed that the farther he went, the more the grid beneath him wobbled and bounced. He drew in a tense, hissing breath and stopped moving.

*Shit! This thing is not meant to support my weight. Maybe this was a bad idea after all.* He looked back over his shoulder, considering going back and forgetting the whole thing. It was too late now.

Suddenly, a metal duct next to him gave a loud hollow *clunk* and whirred to life. Freddy jumped, felt the grid beneath him buckle even harder. He breathed in little tense gasps, his heart was pounding wildly.

*Get a hold of yourself, goddammit! It's just the fuckin' heat turning on.*

Freddy thought he heard the air ducts clunking in all directions, filling up with hot air all over the ceiling. He could already feel the heat radiating off of the duct, warming up the air up here. The combination of the heat and the dusty air was already starting to make him feel claustrophobic. He felt beads of sweat popping out on his forehead.

*Time to get moving*, he told himself. *The sooner I get going, the sooner I get out of here and get some fresh air.*

Freddy started sliding forward again, but his progress was short-lived. One of the thick steel beams supporting the roof seemed to materialize out of nowhere in the darkness, and he bumped face first into it without even slowing down. He hissed in pain and inched backwards. With one hand, he rubbed the sore spot on his aching forehead. He shook his head, trying to will away the dull thud. As soon as the pain began to subside, he felt along the bottom edge of the beam for any kind of opening and found none. The beam felt completely solid, blocking his path from the roof down to the ceiling grid.

*Shit! Why hadn't I thought about the damn support beams? Now how am I gonna get across? What a stupid idea this was.*

Freddy stubbornly refused to believe that this roadblock could stand in his way. There had to be some kind of opening somewhere, just had to. As he ran his hands along the bottom edge of the beam, he found a slight gap, no more than an inch wide, on his far right side. He leaned to the right, slid his hand through the gap, and felt an opening on the other side of the beam. *Were the beams angled up toward the middle of the building?* he wondered. He crab-walked over to the right, being careful to step over the next row of ceiling tiles, and continued to run his fingers along the bottom edge of the beam. Just as he had suspected, the gap under the beam widened. They *were* angling up toward the middle of the building. If only he could get out to the center of the rink, the gap between beams and the ceiling grid would be widest out there. Out near the center, he might have just enough room to slide underneath and continue along to the far side of the building.

*Well, I don't like it, I'll probably end up falling through the damn ceiling, but it's the only chance I've got.*

Freddy slowly turned his body to the right, putting the beam on his left side and the center of the rink in front of him. He tried to be quiet and keep the ceiling grid as still as possible. At first, he attempted to position himself like he had been before, spread out over the width of one row of ceiling tiles, but now that he had turned sideways, the ceiling tiles were lengthwise, and four feet was too far of a stretch. All he could do was keep his left side sliding along the ceiling grid like before, while his right hand and foot now had to reach over each tile before coming down on another bar of ceiling grid. He tentatively began his weird slide-crawl out into the middle of the building.

Left hand slide, right hand stretch. Left foot slide, right foot stretch. Each time his right foot came down on the grid, it gave an alarming bounce. More and more, he thought that once he got out into the middle of the rink, the whole damn ceiling would collapse and send him to the floor in a heap of dust and broken ceiling tiles. As he moved forward, he also had to brush random hanging electrical cables and thin strands of spider-web out of his way.

Periodically, he stopped and felt underneath the beam on his left side, the gap between the beam and the grid was getting wider and wider. It was now almost a foot wide, still too narrow for him to slide under, but it was getting there. This encouraged him and he sped up his pace a little. His left sock slipped in the dust on the ceiling grid. Instinctively, his right foot overcompensated and quickly came down past the ceiling grid. It stepped down too hard on a ceiling tile, and even over the loud whirr of the air ducts, he heard a soft crack. He stopped immediately, lifted his foot, and held it in the air. He was deathly afraid to set it back down in the wrong spot and break the ceiling tile out completely.

*It's okay. Just take it easy. No rush, just go nice and slow.* He forced himself to crawl forward again, and wondered just how far out into the center of the ceiling he had crawled.

Four ceiling tiles later, he bumped into another roadblock.

*For fuck's sake, what now?!*

This roadblock hadn't felt as hard and unyielding as the metal beam had though, this had a hollow feeling to it. He ran a hand along its papery surface, it felt like drywall. It curved in a wide arc in front of him and joined up with the beam on his left side. He stopped and tried to figure out where he was, mentally visualizing the geography of the rink. Up here in the dark, it was so hard to tell where anything was. Then it came to him, he was just outside the dining area, the TVs were mounted right on the other side of this curving wall. He blindly ran his fingers over the ceiling tiles directly in front of him and found a small triangular tile about the size and shape of a slice of pizza. He gently lifted it up.

Blessed cool air rushed up through the hole. Freddy hadn't realized how hot and stuffy the air had gotten up here until now. Those heat ducts were still running, wastefully working hard to warm up all those cooling bodies below.

The rink lights were usually pretty dim, but the pink and blue light that flooded in from that small gap was almost blinding to Freddy's dilated pupils. Once his eyes adjusted, he looked straight down and saw the curve of the short white cinder block wall and the wood floor of the rink on its left. To the right of the low wall, he could see the dark wood of one of the tables in the dining area. On the table he saw some rather saggy looking New Year's Eve balloons attached to a black plastic napkin holder. Mrs. Bauer had been still alive and sitting at this table reading only a few hours earlier, her paperback book was still there.

Using the light from the hole, he looked off to his left and saw the dark, eighteen-inch gap between the beam and the ceiling grid. It looked like an incredibly tight squeeze.

*How the hell am I gonna slide under that thing?*

Freddy replaced the triangular ceiling tile, shutting out the bright pink and blue light. He turned his body to the left, back in his original direction, pressing his right side up against the curving drywall. He stretched out into a push-up position and lowered himself until he was lying flat and centered over one length of the ceiling grid. The gold chain and the medallion around his neck clinked against the metal frame of the ceiling grid, and with one hand he tucked it into his shirt. He reached out, grabbed hold of a horizontal crosspiece in the ceiling grid in front of him, and pulled himself underneath the beam. The thin ceiling grid dug uncomfortably into his chest, making him wince. His back brushed against the beam's dusty metal surface. It was tight, but thankfully he managed to fit. At one point, his legs began to drag and bump against the ceiling tiles, so he crossed them and held them up in the air just above the grid.

Finally, he made it all the way to the other side of the beam. He lifted himself back up to that push-up position, and the ceiling grid bounced hard, the air ducts even gave a sympathetic rumble. He stopped moving and cautiously examined himself. Both his arms and legs were on the grid, not touching the ceiling tiles.

*Whoa, gotta be more careful,* he thought. *Don't wanna give myself away.*

He waited for a second, then took his time, slowly getting himself back into position squatting over a row of ceiling tiles. He took a deep breath, started sliding forward, and the grid bounced again.

S*omeone's up here with me.*

He froze and felt his blood run cold. Surely that couldn't have been him making the grid bounce like that. It was starting to get wobbly out here near the middle of the rink, but it wasn't *that* wobbly. He wasn't even close to the DJ booth yet. Was someone else up here hiding? He inhaled, meaning to call out; *Who's there?* His lips even formed the O shape before he caught himself.

*Wait! Don't, you idiot! What if it's him? What if it's Charlie Hart?* His heart sped up, he could practically hear it pounding in this cramped, dark space. That eerie feeling that he wasn't alone began to creep into his skin. He could feel someone else's presence nearby, it was just like all those late nights working here. There had always been something nasty about this place, he could never quite put his finger on it until now. You could feel it in the walls, feel it in the floor. Were there dead people buried underneath that floor? *Of course* there were. Dead people under the floor. Maybe there were even dead people up in the ceiling, crawling around.

Freddy glanced over his shoulder, getting ready to turn back around. He would just turn around and go back the way he came. *If I can even find the way back again.*

He felt another tremor in the grid and a metal air duct next to him made a soft, hollow boom. Freddy whipped his head towards it. All he could see was darkness.

He sat still, barely breathing, trying to decide whether he should continue forward or turn back. The ceiling grid was still now, yet the ducts continued to make little thumps and booms.

*Maybe it's just the heating system doin' somethin.' Christ, the damn thing's been on forever. It's fuckin' boilin' up here. It's probably about to shut down. That's all. Stop givin' yourself the creeps!*

Freddy warily began sliding forward again, taking his time, and paying extra attention to the noises in the ducts and any movements in the ceiling grid. There wasn't anything he could do to shake off that creepy feeling. He was trying to escape from a masked psycho murderer and crawling in the dark high above dozens of dead bodies. Wouldn't anyone get creepy feelings in a situation like this? He began to consider the bodies as he slid along the grid, asking himself: *How soon would a restless spirit start haunting a place after it was murdered anyway?*

*Just shut up and move. Stop thinkin' fucked up thoughts like that and just get the fuck outta here. Concentrate on what you're doin.'* He forced himself to think about the ceiling itself. He focused on harmless questions like: *Just how many more beams will I have to slide under like that? How far have I actually gone?*

Freddy sensed a stillness in the air only a few

inches in front of his face, it was the next beam. He reached out with his hand and his knuckles knocked against it. He let out a sigh of relief, grateful that he hadn't bumped his head a third time.

"Okay, round two," he whispered to himself.

Again he lowered himself down into that push-up position and pushed his way forward. The closest grid crosspiece was on his side of the beam this time, so with both hands, he pushed himself face first through the gap. As he slid forward, sticky strands of thick spider-web stretched across his face. Freddy gagged and closed his mouth tight, not wanting any of the nasty stuff to touch his tongue, it was bad enough that it coated his lips.

A second later, he felt the creepy-crawly sensation of tiny legs scurrying through his hair. Freddy desperately shook his head like a dog, shuddering with revulsion as the spider crawled to the back of his head. He felt the ceiling grid bouncing violently beneath him and he forced himself to stop moving. The little legs crawled out of his hair and dropped off somewhere else. With gasping little breaths, Freddy slid underneath the beam, ignoring the spider-web on his face for the moment. He hurried as fast as he could to the other side, desperately hoping the spider wouldn't crawl inside his shirt.

Once he was on the other side of the beam and back up in his forward position, he was able to reach up a hand and wipe the nasty spider-web off of his sweaty face. He gasped and pulled the little lingering strands off his ears and out of his hair. He let another revolted chill shudder its way violently down his back.

After his breathing calmed down a bit, he continued forward. He wished he could just shut off his brain entirely, wanting to just make it through this horrible night without having to think about it so much.

He came to the next beam, and this time he spread his hands out underneath it to brush away any spider-webs that might have been lurking. This time the gap underneath the beam was clear. He slid underneath the beam like before.

As he was hauling himself up into that push-up position again, a blinding white glimmer of something flashed in his eyes. He stopped dead.

*Whoa, what the fuck was that?* Freddy let his pupils adjust to the darkness again and saw a thin sliver of light shining up from the ceiling tiles about eight feet ahead of him. A few seconds later, that white glimmer flashed through again. It was one of those leopard-spot reflections off the big spinning disco ball.

*Jesus! Am I really only that far across the rink? Only halfway? I've been up here forever, I should be almost all the way across by now.*

Freddy slid forward toward the sliver of light. Upon closer inspection, he could see that it was a small corner broken off of one of the ceiling tiles. He stopped right above it and peered down through the hole. From his straight-down vantage point, he saw that he was now in between the DJ booth and the disco ball. Down on the floor below, he saw the stiff, bloodstained body of the goofy kid that had been wearing that New Year's Baby costume lying in a dark puddle next to a few other mangled teenage girls. The kid's skin was now as white as that stupid diaper he was wearing.

Freddy's stomach dropped at the gruesome sight below, and he turned away to his right, holding the back of his hand up to his mouth. In the dim light, he concentrated on the few things he *could* see. The biggest thing up here was the curving metal air duct that kept making those booming sounds. In front of the duct were electric wires that hung down inside a silver line of flexible metal conduit attached to the ceiling. They must have been the electric lines that connected down to the disco ball's spinning motor that was mounted on the other side of the ceiling tile. Metal bolts also hung down from the roof to help support the ceiling grid against all the added weight of the disco ball. He remembered that his uncle Geno had wanted to ensure that the heavy disco ball wouldn't fall to the floor and shatter, or even, God forbid, kill someone. Freddy stared at these things, only vague shapes in the dim light seeping in from that broken ceiling tile corner.

Just then, the heat finally turned off. The heat ducts shuddered, the whirring air sound faded down to nothing, and the entire place was left in thick silence.

"About time," he whispered to himself.

That was when he heard the breathing. It was shallow and muffled, blocked by rubber. It was right behind his head.

Freddy turned to his left and looked directly into the rotting skull face of death. A black gloved hand shot out and clamped tightly onto Freddy's throat. He uttered a choked, parroty scream and fell backwards. He landed on a thin intersecting X of ceiling grid, barely feeling the pain as it dug into his back.

The killer crawled on top of him in a second, feet braced on two lengths of ceiling grid. Both hands were locked on Freddy's neck, squeezing his windpipe. He gagged and dug his nails into the leather of the black gloves.

He writhed, struggling to kick backwards and out of the killer's tight grasp. He kicked jagged holes in the ceiling tiles, then his feet got stuck, thumping the tiles against the grid. His head crashed backwards against another tile, knocking half of it out. From a crazy upside-down point of view, he saw the broken chunk of ceiling tile tumble through the air, then splash into a dark puddle of blood on the floor. His head hung backwards in open air above the rink, cutting off his windpipe even more.

Bony fingers inside the gloves dug tighter and tighter into his throat, shaking with effort. Freddy's head shook with the cruel hands as they cut off his air and circulation. He felt his neck bulge with blood as it pooled in his head with nowhere to go. He could even feel his eyes beginning to swell up. Pinpricks of tiny colored lights seemed to twinkle in his eyes as he suffocated. He couldn't let go of the killer's hands around his throat, not even to grab something to defend himself (not that there was anything up in the ceiling he could use for defense anyway).

Freddy lifted his head back up into the darkness and looked at the death skull with its crooked teeth, black gums, and gray flaps of skin. His lungs began to burn and he panicked even harder. He clenched his hands into fists and beat at the killer's skinny arms.

One of the hands around Freddy's throat pulled away, and he felt a thin, but blessed, rush of air flow into his lungs. Some of the blood began to drain back into his body, making him feel all dizzy and light-headed.

The killer leaned forward and shoved Freddy's head out into the broken ceiling tile hole. His neck creaked painfully as it bent back in an impossible angle. A black gloved hand reached out, grabbed the long metal flex conduit, and yanked it forward. The killer let go of Freddy's neck and looped the conduit around his throat three times. Through his swimmy haze of consciousness, Freddy felt the metal circling around his neck. The black gloves crossed, grabbing opposite ends of the conduit, and tugged them tight.

Freddy began to struggle and jerk even harder as he realized what was happening. The conduit was even sharper and tighter than the bony fingers had been. The harder he thrashed, the tighter the killer pulled. He even felt the coiled metal break in a few places, cutting into the soft skin of his neck. With each of his convulsions, the grid bounced and bucked under his back. The long bolts hanging down from the roof did their job reinforcing the grid and it refused to give way.

The skull mask came forward, filling Freddy's vision. He could hear the panting animal breathing behind the mask as the killer held him in a death-grip.

"*Charlie*," Freddy choked out in little struggling squeaks. "*Please!*" The killer didn't respond, only kept a tight grip on the conduit.

Waves of gray and more tiny colored dots began to cloud Freddy's vision. He opened his mouth and closed it over and over again like a fish gasping for oxygen.

He had time to think, *Oh God, no. Please no! This can't be happening to me. I'm supposed to be driving outta here to rescue everyone. It was supposed to be me....*

The gray waves flooded out that awful skull. Its jutting upper teeth were the last thing Freddy saw. He felt the strength draining out of his arms and legs. He felt his brain growing sluggish as he continued to deny that this was happening to him. The gray became deeper and deeper, and the sounds of those animal pants behind the mask faded away into nothing.

Freddy passed out, and after another few minutes, he was gone.

As Freddy's body slumped, the killer loosened the grip around the conduit, and let his head hang down limply from the hole in the ceiling tile. The thick vein in the middle of Freddy's forehead slowly began to shrink as the blood drained to the back of his skull. The killer watched the leopard spots of light spin and dash across Freddy's purple, sweaty chin.

After a moment, the killer left Freddy up there,

slinking back into the shadows again. The black gloves reached down and pulled up the broken corner of ceiling tile, sliding it away to the side. This was just the reverse of what had been done earlier, when the killer had followed the sounds of Freddy up into the ceiling. Black clad legs dropped back down onto the desk in the DJ booth. The killer brushed the ceiling dust off the gloves. Without bothering to put the ceiling tile back into place, the killer hopped down off the desk and walked toward the carpeted steps leading down onto the rink, the scythe was leaning there. In one hand, the killer scooped it up, and walked off in search of the others.

## Chapter Eleven:

## Bus Ride

**1**

Jim and Gary were not getting along with Tony Tanner. They didn't like him, and didn't trust him. He was territorial and petty, making them feel that they were unwelcome in his precious hiding spot. He constantly gave them suspicious glances, as if he were ready to kick them out of the room at any second. Thankfully, Suzanne and Lindy were there to diffuse the situation.

Right after they had escaped the midnight massacre out on the rink and ran into the skate rental storage room, Tony had been trying to shove them back out the door. The sight of the crying girls stopped him dead in his tracks. Seeing them clutching each other like that made him feel ashamed that his first instinct had been to lock them out and leave them to die at the hands of that raging psycho.

Gary had frantically twisted the tiny lock in the metal door handle, and gave it an experimental tug.

"I hope to God that holds," he said, staring

skeptically at the door handle.

"Somebody call the police! We have to call 911!" Lindy cried.

Tony couldn't take his eyes off Lindy. At first glance, he thought she was his girlfriend, Michelle. Her face had an odd red and green Christmas-Noir look under the glowing green light from the Emergency Exit sign above the door, and the single red emergency light bulb mounted high up in the middle of the ceiling above the racks of skates. In the light of those weird, dim colors, he noticed all the features Lindy had that made her look similar to Michelle. She had the same red hair, the same freckles, and the same thin body. If the light had been brighter and more naturally colored, he would have seen the differences between the two of them much more easily.

Jim and Gary approached Tony, blocking his view of Lindy. "Is there a phone in here?" Gary asked frantically.

"The phone, where's the phone?" Jim demanded, without even giving him a chance to answer.

"The wall. On your left," Tony answered. They both looked over, saw the battered, old rotary dialer on the wall, and ran to it together. "It's dead though. I already tried it. It's been out for the past hour at least."

Jim ignored him, ran over to the phone, and yanked it off its cradle. Gary hung back and listened as Tony explained that it was dead. He looked over at Jim hopefully, but felt sick when he saw him jiggling the useless phone cradle.

*"Fuck!"* Jim screamed and slammed the phone down hard enough to make the ringer ding once in protest. He turned and glared at Tony between two shelves on the skate racks with an accusatory expression on his face. Tony responded by narrowing his eyes at him. That set Jim off, he stormed toward Tony. As Jim

passed the skate racks and turned to meet him, Suzanne reached out with clutching hands, wanting him to hold and comfort her. Jim was too mad though, he brushed past her, his eyes focused solely on Tony.

*"You!"* Jim began. Tony instinctively backed up a few steps. "You were gonna lock us out. We could've been *killed* out there! What the *fuck* is wrong with you?" He growled out the word *fuck,* and shoved Tony hard as he said it. Tony stumbled backwards only for a second, then his mouth twisted into a sneer. He caught his balance, rushed forward, and shoved Jim back as hard as he could.

*"Fuck you!"* Tony screamed. Jim flew back, his heels skidding against the floor. Luckily for Jim, he had taken his skates off to sit with Suzanne, and was in socks. If he'd had his skates still on, he would have fallen flat on his ass from that shove. Gary turned his skate wheels sideways and caught Jim, he was just barely able to help keep him on his feet. Jim recovered quickly, bounced back up, and ran back toward Tony again. This time Gary followed him.

*"Jim! Gary! Stop it!"* Suzanne screamed.

Jim and Gary slammed into Tony. The three of them were a mass of shoving, grabbing hands and fists. Lindy didn't stop to think, didn't even stop to take off her skates. She half-rolled, half-sprinted across the room, then wrestled her way in between the three of them.

*"Hey! Knock it off, you guys! Cool it!"* she shrieked fiercely. She shoved Tony back and all the fight went out of him. He had no desire to lay a forceful hand on her at all, or any girl for that matter, especially one that resembled Michelle so much. She held Gary back, and he tried to twist away briefly. *"Gary! Stop!"*

Jim was ready to launch himself at Tony again, but Suzanne had now joined in and was tugging one of his arms back as hard as she could. Suzanne outweighed him by fifty pounds and was able to hold his skinny frame back. Jim whirled on her, then stopped himself at the sight of her pale, tear-streaked face. Gary also stopped fighting and looked at Lindy questioningly.

Lindy stood with her arms out in the middle of their tight little circle in the back of the skate rental room.

"Do you realize that he could've left us for dead out there, L--" Jim began loudly.

"That's bullshit!" Tony retorted.

*"Shut up! Everyone just shut up!"* She interrupted the both of them, then fell silent. "Lower your fucking voices. Listen," she continued at a much lower volume.

As they sat there listening, the muffled sounds of agonized screams dwindled down from a half dozen people, to two or three, then down to one. Finally, silence.

"Don't anyone say another word," Lindy whispered gravely.

None of them had experienced silence like this in hours. The last time they'd had any peace and quiet had been late that afternoon. Now the quiet wasn't a relief, it felt wrong, full of evil omens. It hammered home the fact that everyone outside this room was either dying or already dead. All their friends, classmates, coworkers, all dead. Except for one. Death.

The five of them stood there in silence for the next few minutes, unsure of what to do, afraid to move or make a sound. Finally, Gary began slowly creeping toward the door, rolling forward and not letting his skates lift off the dirty concrete floor.

"What are you--" Jim whispered. Gary cut him off with a sharp snap of his index finger, and continued silently and cautiously towards the door. He approached it, turning his body sideways, preparing to run to the back of the room at the first sign of trouble. He leaned forward, pressed his ear to the door, and listened for any signs of life. There was nothing but empty silence. He turned back to the others and shrugged his shoulders. They glanced at each other in anticipation.

Gary turned back to the door, and suddenly the bright, white florescent lights flickered to life overhead. He gasped and jumped back. Suzanne clutched Jim tightly and whimpered. They all looked quickly up at the lights, then down at the door.

"Did he see us come back here?" Jim whispered. He turned to Gary and Tony for an answer, but they had none. "Did he?"

Gary backed away from the door and stood up straight when the ghostly crooning sound of Guy Lombardo's big band began oozing through the walls. Listening to that eerie music, he felt like someone had just walked over his grave. He grabbed Lindy's hand and held it tight. A few moments later, they heard the first of the screams. Gary felt sick as he recognized another one of the screams coming from their English teacher Mrs. Bauer. They had no choice but to lower their heads and endure the awful sounds of murder and old music.

**2**

The next few hours felt like they lasted all night. They sat around on the floor near the back of the skate rental storage room in morose silence. Suzanne had finally calmed down and was now dozing, lying sideways with her head in Jim's lap. He lightly ran one soothing hand over her dark hair, brushing her curled bangs off her forehead, and held his other hand up to shield his dry, exhausted eyes from the glare of the florescent lights. Tony sat in the back of the room with his knees up and his arms resting on them. Whether or not his girlfriend was drunk and off with some guy was the least of his concerns now, yet he still thought about her.

*Why couldn't I have just called in? Or left when I had the chance? We would be together now. That girl over there that looks like Michelle could actually be Michelle, and that guy would be me, and we'd be far away from this shit hole. And we would be fine and safe and....*

Gary sat with his back against the one of the racks of skates. Lindy was leaning on him, resting her head on his shoulder and gazing blankly down at the floor. They had both taken off their skates, located their shoes on the skate racks, and put them back on. Jim and Suzanne had found their shoes also. Everyone had agreed that it would be safer if they were all able to move comfortably in their own shoes.

Gary kept his eyes focused mostly on the door since no one else seemed to want to look at it. Fifteen minutes earlier, he had heard some strange bumping noises out on the other end of the rink. It had actually been the sound of Freddy's death struggles up in the ceiling, but Gary didn't know that. No one else had reacted to the sounds so he shrugged them off, hoping that they were just strange noises made by the heating ducts settling.

His neck was stiff from looking over to the right, so he turned his head the other way to even things out. He tilted his head and felt several satisfying cracks in his neck. Over on his left side against the far back wall, he caught Tony staring at Lindy for about the tenth time. He felt his blood boil watching the guy stare at Lindy like that.

"Hey," Gary whispered to him. Tony broke out

of his daze and looked up at Gary. "What the fuck are you starin' at? Why don't you take a picture, it'll last longer."

Lindy broke out of her own daze now and looked up at Gary with bleary eyes.

"Stop it. Don't start up again. Hey." She shook Gary's arm, but he refused to look back at her and break his glare with Tony.

"I'm sorry, okay? Jesus," Tony muttered in a low voice, then he turned to Lindy. "It's just that you remind me of somebody I know."

"Who?" she asked. Gary glanced at her, then narrowed his eyes suspiciously at Tony.

"My girlfriend." Gary softened a little bit at the mention of Tony's girlfriend, somehow it made him seem more human, and less of an asshole. "Her name is Michelle Connel. You wouldn't know her, she's--"

"My cousin!" Lindy finished for him. "Michelle is my cousin."

Tony's eyes lit up. "Really? That makes perfect sense now. You look a lot like her."

"Yeah, I hear that a lot. When we were kids, everyone always thought she was my older sister."

"I can see why. You wouldn't happen to know anything about that New Year's party, would you? The one at Leslie's house? I mean, who was planning on going? How crazy it's supposed to get? Stuff like that?"

Lindy shrugged and shook her head. "Honestly, I never really see Michelle anymore. We live a few blocks away, but we never see each other, or talk to each other, or anything. I don't know why."

"Oh." Tony looked disappointed. "I guess that would explain why I've never met *you* before."

"Yeah. It all seems so stupid now, after tonight, I mean. Living that close to your own family and not ever seeing them. I didn't even see her on Christmas."

Lindy looked ashamed and Tony made no reply. "I wish I was with her now instead of stuck in here."

Tony gave a brief, bitter laugh. "That makes two of us."

They fell into silence again, everyone lost in their own grim thoughts. Jim hadn't been paying much attention to their conversation, it didn't concern him or anyone he knew. He was thinking about Dan and how they had lost him tonight. He remembered how he had met Dan in seventh grade Home Ec class sewing tote bags. They had finished the bags early, then walked around stealing other people's school supplies, putting them in the tote bags, and dropping them off on other people's desks. They had laughed so hard back then, and to this day, if it came up in conversation, they still laughed hard about it. But now Dan was gone, his body lying out on that wood floor somewhere with all their other friends and classmates.

Jim felt his eyes welling up with tears and his lower lip began to tremble.

*Oh God, I don't wanna lose it here in front of everybody. Please don't let them see me cry.* Jim casually looked up, not to see anything, but to dry his eyes out. He bit down on his lower lip and tried to will away the tears, it seemed to do the trick. He blinked several times, and when his vision cleared, he was looking up the side of a wall-mounted metal ladder that went all the way to the ceiling. Two feet above the ladder's top rung, was a square hatchway with a metal handle.

"Hey, does that go all the way up onto the roof?" Jim asked Tony, being careful to keep his voice low.

Tony looked over at him in surprise, then looked up at the roof hatch. "Uh, yeah. What about it?"

Jim looked back up at it again and shrugged.

"Just wonderin.'" He continued to stare at the roof hatch, the wheels in his mind slowly turning. "But..." he added, "we could get out of here if we absolutely had to." He looked over at Gary for approval.

"What are you talking about?" Gary asked.

"I mean, we could get out onto the roof and go get help."

Suzanne sat up, Jim's voice had woken her up. "It's a blizzard out there. And the bus picked us up, remember? None of us have cars."

"*He* does." Jim pointed at Tony.

"I do," Tony replied. "There's only one problem though."

"What's that?"

"No keys. They're in my jacket pocket, and that's hanging up way on the other side of the rink. No coat, no keys. If this was July, I'd say we just walk, but none of us are exactly dressed for the weather if you know what I mean." Jim looked down at his own thin Ramones T-shirt and fell silent. Suzanne's low cut blouse was even thinner, and left more bare skin exposed than his T-shirt. Lindy's thin purple shirt didn't even have sleeves. Gary's orange and white striped polo shirt, and Tony's red button-up work shirt didn't look like they would do much against those howling winds either.

Jim almost decided to drop it and return to his sullen silence, but the image of that psycho in the black cloak and skull mask popped into his head again. In his mind, he saw Death tearing across the rink, slicing kids down with that long, razor sharp scythe blade.

"But if we had to go, I mean, if he comes lookin' for us, we might not have a choice."

Tony shrugged. "Key for the roof's right there above your head." He idly pointed above Jim's head with one finger.

Jim turned and saw the small metal lock box

mounted on the wall above him. He stood up and opened the box. Inside were half a dozen keys with flimsy white tags hanging up on pegs. The tags were labeled in handwritten blue ink. It only took a second for him to find the one with the word *ROOF* scribbled on its bent white tag. He lifted the key off its peg and looped the key-ring over his index finger.

He was about to turn away when he noticed another key hanging next to where the roof key had been. It was shaped like a car key, long with a large flat head. The scribbly blue word on its tag read: *BETTY SPARE*. He took out the key and held it for Tony to see.

"What's this?" he asked. "What does *BETTY SPARE* mean?"

Tony squinted at it for a second, then gave a little amused laugh. "Oh Betty, right. That's the bus. My boss calls it Betty for some reason, I have no idea why. He comes up with stupid names for shit all the time." Jim stared at Tony and the others, waiting for them to make the connection.

"Don't you guys see?" he asked. "We *could* drive out of here. We could take the bus."

Tony looked doubtful. "Have you ever driven a bus before? Have *any* of you?" They all shook their heads.

"No, have you?" Gary replied smartly.

"No, only Geno drives the bus. He doesn't trust anyone else to drive it."

"Well, how hard could it be?" Jim asked.

"Maybe in the snow it'd be harder, but I bet we could figure it out," Suzanne added. She gave them all a hopeful smile. Tony sighed, he had been about to make a cutting comeback, but Suzanne's shining smile made him soften his response. It was always so much easier for him to be a jerk to guys rather than girls.

"I don't know," he said doubtfully. "There's

gotta be a better way of getting out of here."

"Fine, you stay here and we'll take the bus," Jim suggested.

"I'm not lettin' you guys take that bus without me. You don't even know how to drive it. You'd crash it in five minutes. Then that would come back on me. No way."

"Then *you* come up with something if you're so smart," Jim said bitterly. Tony sat silently for almost a full minute, honestly giving the situation some careful consideration.

"You think he's gone yet?" Tony finally asked. "That psycho out there, I mean. It's been a while since we've heard anything. Maybe he left."

"I thought I heard something just a little bit ago," Gary said, remembering the sounds he had ignored. "It sounded like something bumping around on the other end of the rink."

"*I* didn't hear anything," Tony said.

"That's because you're sittin' way over there. And you're off in La-La Land."

Tony was starting to get irritated with these kids again, but he decided to try to take the high road and keep his cool.

"Well, what if that guy took off hours ago and we've just been sitting here this whole time for nothing? Did you ever think about that? What if he killed as many people as he could, then ran away to try to get ahead of the police that are gonna be hunting him down?"

"If he was gonna run away like that, then why did he turn the lights back on and play that creepy record?" Gary retorted.

"So he could see better and because he likes shitty old music," Tony replied sarcastically. "How the fuck should I know? And so what if he is out there? The five of us could go out there and take him down."

Gary and Jim both frowned at him. "What are you talking about? You want us to fight him?" Gary asked.

"You can't be serious. I'm not gonna fight that guy."

"Why not?"

"Oh gee, I don't know. Maybe because I don't want to get *stabbed!*"

"Look all I'm saying is that we might just be wasting a whole bunch of time sitting here when we could be getting the hell *out* of here." None of them responded, they only cast doubtful glances at one another. "I'm gonna go check it out, you stay here if you want to."

Tony stood up and began walking over to the door. Gary immediately got up and stood in his way.

"Don't go out there, man," he pleaded. "We don't know what's going on out there."

"Either come with me or get the hell out of my way," Tony said in a bored voice, trying to sidestep around him. Gary blocked his every movement. Jim also stood up, getting ready to step in if things escalated to a fight again.

"Did you ever stop to think that you might just be giving us all away?" Gary whispered through gritted teeth. "What if he's standing right outside the door waiting for us, huh? I'm not gonna let you get us all killed." Gary pointed an angry finger into Tony's chest, and Tony looked down at it as if it were a troublesome fly. He was four inches taller than Gary and outweighed him by at least seventy pounds.

"You take your fuckin' hand off me right now," Tony threatened. "Or I'll throw your ass out that door and you can find out for yourself."

Lindy stood up, getting ready to step in between them again, but stopped when she heard the door handle begin to jiggle slowly. They all whirled around and stared at it with wide eyes. When Suzanne heard it, she sprang to her feet and clung to Jim. The five of them stood still, clustered in a little group, watching the handle jiggle slowly up and down.

Then it began to rattle violently. The whole door thumped against its frame as if the killer were outside pulling it, trying to force it open. Lindy wrapped both of her hands tightly around one of Gary's. Suzanne buried her face in Jim's shirt.

The door thumped and shook, then fell silent. They stood there waiting for the door to start rattling and thumping again, but nothing happened. They all held their breath, not moving a muscle. Nothing happened for almost a full minute.

Tony turned to the others, giving each of them questioning glances. Jim finally broke the silence, whispering in his quietest voice, almost mouthing the words.

"Still wanna go check it out?" Jim asked. Tony only gave him a worried look.

"Do you think he heard us?" Gary asked, matching Jim's barely audible volume.

Before anyone could answer, the long scythe blade ripped through the thin door jamb with a crack. It sliced forward eight full inches just above the door handle, and stopped with a wooden, protesting squeak. The sides of the blade were covered with dark brown blotches of dried blood. It began to wiggle around, working its way down to the latch to try and unlock the door.

The group jumped back a few steps, all their faces had gone pale white. Suzanne and Lindy whimpered, and the boys began to breathe in short gasps. They glanced at each other, scrambling to figure out what to do. Tony looked up at the roof hatch and knew that the time had come.

"The roof," he said. "Time to go." He made no attempt to lower the volume of his voice, it was too late for that. Without another word, he took off, racing up the ladder to the roof.

*"Wait!"* Jim shouted, and followed him.

*"Go!"* Lindy cried and shoved Suzanne towards the ladder. Gary followed close behind Lindy, his eyes still on the door. The scythe blade still wiggled furiously in the door jamb, squeaking and scraping against the lock. The killer now began to kick the outside of the door with the thick rubber toe-stops on the end of blood-spattered skates. Gary watched Suzanne and Lindy slowly make their way up the ladder.

"Come on, come on. Hurry!" he urged.

At the top of the ladder, Tony came to the hatchway. The padlock near the roof's access handle was locked. He looked down at Jim.

*"The key! Gimme the key! Now!"* He held out his hand and Jim didn't hesitate to hand him the roof key. With trembling fingers, Tony fumbled the key into the padlock's keyhole, trying to keep an arm looped around the ladder at the same time.

Down below, Gary watched as the scythe blade slid out of the door frame and sliced back in again. It angled down and wiggled more fiercely than ever. Up above him, he could see Tony still clumsily trying to work the key into the padlock.

*If he doesn't hurry his ass up, I may not make it out of this room alive.*

Gary looked around the room for a weapon and saw nothing. There was a broom, a few dingy old towels used for polishing the rental skates, a box of spare shoe laces, a box of spare orange rubber skate wheels. His mind worked frantically, trying to figure out a way to use any of these things to their advantage. A vague plan was forming itself in his mind, it certainly wouldn't save them, but it might buy them some time.

Tony finally steadied his hands, slid the key into the padlock, and it popped open in his hands. With shaking eager fingers, he slid the padlock out of roof hatch's handle and let it drop to the floor. He gripped the icy handle of the hatch and turned it, expecting the door to swing open, but nothing happened. Earlier that fall, when he and Geno Atkinson had gone up there with a maintenance guy to fix one of the air handlers, it had swung open easily. Now something was wrong.

Placing his hand flat against the ice-cold, metal hatch, he yanked on the handle as hard as he could and pushed up at the same time. As he pushed against the hatch, he heard the thin brittle snaps of ice breaking.

*"What's wrong?"* Jim asked below. *"Hurry up, man!"*

*"I can't! The damn thing's frozen shut!"* He hammered it with his fist and felt it give a little with each hard thump.

The killer continued to pummel the door with pounding fists and heavy kicks. Gary could see the door frame shaking more and more with every kick, getting weaker by the second. That maniac was going to break through any second, and they were still stuck inside.

*"Hurry up! The door's not gonna hold much longer!"* Gary screamed. He picked up the box full of skate wheels, getting ready for step one of his plan.

*"Go! What are you waiting for?"* the girls screamed from halfway up the ladder.

Tony climbed up one more rung on the ladder, getting his body into a crouching position beneath the roof hatch. In one solid push with his legs, he jammed his whole body, shoulder first, into the door. He cried out with effort and felt a sharp pain in his shoulder.

The ice around the hatch gave a loud crunch,

and it lazily bounced open. A thick cloud of steam rose up into the night, while an icy swirl of snow and wind howled down into the skate storage room from above. To Tony, the hatch felt much heavier than normal because of the weight of two feet of snow that had piled up on top of it. He pushed the door open as high as it would go and felt some of the snow slide off. Now the full force of the snowy blizzard winds whirled down the ladder, dusting their heads and shoulders with fat snowflakes that melted almost instantly on their warm skin and clothes.

Tony scrambled out into the blizzard. Jim followed him up as quickly as he could, half preparing himself for the possibility that Tony would slam the hatch closed in his face. But when he reached the top of the ladder, he looked up and saw Tony's hand held out to help him up. He grasped it gratefully and hauled himself up onto the snowy roof.

Gary saw that they were finally moving and dumped the box of skate wheels out onto the floor in front of the door. He watched as they bounced and rolled toward the door like a rubbery orange river. He hoped the killer would trip on the skate wheels and fall, giving them some extra precious time to escape to the bus. He snagged the polishing towels off the hooks where they hung, slung them over his shoulder, and rushed up the ladder behind Lindy. Halfway to the top, he looked up and saw Jim's face peering down from the roof, his eyes squinting against the freezing blasts of wind and snow. Jim and Tony grabbed Lindy by the arms and hauled her out. Gary reached the top of the ladder and his hand slipped in the melted snow on the metal rungs. Tony and Jim reached down and grabbed his arms before he could fall back down into the skate rental storage room. With straining grunts, they yanked him up into the storm.

The door frame to the skate rental storage room

cracked and the door flew open, banging against the wall. They all heard the crash from up above. Gary clumsily gained his footing in the deep snow and turned around to see if the killer was coming up after them. Before he could see much of anything, Tony tackled the back of the snow covered hatch like a football player, slamming it shut. The last of the rising heat from the storage room was instantly whisked away by the wind, and the five of them were left out in the cold.

### 3

They could all feel the icy wind ripping into their bare skin, chilling them almost immediately. Suzanne and Lindy stood huddled together, it had only been a few seconds, but their teeth were already chattering. Gary went over to them and wrapped a towel around each of their shoulders.

"It's not much, but it'll help a little," he shouted over the howling wind. Thick clouds of steam rose from his mouth and were whipped away immediately with the wind and snow. The girls nodded gratefully at him. Lindy mouthed the word *Th-th-th-anks* through her chattering teeth, but none of them heard it.

*Thank God we all switched back into our shoes,* Jim thought. *No way I'd be able to handle this in bare feet.*

Tony pushed himself up off the closed hatch and stood up. He brushed clumps of snow off his red work shirt and shuddered as the cold wet fabric clung to his skin.

*"Come on, you guys! Don't just stand there! He's right behind us!"* Gary screamed.

*"But where do we go?"* Lindy yelled.

*"The front of the building! Come on!"* Tony answered back. He didn't wait for them to follow. He took off running across the roof toward the opposite side of the building. He waded his way through snow piled two feet high, his pumping legs kicking up clouds of powdery snowflakes. The others followed him, panting out plumes of steam. The thick snow bogged them down so much that even though they were pushing themselves hard enough to be sprinting across the roof, they could only manage the speed of a fast walk. Up ahead, they could just barely make out two faint cones of orange light high in the air, they were the streetlights shining down on the parking lot. From the back side of the roof where the hatch was, the swirling snow had masked those streetlights from view completely.

They ran past huge snow covered mounds that Gary assumed were the heating and air conditioning units. He barely noticed them, trying to keep up behind the girls and stay on his feet. He glanced over his shoulder, expecting to see the roof hatch opening up and the grim figure of Death climbing out after them. He saw only fat flying snowflakes.

While his head was turned, his foot slid underneath a two-inch gas pipe that fed into the heating units, and he fell sprawling into the snow. As he hit the roof, he slid forward, his face grinding painfully on chunks of ice. It burned against the hot skin on his cheeks, and soaked his jeans and striped polo shirt. The others felt the roof bounce slightly as Gary went down. Lindy turned to see him land hard, the deep snow had almost buried him as he skidded forward.

*"Gary!"* she screamed and turned back to help him up. She fell to her knees beside him and began tugging at his shoulders. *"Get up! Come on!"* Gary slipped in the snow and struggled to get back up on his own two feet. Lindy only succeeded in pulling him even

more off balance, making it harder for him to get up.

*"Just go, I'm fine! Go, goddammit!"*

Lindy ignored him, refusing to let go until he was on his feet and running with her.

Tony came to a sliding stop at the far edge of the roof. A cascade of snow fell past the glowing red neon Rollerville sign and dusted the top of the five foot high snowdrift that had piled up against the front of the building. There was the bus, a snow-covered hulk less than fifty feet away in the parking lot. Two feet of snow had piled up on its roof and deep snowdrifts were now almost to the tops of its wheels. He could see that Geno's plow truck had cleared most of the snow around the bus, the fire lane in front of the building, and through most of the empty parking lot, but eight or nine inches of fresh snow had already covered up his work. Tony spotted his car, a battered, ten-year-old Gremlin, on the far left side of the lot where the plow truck hadn't gone. It was just a white lump, completely buried in snow. Even if he'd had his own car keys with him, it would take a good twenty minutes to dig it out, and they were short on time. Also there was no guarantee that it wouldn't get stuck in deep snow out on the road somewhere.

Jim slid to a stop on Tony's right side and looked down at the parking lot. Suzanne slowed down, took small baby steps up to the edge beside Jim, and grabbed onto his arm. The red from the neon sign at their feet lit up their faces like the glow of a car's taillights.

"What now?" Jim asked Tony.

"How do we get down from here?" Suzanne asked, pulling the towel tightly around her shoulders. "Is there a ladder or something?"

"No," Tony said flatly, and turned around to see Gary and Lindy running towards them. "Is he coming?" He craned his neck to look back behind Gary, but the far side of the roof had disappeared behind a veil of falling snow and darkness.

"I don't know! I can't tell!" Gary shouted, panting as he ran up and joined them on the edge of the roof. Tony looked back and forth from the far side of the roof to the high snowdrift below.

"No time to find out," Tony replied gravely.

Without another moment of hesitation, Tony suddenly jumped off the roof. He screamed as he plummeted to the ground below. That red taillight glow from the neon sign flashed against his back as he fell. Their mouths dropped open and they cried out as he went down. Tony hit the snowdrift feet first and a huge dust cloud of snow plumed up all around him. After a second, he shook his head, then climbed out of the high drift.

"Jesus Christ!" Jim said. "He's out of his fucking mind."

*"Come on!"* Tony shouted from down below.

"There's gotta be another way down," Gary began. "Maybe we could--"

Then Lindy jumped off the edge of the roof, screaming into the wind. The dirty towel around her shoulders flapped in the air like a dingy superhero's cape. Her red hair flew out behind her.

*"Wait! Lindy!"* Gary and Suzanne both screamed after her.

She landed in the snowdrift next to where Tony had crashed down. A smaller dusty plume of snow blew up around her, but she began crawling her way out of the drift and into the parking lot a second later.

"Holy shit!" Gary laughed. He threw up his hands in a surrendering gesture and grinned at Jim and Suzanne. "I admit it, my girlfriend is braver than me!"

*"Come on, you guys!"* Lindy shouted from down below. She stood with Tony in front of the building, looking up at them and brushing snow off her

arms.

*"We don't have much time! He might be coming any second!"* Tony shouted with his hands cupped around his mouth.

"Okay," Gary whispered to himself, psyching himself up for the fall. He had always hated heights and had to work himself up to going on the roller coasters at amusement parks. "One, two, *three!*"

Gary launched himself off the edge of the roof, holding his breath as he fell down. He watched as a fat snowflake fell slowly right in front of his face, going slightly slower as they both fell. He crunched into the snowdrift, inhaling some of the snow cloud that billowed up around him. It stung in his nose like he had inhaled water while swimming, and he began to cough. He shook the snow out of his hair and face, and began crawling his way out of the thick snow.

Up above, Jim took another look behind them, there was still no sign of the killer.

"Jim, please don't leave me alone up here!" Suzanne pleaded through chattering teeth. She was shivering all over.

"I won't. I promise I won't, but you have to jump now."

"I can't. You know I hate heights." She looked down and backed away from the edge a step.

"Yeah, I know you hate heights, Suze, but you don't have a choice," Jim said, putting both of his hands on her shoulders, he could feel the thick goosebumps that covered them. He looked deep into her eyes, urging her to be brave, trying to mentally send her some of his own strength. "That guy is coming and he will *kill* you if you don't go now!"

*"Come on, Suze!"* Lindy shouted. *"You can do it!"*

*"You'll be okay, Suzanne!"* Gary shouted. *"It's

*not that far at all!"*

Tony rolled his eyes and prayed that he hadn't made a mistake by not grabbing the keys from that goofy punk-rock kid up on the roof. They couldn't get on the bus until he came down.

"I...can't. I'm sorry, but I just can't," Suzanne wailed, looking miserably into Jim's eyes. Jim stared at her for a second, reading the expression on her face. He saw that she really meant it, there was no way she would jump. He looked back and forth for an easier way down, but there were no other options. Time was running out. That psycho might be climbing onto the roof right now, coming for them.

Jim saw the tears welling up in her eyes, and became angry at her all over again. It was just like the skates that hurt her ankles. He hated to be angry at her, but he couldn't help it. *Why did she have to hate heights? Of all the girls I could go out with, I had to pick the biggest 'fraidy cat of them all. I can't even pick her up one foot off the ground without her freaking out.*

He remembered Gary picking Lindy up earlier that night, thinking that he would never have been able to do anything like that with Suzanne. The memory gave him an idea. He had no time to think about it though, he just went for it.

"I'm sorry to have to do this to you," he said.

*"No!"* she wailed, thinking he meant to jump off the roof without her. Before she could stop him, he bent down and swept her up off her feet like a firefighter. She immediately started screaming and thrashing around. He took two steps forward and jumped into the air.

Down below, the others gasped as Jim came dangerously close to hitting the neon sign. Suzanne shrieked in terror the whole way down, her legs kicking feebly in the air.

They crashed down into the snow, a white cloud

exploded around them. Jim's legs went deep into the snowdrift, almost hitting the pavement at the bottom. Suzanne barely made a dent in the snow. Jim let go of her as they landed, and she rolled forwards, tumbling down to the shallower area at the foot of the snowdrift. Lindy and Gary rushed over to help their friends up.

"Hey, you okay?" Lindy asked Suzanne, crawling in the snow toward her. Suzanne mumbled that she was fine. She was in too much of a daze to say much else.

"Dude, that was amazing! You looked like fuckin' Superman!" Gary yelled excitedly, as he helped pull Jim out of the deep, now packed, snow. Jim smiled back at him in dazed relief. He finally stood back up on two feet, brushed himself off, and walked over to Suzanne.

"Hey, you okay?" he asked softly.

Suzanne stared at him incredulously for a second, then launched herself into his arms, kissing him deeply on the mouth. He was forced backward a step, not expecting it at first, then he gave in. She broke away from him, then smacked him hard on the cheek with her clammy snow-covered palm.

*"Don't you ever do that to me again!"* she shouted in his face. He looked horrified and clutched his burning cheek with his own numb, ice-cold hand.

"Come on, come on," Tony urged from the front of the school bus. "Time for that shit later! We gotta get the fuck outta here!" He was already running around the front end of the bus to the folding door. The others followed him, freshly aware that they hadn't escaped yet.

# 4

Tony led the charge around the front end of the bus. It was one of the few vehicles in the nearly empty parking lot, and it had been parked facing south. Even though Geno had plowed around it, the wind and snow blasting out of the west had piled up a smooth snowdrift against its right side. It made the bus look like it was partially buried by a white sand dune.

He dug his way through the snowdrift, pawing away huge handfuls, digging a trench to the door. He thanked God that Geno had at least plowed some of the snow away, otherwise they wouldn't stand a chance of getting out of here alive. As the others came around the front end, Tony was already brushing away snow from the left side of the door, searching for the access panel. He finally found it and tried to pull it open, but his fingernails only scraped across ice. The panel was almost totally frozen over. Tony stuck his numb, clumsy hands in his pockets, feeling for the bus key, then remembered that Jim was the one who'd picked it up back in the storage room.

"Please tell me you brought the key," he yelled over another gust of icy wind.

Jim jammed his own numb fingers down into the thin pockets of his jeans, also feeling around for the key. It didn't help that his fingers were wet, ice cold, and he could barely move them. His jeans were soaking wet, caked with clumps of snow, and clinging to his goosebump-covered legs. There were even a few small clumps of melting snow down in his pockets. He finally scratched his fingertips against the ridges on the key, fished it out, and gave it to Tony.

"Oh, thank God!" Tony sighed. "Is he

coming?" Gary, shivering and crossing his freezing arms over his chest, squinted up at the roof and saw no one standing at the edge looking down on them. He looked down and saw no one running out the front door.

"No. Unless he's standing there in the dark. Can't see in all this fuckin' snow."

"Don'even think like that, man," Jim said to him. His face felt numb and stiff in the frigid cold, it was a struggle to get his lips to form the words properly. The girls gave each other a worried look as they stood huddled together with their teeth chattering and their lips turning blue. Their hair was soaking wet and the tops of their heads were completely white with snowflakes.

Tony chipped away at the ice with the key, then pulled the access panel open. To gain some of his dexterity back, he flexed his fingers, held his hands up to his mouth, and blew his own warm breath on them. He had to use both frozen hands to pinch the key and steady it enough to insert it into the little keyhole inside the panel. It finally slid in with a crunch, and he twisted it hard to the right.

With an icy ripping sound, the bus's front door folded open only a few inches, jamming up in the thick wet snow. Tony brushed away a giant scoop of snow from the bottom of the door, then yanked it open halfway with a grunt. Frozen clumps from the snowdrift fell in and covered the lowest step.

"Go'head! Hurry!" he said as he held the door open. His frozen lips caused him to slur his words too. Suzanne was the first on board, then Lindy, Jim, and Gary followed behind. Tony took one suspicious glance around the parking lot, saw no one, then climbed on board himself.

The inside of the bus was just as cold as it was outside. Without the wind relentlessly hammering them, their steamy breath lingered in the air. The girls stood near the front row of seats, held tightly in their boyfriend's arms. Everyone was soaking wet from the snow, Jim's heavily gelled hair had flattened and fell down over his forehead. All of their faces wore the same tense expression: red cheeks, bluish-purple lips, and wide eyes.

Tony glanced at Lindy and thought of Michelle. Soon he would be with her, he was on his way. He rubbed his hands together and blew on them again, it helped a little. He clumsily stuck the key in the ignition as he sat down at the driver's seat, and scanned the console for the lever that would close the door. At first, he saw nothing that would control it, then he looked off to his far right and saw the upturned lever sticking out of the lower part of the dashboard. He held onto the steering wheel with his left hand, leaned over, and pulled the lever towards him. With a squeaky metallic scrape, the door slapped itself closed and shut out the storm. The interior of the empty bus was now silent and echoey, their panting, nervous breaths seemed to reverberate off of everything. The howling wind outside rocked the bus and whistled in small crevices.

Tony twisted the key in the ignition. The bus's engine gave a few lazy turns, then stalled.

"Shit!" Tony whispered under his breath. Suzanne and Lindy looked at each other with matching expressions of dread, their teeth were still chattering. Tony gave it another crank and the engine struggled. It turned and turned, but wouldn't catch, making a lethargic *RrrRrrRrrRrr* sound. Jim and Gary kept their mouths shut and their eyes on Tony, praying that the engine would start.

"Pleasepleasepleaseplease!" Tony mumbled.

He let go of the key for a second, then gave it a third turn. Again it lazily turned, failing to catch, but Tony held the key tight. After twenty fruitless turns of the engine, he lost his patience, grabbed the wide steering wheel and shook it hard.

*"Come on, you fuckin' piece of shit!"* He turned the key again and suddenly the engine roared to life. *"YEAH!"* Tony screamed triumphantly, and clenched his clammy fists tight.

The four passengers exhaled steamy sighs of relief. Geno hadn't bothered to turn the heat controls off when he parked, and they blasted out cold air from the floor vents. They shuddered at the unpleasantly cold air now, but they knew it would turn warm in the next few minutes or so.

"Thank God!" Lindy said.

Tony revved the engine a few times to warm the bus up. He didn't want to put it into gear only to have it stall out. Once they were moving, he wouldn't stop the bus at all until they pulled into the nearest police station. Not red lights, not stop signs, nothing. He searched the controls for the windshield wipers, found them and flicked them on at high speed. The wet wipers broke away from a thin layer of ice and weakly pushed the thick snow off to one side of the bus. The visibility through the windshield wasn't great, but Tony could see enough to get going. Once the air from the defrost vents warmed up, he would be able to see a lot better.

"Okay, you guys might wanna sit down. I'm gonna have to punch it to get out of this snow," Tony warned them. They all obeyed. Jim and Suzanne took the seat on the left behind the driver's seat, Gary and Lindy took the opposite seat on the right behind the steps.

Tony revved the accelerator, then let his foot off the clutch fast. The bus jerked forward, and they all slammed back against their seats. A huge pile of snow slid off the roof and the hood. He made a hard right and gunned it toward the graveyard.

The four passengers flopped around on their seats like ragdolls.

"Jesus, man!" Gary exclaimed.

"Yeah, what the fuck are you doing?" Jim yelled, leaning over his seat.

"Shut up! Just shut the hell up and let me drive!" Tony fired back defensively. He shifted into second gear too quickly, and knew that was a mistake almost immediately. The bus jerked and its back end started to fishtail to the right. He braked hard and shifted back into first.

"You want me to drive?" Jim asked. "I can do a much better job than you."

Luckily, the wheels caught and they moved forward toward the graveyard fence. In the glow of the headlights, Tony could see several snow-covered headstones on the other side. He stared at the graves, hypnotized for a second, then realized the fence was coming up fast. He had forgotten that he was in this long beast of a bus, not his own tiny Gremlin.

He braked hard again and started making a wide turn back toward the road that ran alongside the parking lot. The bus's big tires crunched over thick snow that had piled up since Geno had last plowed. Suzanne leaned over and looked out the window, they seemed to be crawling along. At this rate, the killer would be able to run out and catch up with them.

"Can't you go any faster?" she asked.

"If I go any faster we'll be spinning out of control when we turn onto the road, honey," Tony snapped. "Then you'll be outside walking again. You want that?" Suzanne said nothing, only sat back in her seat. Jim saw Tony's eyes flick up and glare at Suzanne in the overhead mirror. "No? Then pipe down!"

"*HEY!* Knock it off!" Jim cried, and stood up out of his seat.

*"Everyone just stop talking, okay?"* Lindy shouted and the whole bus fell silent.

The bus almost made it through the turn onto the main road before the back end started sliding out of control again. Tony over-corrected and the bus started sliding in the opposite direction. He spun the wheel madly back and forth trying to get the bus going straight. The four of them clung to their seats with white knuckles, half certain that they'd spin off the road. Somehow, Tony got the bus on the straightaway though, leaving four long snaking tracks in the deep snow behind them.

Gary finally allowed himself a sigh of relief as the bus straightened out and began to drive confidently forward on the road that ran alongside the graveyard. The floor vents were even beginning to pump out blessedly warm air, and the temperature was already rising noticeably.

"We made it," Gary sighed.

"Yes!" Jim exhaled and hugged Suzanne tightly. She began to cry tears of relief. Tony wasn't so optimistic, and wouldn't be until they had safely reached a police station. He was still in the driver's seat, all five of their lives were still in his hands. They had escaped Rollerville and that maniac in the death costume, but they weren't safe yet.

*At least, I hope we escaped him.* The thought left a nagging flicker of doubt in the back of Tony's mind.

He turned to the driver's side mirror, looking back at the Rollerville parking lot. After a moment, something caught his eye, a flap of black in the middle of all that flying snow. It had flashed under one of those orange cones of light from a streetlight, then it was gone. He glanced back out at the road in front of him and saw nothing but fat snowflakes swooping down from the sky and flying straight at the windshield. The windshield wipers were having to work fast just to keep the glass clear.

Turning back to the mirror again, he saw nothing but the icy road and falling snow for a few seconds. He almost turned away when that flap of black caught his attention again. Now it wasn't just a vague flash, that black flapping shape was coming after them. It was Death running down the street, sprinting after them through the snow with that black cloak whipping back in the wind. The sight made his blood run cold.

"Oh shit," he whispered to himself.

"What is that?" Lindy asked. Tony didn't even hear her, he was so engrossed in watching the killer chasing them in the mirror. The only thing that pulled him out of it was Gary's cry of fear.

*"Holy shit! Look out!"*

Tony snapped forward and saw what stood in the road directly in front of the bus. At first he thought it was one of those big headstones from the graveyard, one with a statue of an angel with its arms spread wide. It led him to briefly believe that he had somehow accidentally driven the bus into the graveyard. Then the windshield wipers cleared away a thick pile of snow, and he saw that it wasn't a stone statue at all. It was a frozen corpse nailed to a thick wooden cross right out in the middle of the road. The corpse was covered in snow, but he could clearly see that its throat had been ripped open. Long red icicles of frozen blood hung down like a bib from the gaping wound in the corpse's slashed throat. Its mouth lolled open and its bluish purple tongue hung out grotesquely.

Tony instinctively slammed on the brakes. Just as the bus began to skid, he was horrified to discover that he recognized who the frozen corpse was. It was Geno Atkinson.

*"SHIT!"* he screamed. On impulse, he yanked the wheel to the left, trying to swerve around the grisly scarecrow that had been left in the road for them. He knew it was a mistake, he should have just hit the damn thing, but the damage was already done.

The brakes locked and the bus spun violently out of control for the second time that night. The four passengers screamed as they were whipped around. The bus tilted up on only the right side's wheels. Tony's foot remained clamped down on the brake pedal, he felt them grinding uselessly under his foot. He cranked hard on the wheel to turn back to the right, but now the bus's momentum and the ice on the road had all the control.

The bus careened toward the green fence around the graveyard, then the front end suddenly lurched forward and down. The front end of the bus went into the irrigation ditch on the side of the road, slamming to an abrupt stop.

Gary and Lindy were launched up out of their seats and crashed into the roof. They crumpled in an awkward heap on the stairs. The hard plastic edges of the steps snapped the bones in Lindy's left shin and Gary's right wrist. Jim and Suzanne slammed forward into the seat in front of them. Jim's head connected with a metal pole between the aisle and the driver's seat, and he was knocked into a semi-conscious daze. Suzanne slammed into the window hard, bruising up both of her arms. The window glass broke and sliced open the skin above her eyebrow. Tony had the steering wheel to brace himself with, and suffered the least amount of injuries. As they made their final jolting stop, he slammed forward and bumped his forehead hard on the steering wheel, then thumped violently back into the drivers seat unscathed.

The crumpled front end of the bus lay steaming in the snow. The whole bus was up at a weird, diagonal, funhouse angle, adding to everyone's sense of disorientation. The back end protruded up in the air, its back wheels spun slowly a foot off the ground.

No one heard the black gloved hand reach up and begin to turn the emergency exit back door handle.

They all lay there writhing in pain, moving around sluggishly, and trying to gain a sense of balance. They all wore the shell-shocked expressions, and their hair looked messy and disheveled. Tony sat in shocked silence, gasping for breath and trying to comprehend what just happened.

The bus jerked a little bit from the back end, pulling Tony out of his daze. He looked around in confusion, trying to figure out what caused the movement. He saw Lindy lying against the folding door in a heap with her boyfriend, grimacing in pain and clutching her leg. He didn't hear her though, he could only register a loud ringing in his ears.

Suddenly there was an angry scream of metal that he heard quite clearly. The emergency door at the back of the bus was ripped open, and the cold wind howled into the bus again. Tony turned back in his seat and saw the black silhouette of Death propping itself up in the emergency exit door frame.

Suzanne turned and peered over the edge of the seat with wide eyes. She saw Death rolling down the middle aisle of the bus on snowy skate wheels. In one hand, Death held a sickle, its curved, C-shaped blade tore into the leather on the back of each seat, foam padding spurted out of each cut. With a purring rip it sliced free and Death rolled forward another few feet. Suzanne shrieked Jim's name and tried to shake him awake. He moved groggily like a man in a deep sleep.

The killer skated down the center aisle, then stopped one row behind Suzanne and Jim. Suzanne slunk down to the floor as the skull-faced figure climbed

212

onto the backrest and slashed down wildly. She ducked, and turned her head away from the swinging sickle. The blade missed her by a few inches, but stuck deep into Jim's throat. She was looking right at him, and saw his eyes fly open as the sickle drove deep into his Adam's Apple. She shrieked as he choked and gagged. His blood rained down on her from above. She wanted to cringe away from him and reach out to help him at the same time. Death ripped the sickle out of Jim's throat and jumped forward.

In a mad panic, Tony had bolted out of the driver's seat, shoved Suzanne and Gary off to one side, and tried to yank the folding door open. Grabbing its bent edge, he tugged on it frantically. The door was twisted and bent, jammed into the sides of the irrigation ditch. Gary and Lindy's weight also rested against the door, but Tony uselessly tried to rip it open anyway. He looked up and saw that black cloak and white skull mask flying down at him like a huge demonic bat. The black wheeled skates slammed into the bus's console and the maniac crouched there. Tony awkwardly spun away from the killer, and fell into Lindy and Gary. Tony's crushing weight on top of their broken bones made them cry out in fresh agony.

The killer slashed at them, and Tony caught the black cloaked arm in both hands. He stared at the grinning skull under the black hood. His eyes flicked to the left and saw the razor sharp tip of the blade inching its way toward his face.

Tony gritted his teeth with the effort of holding that powerful rage-filled arm away. He took one last glance over his shoulder into Lindy's face, that face that was so similar to his girlfriend's. Bracing his feet against the sides of the stairs, he stood up, holding himself up like a shield in front of her. The killer yanked out of Tony's grip and drew the sickle back. The sickle slashed two diagonal rips across Tony's face, forming a bloody X. One black glove reached out and grabbed Tony by his dark sweaty hair. The blade tilted sideways and sliced his throat open. The killer let go of his hair, and kicked him backwards. He flew back limply against the left side of the shattered folding door, his blood splattering against the cracked glass.

As Tony had struggled with the killer, Gary and Lindy had been struggling to climb over the seat. They hadn't made much progress with their broken bones. Death grabbed both of them by the arms, threw them back down against the folding door, and began slashing mercilessly. They shrieked with each cut.

Suzanne had crawled over the seat while Death dealt with Tony, Gary, and Lindy. Now she was desperately crawling up the tilted center aisle, slipping on the wet plastic, and sobbing in panicky little gasps. The killer heard the rubber of her shoes squeaking against the floor and saw her crawling up the aisle towards the emergency exit. The blade lashed out and stabbed into Suzanne's ankle, the one she had said hurt her all night while she was wearing the wrong skates. She shrieked hoarsely as she was yanked back down the aisle. Her fingernails scratched grooves in the linoleum floor as she was pulled down to join her friends.

A short time later, the killer finally finished with the five of them. The black skate wheels left a bloody trail all the way up the center aisle. The black cloaked figure jumped down out of the bus and walked calmly back into the graveyard.

Blood was seeping out from the bottom of the bus's folding door, and in the freezing, sub-zero temperature, it was already crystallizing into red icicles.

**Part Three:**

**Resolutions**

**January 1, 1981**

# Chapter Twelve:

# Under the Rink

### 1

It was the thumping sounds overhead that woke Dan up again. He and Denise had been dozing sitting up; Denise's head resting on his shoulder, Dan's head on top of hers. Over the last couple of hours they had sat there making out, talking a little bit, making out again, experiencing a roller coaster of adrenaline. They gave in to the thrill of infatuation with each other, then something would remind one of them that they were still trapped in a pantry hiding from a psycho killer, and they would be afraid for their lives all over again. But once they rested their heads on each other, they almost immediately felt their eyelids growing heavy. All those raging emotions had finally sapped the last of their energy, and within five minutes, they simply passed out.

Forty-five minutes later, Dan jerked awake, tense and disoriented. It sounded like something heavy had fallen against the ceiling right over their heads. Denise inhaled sharply as Dan's jerking movements woke her up, she gazed around the room confused. Just then, she remembered where she was and what had happened that night. She grabbed onto Dan's arm and followed his eyes up to the ceiling tiles overhead.

"What was that?" she whispered.

"I don't know," he tensely replied without taking his eyes off the ceiling.

*This is it*, his mind yammered. *He's come for us. Oh God! Why didn't I just stay home tonight? Shit shit shit!*

Dan and Denise waited in breathless silence for another overhead crash, or for Death to burst into the pantry and rip their guts open with that long, deadly blade. Nothing happened though, the ceiling remained still, the pantry door remained closed. Dan and Denise glanced curiously at each other, waiting for the end, but still no end came.

Finally, they heard the muffled growl of an engine starting up outside the building. They could almost feel the low rumble through the cinder block at their backs.

"What the fuck?" Dan said.

They listened to the engine rev a few times, then there was rubbery whirring sound of tires spinning on icy snow. The sound faded away as the vehicle drove off, leaving Rollerville in dead silence again.

"Did he just...leave?" Dan asked in a quiet, hesitant voice, not wanting to jinx their possible good luck. He didn't quite dare to speak at his regular volume, but it was the loudest voice he had used since they first ran into this claustrophobic little pantry.

"I don't know. It sounded like it," Denise replied in the same low voice. "What if it's a trick?" Dan gave her a shrug that said he didn't disagree with her, it damn well could've been a trick and they both knew it. They sat quietly, trying to figure out what they had just heard. Denise looked up at the ceiling again, then turned to Dan.

"What was that noise that woke us up a few minutes ago?" she asked. "What did it sound like?"

"I don't know. It sounded like something was falling through the damn ceiling on top of us. You know what it reminded me of?"

"What?" she asked a little distractedly. She was thinking hard, trying to come up with some kind of logical explanation for the mysterious noises, and really only half listening to Dan.

"It reminded me of this one time a few years back, when this big fucking cupboard thing fell on me at my house."

"A cupboard *fell* on you?" she asked.

"Yeah. We have this big freestanding cupboard in our kitchen at home, it's got all the pots and pans in it, and breakfast cereal and flour and all kinds of shit. One morning I was kind of hanging on the doors trying to pick out a cereal to eat, and the damn thing just tipped forward and fell on top of me."

"Jesus. Did you get hurt?"

"No, I got lucky. All the pots and pans fell on me, and all these glass jars broke around me, but all I got was a welt from where one of those stupid doors pinched my arm. I was able to push the cupboard off of me before my mom got up to see what was going on. Anyway, when I heard that noise I first thought I was asleep in my room at home and that thing fell again." Neither Dan or Denise had any way of knowing that they had heard the sound of Gary tripping and falling on the roof above them.

She continued to sit silently, trying to figure out what that crashing noise was, and Dan could practically see the wheels turning in her head. "What are you thinking?" he asked. She hesitated for a moment, gathering up her thoughts.

"What if someone got away?" she suggested. "What if that was what that the noise on the roof was?"

"Got away? How? We're locked in, remember?"

"The doors aren't the only way in and out of the building. Remember I told you there was a roof access in the skate rental room? What if Tony, or whoever was in there, got out through the roof? Maybe that noise we heard was them running across to the front of the building? Maybe they got down somehow and drove off to get help."

"It's possible," Dan agreed. "Now that I think of it, that noise up there could've been some footsteps running. So what now? Should we go out there?" Dan stood up and began walking toward the door, eager to get out of this cramped space. Denise grabbed his hand and pulled him back.

"No, wait. We don't know for sure what that was. For all we know, that car noise was just a snow plow truck driving by or something, and the noises on the roof could've been a big chunk of snow falling off one of the air conditioners."

"Oh come on, Denise. Someone drove away. That engine started up in the parking lot. Didn't you hear it?"

"Do you really wanna take that chance?" She looked gravely at Dan and he hesitated. "If someone actually did get away, they'll bring help. And until they get here, we won't have to take a chance on anything. We'll just have to wait until we can hear the police inside the building. Then we'll know for sure that we're safe."

Dan sighed. "You're right." He sat back down in his spot again, it was still warm from his leftover body heat. "We've waited this long, might as well wait a little longer."

"Right."

At that moment, as Jim and Gary were being murdered in the crashed bus outside, Dan thought of them. They seemed to pop into his mind out of nowhere, and with them came a sick feeling of dread deep down in his stomach. He figured that they were probably dead out there on the rink somewhere, but a part of him wondered if they were still alive, if there was any chance at all of saving them. *If only the killer had been the one that drove away, I could....*

"But, wait a minute. What if it was that psycho driving away instead?" Dan speculated. "I mean, maybe he figured he got everyone, and then he couldn't find the keys to the doors or something. So he took off through the roof."

"So what if he did?"

"Shit, Denise, there could be people still alive out there. What if they need help? You wanna just sit here and let them die?"

Denise looked down guiltily. "I guess I hadn't thought of that." They sat in silent contemplation for a moment, then Denise came up with a plan. "Here's what I say we do, we wait for an hour, then if we don't hear anything at all, we'll go and check it out. If Tony or some of your classmates *did* get out and drive away, they should be able to get some help back here within an hour. But if nothing happens after an hour of waiting, we'll have to assume that there's no police coming, and it was that psycho driving away. Either way, we'll be safe...I hope."

"Makes sense. Wait for an hour," Dan repeated. He hoped that if anyone was still alive out there, they could hold out for at least another hour. "We can handle that. Boy, I sure can't wait to get out of this fuckin' pantry though. I feel like I can't breathe in here."

"Yeah, I know what you mean. It's getting

really stuffy in here," she agreed.

"At least we've got good company," he said with a smile and leaned in to kiss her again. She smiled and leaned in herself, sharing another long kiss with him. Finally, Dan broke away from her.

"How do you do that?" he asked.

"Do what?" she asked, thinking he was asking about how she kissed. She didn't think she was doing anything out of the ordinary at all. In fact, at one point that night, the thought had even crossed her mind that she might be a boring kisser.

"I mean, how do you figure things out, and, like make...I don't know, mental connections like that? You figured out who he was, you figured out what to do. I never could've thought of that stuff on my own, well I mean, not as fast as you can."

"I don't know, I'm just thinking. Nothing special about that," she said, trying to be modest, but feeling the flush in her cheeks rising.

"You're pretty smart, Resolution Buddy. A hell of a lot smarter than me."

Denise rewarded his compliment with a long, deep kiss. One kiss turned to two, then before they knew it, they were making out again, loving the feel and the taste of each other. Dan couldn't wait to get out of the pantry and get some fresh air, but as they made out, a small part of him wished they could stay in here all night.

## 2

A little over an hour later, there was a tiny click as Dan unlocked the pantry door. The knob slowly turned and the door opened with a low wooden thump.

The door slowly swung open, revealing Dan standing tense and alert with Denise behind him. He slowly lowered his right hand after pushing the door open with the flat of his palm. In his other hand, he held the heavy metal flashlight up defensively, ready to take a swing at anything that moved.

Before opening the door, they had settled on a game plan. The first step had been to look through the crack under the door to see if there were shadows from feet or skate wheels standing outside waiting for them. They saw nothing but the dim, dirty brick floor behind the snack counter. The little alleyway behind the refrigerators, microwave, and oven was too high and too tight for anyone to be standing off to the side of the door, waiting to ambush them.

The next step was to open the door and stand back, ready to slam it shut again if the killer was out there somewhere and happened to see them. From where they stood, just inside the pantry doorway, they didn't see anyone standing out there at all. The place was as still and quiet as a tomb, and with all the bodies lying around, that was exactly what Rollerville had become.

Dan took the first soft, silent steps out of the pantry. He walked in only his socks, he had taken off his skates in the pantry hours ago, and left them in a corner. Denise followed right behind him, holding onto his shirt. He made a careful effort to breathe only through his nose and take slow, shallow breaths. Once outside the pantry, he turned his body to the side and stepped back against the oven. He noticed that the rink had taken on a nasty smell, it was like a combination of sweat and blood.

They reached the corner of the oven and stopped. Dan glanced back at Denise as if to ask if she was ready to turn the corner. She gave him a nod of encouragement. He tightened his grip on the heavy flashlight in his hands. Inching his head forward, he peered around the corner. Only his nose, eyes, and a sliver of forehead were visible from around the other side. He half expected to see that psycho in the death cloak standing there waiting for him. Denise saw his fist shaking slightly as it clenched tight around the flashlight.

To Dan's relief, no one stood on either side of the snack counter. He let out a silent sigh, and let his tight fists relax a little. He looked back at Denise and nodded at her again to tell her that the coast was clear.

They snuck through the little cashier's area behind the snack counter. Dan scanned the entire rink, looking for the killer or any other signs of life. Out on the rink nothing moved, yet Dan couldn't help but feel like they weren't alone. The whole rink was splashed with dark red. His eyes locked on the mess of blood and bodies that lay in tangled heaps against the emergency exit doors. He wondered who was tangled up in those piles. Was Jim over there? Or Gary?

Denise stopped behind Dan, glanced over at the rink, then quickly looked back at him. She thought it was better not to look at that mess unless they absolutely had to. The brief glimpse she had gotten of still, bloody arms and clawed fingers gave her the chills. Looking at Dan's pale, disturbed expression, she could almost see the color draining out of his face. She nudged him with her elbow. He jumped a little and turned towards her.

"Don't look at them," she mouthed. "Stick to the plan." He nodded and swallowed a dry lump in his throat.

They continued on. At the far edge of the snack counter, there was a hinged section that you could lift up to walk out into the dining area. Dan lifted the counter as slowly and quietly as he could, holding it up for Denise to sneak out in front of him. Once she was out, he crept out himself. He gently lowered the hinged counter back down again, and linked hands with her.

The next step of their plan was to walk out to the front lobby to see if the doors had been unlocked by anyone, and also to see if the payphone was working. They figured the phones must not have been working or else the group that they heard get slaughtered in the front lobby would've used them. Dan prayed that either the phones worked or the doors were unlocked so they could just get the hell out of this creepy crime-scene roller rink. He had a sinking suspicion that it wouldn't be so easy. He and Denise stayed close together as they crept through the dining area. The rink was so silent they could hear their ears ringing. They peered around, expecting to see that grim reaper maniac around every corner. They were alone, but that feeling of being watched continued to prickle the backs of their necks.

They reached the carpeted doors leading into the front lobby and stopped. Dan mentally prepared himself for the very real possibility that they were walking into a trap. There was a slight crack between the two doors, Dan peered through, but couldn't see anything. He held the heavy flashlight up at the ready again, took another slow, deep breath, and pushed open the door on the right with his flat palm.

From the doors, they saw a trail of mangled bodies leading toward the glass exit doors, Dan winced at the sight of them. They went in, taking tiny baby steps. Denise kept her back pressed against Dan's, watching to make sure no one would sneak up behind them. Dan quickly turned toward the glass doors, then lowered the flashlight, the coast was clear. There were streaks of blood running down the metal edges between the two doors, starting at about four feet off the floor. He couldn't help but let his eyes follow those streaks down to the dark skinned hand near the floor with the meaty stubs that had once been fingers. Dan recognized him as that skate monitor guy with the Afro. He remembered that the guy had pointed to him hours earlier with one of those now-missing fingers while Dan had been trying to flirt with Denise, skating around with a big grin on his face. His own fingers seemed to ache sympathetically, and a chill scurried down his back. He hissed and shook his head to will away the thoughts of how much it must hurt to have your fingers chopped off between two metal doors.

"What is it?" Denise asked.

"You don't wanna know," he replied. He gave his head another brief shake and forced himself to look back at the front doors one more time. To his dismay, the chain and the padlock were still in place. Apparently, no one had been in or out through the front doors.

"Still locked," Dan whispered. He reached over and pulled the payphone off its cradle. There was nothing but dead silence on the line. "Phone's out too, just like we thought. Shit!"

Denise gave him a disappointed frown. "I was afraid of that," she said. "I guess that means we'll have to go find those keys after all."

Dan let the carpeted door swing shut, escaping through those doors would have to wait. He looked past Denise at the blood-spattered rink and sighed, dreading the next step in their plan.

## 3

Dan stopped himself before stepping out on the rink, and taken a look at the thick, congealing puddles of blood on the wood floor.

"This stuff is gonna soak right through my socks. You mind if I get my shoes?"

She agreed and they both went over to the table.

A few minutes earlier, Denise had made a small side trip to Geno's office and checked the phone in there, it was also dead. She cautiously went to the employee coat closet, grabbed her white winter coat, and put it on. She tucked her car keys safely in the inside pocket.

Back at the table, where all of Dan, Jim, Gary, Lindy, and Suzanne's stuff still sat, Dan put on his blue Adidas sneakers. As he tied his shoelaces, Denise looked over and saw the blood trail that led off the rink and into the bathrooms. She wondered if the killer could be hiding in there waiting for them. Maybe it would be a good idea to check the bathrooms out just to be sure.

*So what if he is?* another part of her mind spoke up. *He'll only kill us that much faster if we go in there. At least this way there's a chance we can find those keys and get the hell out of here if we're fast enough.* She forced herself to turn away from the ominous, bloody trail and focus on Dan's shoes. He pulled the last knot tight, stood up, and joined her. They both looked grimly at each other.

"First find Coach Richards or Mrs. Bauer," he whispered, reiterating their plan.

"Then if they don't have the keys, find Geno, my boss," Denise continued. "You ready, Resolution Buddy?" She hoped that would get a smile out of him and lighten the mood. Dan only gave her the briefest smile he could manage.

"Yeah, Resolution Buddy. Let's just get this over with."

They grasped each other's hands again, both felt cold and clammy, but it was still more comforting than walking by themselves. They walked back to the main rink entrance between the dining area and the DJ booth, and stepped out onto the wooden floor. Out there, the sweaty, bloody meat smell was much worse. Both Dan and Denise grimaced and covered their mouths and noses with their free hands. For the first few yards they were able to step around the few scattered bodies lying haphazardly on the floor, they were even able to avoid the splattered pools of dark drying blood. It wasn't long before the muck and bodies became too thick to avoid.

Dan's shoe came down in a sticky pool of dark red wine colored blood, and his foot slid forward against the smooth wood floor with a loud squeak. He gave a slight gasp, his arms pinwheeled wildly for balance, and he almost dropped the heavy flashlight. He wobbled a little, almost stepping on the corpse of a guy laying face down on the floor, then he regained his balance.

"You okay?" Denise whispered.

Dan nodded. "Fine."

Towards the middle of the rink in front of the DJ booth, the floor was thick with bodies. They had all been standing there at midnight, and fell down on top of each other as they were attacked. Now they lay heaped over one another, arms draped over chests, legs splayed, open mouths contorted and grimacing, open eyes dry and glazed. Dan squinted, trying to spot Coach Richard's big, beefy body. He thought the coach should've been easy to find, yet he was having trouble recognizing any of them. There was just so much blood, flaps of jagged skin, and pieces of the human body that he didn't care to identify strewn everywhere.

Denise kept close to Dan, keeping an eye out for the killer and also looking down in search of Coach Richards or Geno Atkinson's bodies. She had no idea if Geno was even out here or not. He usually didn't spend much time out on the rink. She hadn't exactly been paying much attention to Geno's whereabouts earlier that night, she had been too focused on Dan.

Three jagged holes in the ceiling tiles near the disco ball caught her eye. In the two holes closer to the DJ booth, she saw a couple of black socks and pant legs.

In the hole near the disco ball, she could see the top of a head with dark hair.

*Freddy?* She wondered. She looked back at the bodies on the floor, not wanting to even know what else was up there.

"Do you see them?" she whispered to Dan.

"I don't know. They're all so, ugh, chewed up," he answered. In the middle of the sentence, he had caught sight of the grimacing face of a kid he vaguely knew from the halls at school. The kid must've been a junior or sophomore, Dan didn't know his name. The dead kid was arched backward over someone else and had a long jagged slash through one deflated eye. The kid's lips peeled back, and the metal braces on his teeth were clotted with drying blood. The sight of that face made Dan gag. He looked away, then turned back to get a better look. Underneath the kid's back, a hairy, muscular arm poked out, its clawed fingers rested down in a puddle of blood. The hand had a large gold ring on the third finger that looked too smooth and shiny to be a class ring. To Dan, it looked more like a wedding ring.

"Wait a minute," Dan said. He bent down, trying to look under the kid. In the dim light under the kid's body, he thought he saw a familiar meaty head with a crew cut hairstyle. "I think I found him."

The coach seemed to be buried underneath three or four kids, but there were several gaps where his gray track suit was visible. Dan looked around for his pockets, but they were either flat against the floor or hidden under the sprawled bodies. There wasn't any other way around it, he would have to roll the other kids off of the coach to get to his pockets.

Dan set the flashlight down on a clean spot on the wood floor. He reached over and began rolling the kid's body by the shoulder. Denise came over and helped, pulling the body by the ribs. The kid's bloody arm, which had been crossed over his chest, fell limply forward and brushed against Denise's bare leg. It felt like she had been caressed by a piece of cold meat. She jumped back in revulsion, and her shoe slipped a little in the blood, making that loud squeak again.

"Shit, sorry. You all right?" Dan asked.

"It's fine," she said, shaking off the feeling of that cold, dead caress. Dan turned back to the corpse and pulled him by the shoulder until he rolled limply off the coach's body. Dan and Denise quickly stepped back out of the body's way, their heels coming down on another dead arm. The bloody braces kid's face fell into a puddle of blood on the floor with a liquid smack. Dan and Denise both squinted and turned away for a second, wincing over all the nasty little details around them.

Dan shook his head and turned back to the coach. With the kid gone, only the Coach's legs were covered by other bodies. "Help me roll him over."

Dan reached down and grabbed the coach by the hip, feeling uncomfortable as hell about doing it. Coach outweighed the bloody braces kid by at least seventy-five pounds, and they had to strain to get him to flip over. His limp, cold body kept wanting to bend at the waist every time they pulled. Finally, Dan put one of his hands down on the coach's blood-soaked chest, and gave him a hard push. His hand stayed with the body as it rolled, and he felt the coach's liquid insides slosh around. He felt like a rubbery CPR training mannequin filled with cold chili.

Dan felt his gorge rising and he had to turn away. He brought his hands up to cover his mouth, then yanked them back when he remembered they were dripping with blood. He held them away from his body so he wouldn't get any of the blood on his clothes.

"Oh, Jesus," he choked out.

Denise knelt down and rummaged through the

coach's blood-soaked pockets.

"Shit," she muttered.

"What's the matter?"

"No keys. Not anywhere. No keys, no wallet, not even fucking spare change."

"Fuck!" Dan hissed. All that awful searching for nothing. Denise stood up.

"Gotta move on. Gotta find Geno." She stood up and scanned the opposite side of the rink, wondering if Geno could possibly be somewhere in the thick jumbles of bodies blocking the emergency exit doors. Then she remembered the noise they had heard from up on the roof. She turned toward the skate rental counter and saw the storage room door hanging halfway open. Even from way over here, she could see that the door frame had a huge splintery gouge near the handle. She began walking toward it to get a better look. Dan followed behind her.

They stopped near the edge of the DJ booth, both staring at the long splinters of wood that poked out from the door frame.

"What the fuck?" Dan mumbled, keeping his voice low.

"It looks like someone kicked the door in, or forced it open with a crowbar or something," Denise said. "How come we didn't hear that?"

"We must've been asleep," Dan suggested. Denise shrugged in agreement.

"I wonder if there were people hiding in there. Maybe that fucking psycho chased them up onto the roof."

"If they were running, that would explain that crashing noise."

A hand suddenly clamped down on Dan's ankle. He jumped back and let out a short scream of surprise and terror. For an instant, he was sure that he would feel the sharp sting of the killer's blade stab into him. He pulled back the heavy flashlight, ready to swing it hard. Denise whirled around. The girl clutching Dan's ankle began to cough and choke on blood. Dan recognized that cough immediately, and lowered the flashlight.

"Mary Anne?"

"D-Dan?" she croaked weakly.

Dan knelt down and brushed back her unkempt mane of dark brown hair. Her face was smeared with blood and her eyes were bleary and red.

"Oh my God. Thank God, you're alive! I can't believe it, you're alive!" Dan babbled. He was so relieved to see Mary Anne still breathing that all the harsh feelings he'd had toward her seemed to vanish.

"It hurts, Dan," she said, her teary voice breaking up. "He cut me across my stomach. I-I had to pretend I was d-d-d... Oh God, Dan!"

"Shshshsh," he whispered soothingly. He wiped his hands on a dead kid's shirt and then brushed back her hair, it was how he had gotten her to calm down a few times when they had been together. "It's okay, it's okay. I'm gonna get you out of here, all right?" It felt so good to feel her soft hair underneath the palm of his hand like that again. He hadn't realized how much he missed the feel of her hair until now.

"How bad is it?" Denise asked her, kneeling down beside Dan. "Do you think you can walk?" Dan turned around and glanced at Denise, he was so relieved to see Mary Anne alive that he had almost forgotten she was there. "Can you walk, even a little bit?"

Mary Anne struggled to move and clutched her stomach. Her arms and abdomen were soaked with so much blood. Her low cut shirt and high athletic shorts, which had both been red to begin with, were now stained with blotches of a darker red. Dan couldn't tell how much of the blood had seeped out from her wounds and how much had soaked into her clothes from the puddles on the floor.

"I think I can walk, maybe a little." Dan helped her get up into a sitting position, encouraging her despite all of her little gasps and grimacing. Dan turned back to Denise.

"I'll stay with her. You go find your boss. We gotta find those damn keys."

"Right," Denise agreed, standing up. She was glad that the girl was alive, but she couldn't help feeling a nasty little part of herself that was jealous of all the attention Dan was giving to his ex-girlfriend. She shoved those emotions aside and stood up to do the right thing.

"Wait," Mary Anne said, holding up a hand to her. "You won't find any keys in here."

"What? What are you talking about?" Dan asked.

"After he...got me, I got all lightheaded and I blacked out," Mary Anne explained. "When I woke up, everyone was dead and I heard this...breathing behind that mask, y'know? So I closed my eyes and tried not to move. He walked past me, and I could hear him jingling a bunch of keys in his hands. I think he took the keys from Coach too. Then he went back down."

"Back down where?" Dan asked.

Mary Anne turned and pointed to a strangely empty spot on the wood floor behind her. It was right in front of the steps leading up to the DJ booth. Neither Dan or Denise had noticed it when they walked out onto the rink, they had been too busy looking for Coach Richards and trying not to step on bodies.

"There," Mary Anne said. "He's got some kind of trap door in the floor. I think it goes down under the skate rink. I think that's how he got in here tonight. Right when the clock struck midnight, I think he must've popped up from under the floor and started killing everyone. That's how he got Mike, and Jack...and me." Fresh tears began streaming down her face.

"Holy shit," Dan whispered in a voice filled with terrified wonder. He stared fixedly at the spot on the floor right in front of the DJ booth.

"I think he has all the keys," Mary Anne continued. She pointed at the bare spot in the floor again. "That's the only way in and out of the building now."

Denise stared at the spot and remembered something that happened earlier that day, it felt like a hundred years ago now. It was the same spot where she had found that black rose. *Of course, it all makes sense now. That motherfucker, Charlie Hart, had this whole thing all planned out.*

"Do you think he's still down there?" Denise asked.

Mary Anne's eyes suddenly rolled back and her eyelids fluttered. She leaned forward as if she were going to pass out again. Dan caught her by the shoulders and looked into her eyes.

"Whoa, hey, Mary Anne. Stay with me, okay? Everything's gonna be all right."

"Tired... So tired... Just go get help," Mary Anne muttered. Dan snapped his fingers in front of her face.

"Hey, stay awake, all right? I'm not gonna leave you here. We're gonna get you to the hospital."

"Dan, we really should go get help," Denise urged.

In his mind he kept replaying the night he broke up with her. She had told him she was sick and that she had to go to the hospital, and he had told her to get her family to take her, he was busy. And earlier tonight he had left her and the rest of his friends out here with that

233

psycho killer. He refused to leave her, or anyone else again. Twice was enough.

"No. I can't leave her. It'll take too long to go get help and bring them back here. We've gotta take her with us. I'll carry her the whole way if I have to, but I won't leave her. I just can't."

Denise looked over at the trap door and felt extremely uneasy about it. *What other choice do we have? Dan's right, the girl's in bad shape. She'll probably die if we don't get her out of here fast.*

"But if that wasn't him driving away--" Denise trailed off.

"Don't say it," Dan interrupted. "Don't even think it."

"Fuck," Denise muttered to herself, resigning herself to the fact that they had no other options. They had to go through the trap door and under the rink.

**4**

Dan and Denise somehow managed to pry up the heavy trap door with their fingertips. The edges of the trap door were staggered just like the layout of the wood floor, and when they looked closely, they could see its outline. It swung upwards toward the DJ booth, and thumped against the carpeted steps leading up to the turntables. A single iron loop was bolted into the underside of the trap door.

A rush of cold air blew up out of the pitch black darkness into their faces, carrying an earthy, musty smell. To Denise, it smelled like something had died long ago in an old root cellar filled with antiques. She picked up the heavy flashlight, clicked it on, and pointed it down into the dark. The walls were bare dirt, dug and chiseled away, then compacted so the rink floor wouldn't collapse. Four feet beneath the floor were stone steps that led down into a dark room that they couldn't yet see. The steps were caked with dirt, as if they had once been buried, but were recently excavated. They led down in the direction of the front of the building, the parking lot, and the old graveyard beyond that.

Dan, Denise, and Mary Anne all sat at the edge craning their necks to the side to see what was down in that darkness. Both girls clung to Dan's arms. They listened for the sound of enraged, echoing footsteps rushing towards them, but there was only silence.

"You be ready with that flashlight," Dan told Denise in a low voice. She nodded stiffly to him. All three of them were scared out of their minds. "I'll go down first, then I can carry you, Mary Anne." Mary Anne looked more wide-eyed and alert now. The cold air and the fear seemed to have revived her, woken her up a little.

"I'm okay, just give me a hand and I can walk a little," she said.

"You sure?" Dan asked, he did not like how uncontrollably shaky his voice sounded. He mentally told himself to hold it together. Mary Anne nodded. "Okay."

Dan dry-swallowed and cautiously dropped his legs down into the dark. He slid forward to the edge of the trap door, then slowly lowered himself down onto the steps. He immediately felt the temperature drop twenty degrees from the drafty, cold air under the rink. It was forty degrees at most down there.

Standing on the topmost step, he turned to Denise. "Give me the flashlight for a second so I can see what's down there." Denise willingly handed it over. Dan got down on all fours on the top step. The stone felt like blocks of ice under his bare hands. He shined the flashlight into the darkness below the skate rink floor. The steps led down to a narrow stone room, like a tiny little mausoleum, only the coffins (if there ever had been any coffins) had been removed. At the back of the old mausoleum, there was a narrow, jagged opening, crudely cut into the wall. Beyond the opening, a dirt tunnel continued on into the dark.

"It's a tunnel," he said, peering up over his shoulder at them. "I'll bet it goes all the way to the old graveyard. I don't know for sure though. It might go nowhere." He looked up at Mary Anne. "You sure you can do this?"

"No," she said softly. "But I'm afraid of what might happen if I don't get help."

"Do you want my jacket or something?" Denise offered, she was the only one of them who had one on.

"N-no. I'm not sure I could even put it on, it hurts too much," Mary Anne replied. Denise thought it was a rather cold response, but she cut the girl some slack. After all, she was hurt pretty bad.

Dan gave the flashlight back to Denise and held up his arms to Mary Anne. "Come on then." Mary Anne slowly scooted to the edge just like Dan had, wincing with every painful movement. She almost constantly held one hand tight against her injured stomach. She dropped her skate clad feet and bunched up rainbow socks (all the colors now were different shades of a murky dark red) down into the hole. Dan reached up and grabbed one of her arms. Up above, Denise set the flashlight down, took her other arm, and helped her down. Together, they gently lowered Mary Anne to the top step. She hissed and grunted in pain.

"Ah...easy...easy..." she whispered. She wobbled a little on her skate wheels when she touched down on the stone step.

"I got you, I got you," Dan reassured her. They

waited until Denise lowered herself down onto the steps with them, then began their slow descent. Dan and Mary Anne lead the way down, while Denise reached up and pulled the trap door closed behind them. Dan looked back as he noticed the light from the skate rink growing dim.

"What are you doing?" he asked as the last of the light behind them disappeared.

"He's got the keys, remember?" Denise explained. "What if he decides to come back through the front door? He'll know that we went down here and he'll come after us."

"Oh yeah, good thinking," Dan said and gave her a little smile of encouragement. He wanted to say something else to her, give her some flirtatious compliment like he had back in the pantry, but it felt too awkward to flirt with Denise while Mary Anne was here and needed help. He hoped Denise didn't think that he just wanted to get back with Mary Anne and forget about her. He wanted to show her that he still liked her a lot, but now was not the right time.

Denise smiled back at him. She didn't take anything from Dan personally. She was solid as a rock, and focused only on the task at hand. Dan turned forward again, and the darkness ahead terrified him. It washed away all of his personal thoughts and left only fear.

They reached the bottom of the steps and faced the crumbling remains of the stone wall. The narrow opening leading into the tunnel looked like it had been chopped out with a pickax, small bits of stone littered the dirt floor all around it. Without a word, they stepped through the hole in the wall and went into the tunnel.

It was narrow and claustrophobic down here, only about six feet wide and six feet high. Denise was careful to keep both hands on the flashlight, ready to swing hard if anyone came bursting out of the darkness. She pointed the flashlight ahead of them, lighting their way. They walked huddled together for safety and warmth. Denise looked ahead mistrustfully at the walls of the tunnel, they were compacted dirt just like right under the trap door. For a second, she thought she saw the black rumpled folds of a death cloak moving away from the dirt wall. She gasped a little, then realized it was just the shadows from the flashlight against uneven gouges in the wall.

"What? What is it?" Dan whispered.

"N-nothing," she stammered. "I'm okay. I'm okay." She repeated it more for her own benefit than his, and kept repeating it in her mind.

It was slow going with Mary Anne limping along between them. She walked with her shoulders hunched over a little, clutching her stomach. She took baby steps so her skates wouldn't roll too much on the bumpy dirt floor of the tunnel. Every now and then she would stumble and inhale sharply with pain. Dan patiently kept his arm around her the whole time, talking her through it.

As they shuffled forward into the cold, dank tunnel, Denise saw something flat and vaguely shiny up on one of the walls ahead. She shined the light on it as they came closer. It had a flat, black wooden side, but the wood was so splintered and rotten that it looked like it was ready to fall apart. It had a rusted rail bolted to it, broken in the middle with one side hanging down. They all stopped and stared at it.

"Is that what I think it is?" Dan whispered.

Denise didn't even turn to look at Dan, her eyes firmly fixed on the coffin buried in the underground tunnel wall.

"All those stories, they're true," Denise whispered. "There really *are* people buried underneath

Rollerville." Her mouth hung open in horror, knowing that she had skated over this grave dozens of times, she and hundreds of others had disturbed the final resting place of whoever was in there. Now she could almost feel a cold, bitter presence seeping out from inside the coffin.

"Come on, don't look at it," Dan urged, he felt the same coldness from the thing as Denise. He wanted to get away from it before whatever was in there decided to start scratching against the sides, inviting them in. He dragged them along deeper into the tunnel.

The farther they went, the colder it seemed to get. All three of them began to notice little wisps of steam floating up out of their mouths as they exhaled. They passed three more coffins jutting out of the dirt walls. One seemed to have fallen out of the wall and lay on the side of the tunnel, leaving a caved-in section in the dirt above it. Another hung out of the wall like a crooked piano key.

Dan's foot clunked into something hard and plastic. He jumped a little. He had been so focused on looking up at the coffins that he hadn't seen the object in his path at all. It clattered away and the sound echoed off the walls, reverberating through the whole tunnel.

"Ah, shit," he whispered impulsively. Denise pointed the flashlight beam down as it rolled to a stop. It was a yellow construction worker's hard hat. Dan knelt down, picked it up, and examined it. Denise kept her flashlight beam on it so he could see while he read the label on the front.

"Excellent Energy. The power company? What the hell is this doing down here?"

In the dim light reflecting off the hard hat's bright yellow surface, Denise noticed a metal box mounted on the wall behind Dan. She shifted the flashlight beam over his shoulder and looked at it. It was a small electric breaker switch with a line of electric conduit pipe that ran back towards Rollerville, and forward towards the graveyard.

"I'm guessing it belonged to whoever put that switch in," Denise said gravely. "That must've been how he cut the power."

Dan turned the hard hat over in his hands, and saw that the inside of it was caked with dark brown dried blood and grayish gobbets of dried meat. They all gasped and Dan almost dropped it in disgust. He set it down again and wiped his hand on his shirt with revulsion.

"Let's just keep going," Dan pleaded. "This whole place just feels...wrong."

Mary Anne was the first to notice a shiny gleam up ahead. The flashlight beam glimmered off a big, dark shape lying directly in the middle of the tunnel floor. They would have to either slide around it or walk on top of it to get to the other side.

"What's that?" Mary Anne asked.

"I don't know," Denise replied. With a growing sense of suspicion and dread, she kept the light on the thing.

As they got closer, they recognized that the shiny shape was another coffin, but unlike the old rotten coffins embedded in the walls, this one was brand new. It had a smooth, black lacquered finish, and a gold rail ran smoothly along its sides.

"Oh shit, what now?" Dan whispered to himself. He was getting tired of all the awful things this night had shown him, and he sensed that this was going to be one more. He gripped Mary Anne a little tighter as they approached the coffin.

They stopped about fifteen feet in front of it, none of them were sure what to do. Should they go around it? Should they climb over it? Standing just behind the coffin was a polished, gray granite headstone in the shape of a cross. It had no engravings, but some small black letters had been painted on it. A long black rose leaned against the headstone, its fresh dark petals rested on the right side of the black letters. The sight of that rose reminded Denise of the one she had picked up earlier that afternoon, that dreadful hint of the horrors to come. Now seeing this new rose, she wondered what other terrible things were in store for tonight.

"What do we do?" Mary Anne asked. Dan shook his head that he didn't know. They all stared down mistrustfully at the coffin. Something wasn't right about it. It was all too perfectly set up, like a display at one of those fake haunted houses. It felt like a trap. They glanced back and forth at each other, wondering what to do. Denise was at a loss for a plan, she did not have any desire to go near that thing.

Dan let go of Mary Anne and took a few tentative steps toward the coffin and the headstone behind it, his eyes focused on that black writing. The girls gave each other a wary glance, then watched Dan intently. Denise pointed the flashlight beam down at the headstone so he could see whatever it was he was trying to see. Silently, he walked right up to the bottom left corner of the coffin and leaned forward to read the words. His chest and face hung in the air over the closed lid. The letters were so small, painted in looping, flowery cursive.

Dan's mouth dropped open as he read the name on the headstone. The blood drained out of his face and he felt his stomach drop. "Wha--?"

"What's it say?" Denise whispered.

Dan turned back over his shoulder and stared at her with a pale, open-mouthed expression of terror on his face.

"It says *Daniel Parsons*. That's my name."

The coffin thumped heavily underneath him. Dan jumped in the air and almost fell down on top of it. Something began clunking around loudly from inside, making the coffin bounce. The girls screamed and backed away as fast as Mary Anne's stumbling footsteps would allow. Dan ran back to the girls and wrapped his arm around Mary Anne's shoulders, preparing to pick her up and run back to the rink. The coffin continued to bang and thump behind them, muffled grunts and slobbering cries soon joined in the cacophony.

Mary Anne's skate wheels got caught in one of the low ridges of dirt, she stumbled backwards screaming. Dan still held onto her and tried to help her stay on her feet, she almost brought him down with her. In his panic, Dan awkwardly bent forward and dropped her the last foot and a half to the dirt. Mary Anne landed on her back, and lay there writhing and clutching her injured stomach silently, as if the wind had been knocked out of her. She was in too much pain to even scream.

The hasp on the coffin broke apart, and the lid suddenly banged open. Death, dressed in his full cloak and rotting skull mask, burst up out of it like some horrible jack in the box. He swung the scythe blade back and forth wildly at them, uttering a weird bellowing scream that was half drunken rage, half sorrow. Despite the fact that his voice was muffled behind the mask, it was as eerie as a ghost's cry.

Denise turned to run and the bright flashlight beam went with her, leaving the rest of them in total darkness.

Dan scrambled to get to his feet and run. He ducked as he felt the wind from the swinging blade swish right behind his shoulder blades. He blindly groped along the dirt floor for Mary Anne, but he had lost her somewhere in the dark.

Denise sensed that the others weren't near her,

and she swung around to see where Dan and Mary Anne were. In the light of the flashlight beam, she saw Death clambering up out of the coffin. He swung the blade hard to his left, missing Dan's back by inches.

*"DAN!"* she screamed in terror.

The blade slammed into the wooden side of a coffin that was up in the wall. The masked man ripped the blade out and the rotted wood of the old coffin collapsed. A dusty, mummified skeleton in a ragged black dress tumbled out in a cloud of dust and fell on top of Dan. He fell to the ground under the weight of the old bones. He screamed as he looked right into the shriveled face of a dead woman who had been buried there decades earlier. Brittle strands of her thin, cobwebby, white hair fell into his face.

Death reared back again and the blade bumped against the ceiling, a little sprinkle of dirt fell down on top of his hooded head. He chopped down at Dan with both hands on the scythe's handle, but he was disoriented in the cramped space of the tunnel. The blade sliced down into the dirt three inches to the right of Dan's face.

*"NO!"* Denise shrieked and ran toward them as the masked man reared back again. Without thinking, she threw the heavy flashlight at him as hard as she could. It tumbled through the air, spinning the bright beam crazily in all directions like some wild disco light.

The heavy handle struck squarely against the forehead of the mask. His bellowing cry choked off and became an injured grunt. The scythe dropped out of his gloved hands, clattering to the dirt floor. He fell to his knees, and the flashlight fell to the ground near one of the walls, filling the tunnel with dim light.

Denise rushed over and knelt beside Dan to help him brush away the tangle of bones from the moldering skeleton. She immediately felt black gloved hands clamping down tight on her calves. She shrieked as

Death came crawling over her. Behind the black gloves, his groping fingers worked their way up her entire body. She tried to crab-walk backwards, beating his head and shoulders with her fists. He shrugged off her blows, and his weight held her down. Before she knew it, the rotting skull mask was peering down into her face and those hard black fingers had encircled her throat. Her scream turned into a gag as they tightened their grip. He yelled garbled, unintelligible words and shook her throat like a rag doll. She clawed into the gloves with her nails as panic set in.

Suddenly, there was a female cry of rage from above, and Denise felt the wind of a swinging blade. The cloaked man made a *hurk* sound under the mask and his fingers slipped away from Denise's throat. She instantly sucked in air and began to cough violently. He rose up on his knees, and Denise could clearly see Mary Anne standing behind him holding the scythe handle. She had picked up the blade and stabbed him right in his lower back. Her face was a contorted grimace, and her dark brunette hair was a wild mess.

He reached behind his back in an attempt to pull out the blade. He tried to turn around and pulled Mary Anne with him. She jerked forward, then caught her balance and yanked the blade out of his back. It pulled free with a squirt of dark red blood. He whirled, lunging for Mary Anne. Now his deep bellow lost all hints of sadness, it was pure rage.

Mary Anne tilted the blade sideways and hacked into his neck. Denise winced and turned her head away just as she saw the sharp tip of the blade slide in under the bottom edge of the mask. The force of Mary Anne's swing knocked him to the ground beside Denise. She watched as he clutched at his throat, gurgling and convulsing weakly. Even in the dim light, she could see the dark blood oozing out from the bottom edge of the mask and soaking into the dry dirt floor. She lifted herself up and crab-walked away from the dying masked man.

Dan gave the skeleton's rib cage a hard heave, and most of the crumbling bones fell against the wall with a puff of stale mummy dust. He sat up and crawled away, brushing dust and small bone fragments off of his shirt and jeans. He joined Denise at her side, surprising her. They grasped each other's hands and watched the crazy man writhe and clutch at his throat. It looked as if he couldn't quite remember how to move his body anymore. To put him out of his misery, Mary Anne yanked out the scythe blade one more time and stabbed it into his heart. He finally slumped on the floor, still and silent. Mary Anne stood there panting, looking down at the fresh bloody corpse in the death costume.

"My God," Dan whispered, looking back and forth at both of the girls. "Mary Anne? Denise? Are you okay?"

"Yeah, I think so," Denise said hoarsely, still coughing a little.

Dan shakily got to his feet. He walked over to where the flashlight had fallen to the dirt floor. He picked it up, turned around, and stood up next to Mary Anne. Pointing the light down at the still body in the black cloak, they watched and waited for any more signs of life.

"Is he dead?" Dan asked.

Mary Anne nodded. Dan could see that she was clearly traumatized, her eyes looked blank and dazed. He looked back at the corpse, and felt a sudden urge to unmask the killer. Slowly, he knelt down and gripped the rubber edge lightly to avoid touching the blood. Working it back and forth, he pulled the mask up over the dead man's face and off his forehead.

A gaunt, haggard man in his late fifties lay there

with glazed eyes staring up aimlessly at the ceiling. His wrinkly skin was cracked and dried out from too many years in the sun. A gray stubble covered his cheeks. His equally gray hair was slicked back on the sides, but wild on top. Dan dropped the skull mask to the left of the dead man's head, it made a rubbery *plop* sound.

"You were right," Dan said to Denise. "Charlie Hart."

Denise stared down at Charlie Hart's dead face, still holding her throat. Mary Anne was clutching her stomach again and limped over to her.

"Are you okay?" Mary Anne asked. Denise had to swallow and take a breath to answer her.

"Yes, thanks to you," Denise said gratefully. Mary Anne gave as nice a smile as she could manage despite her pain, then she winced again and tightly held her stomach. Denise noticed this and remembered that they had to hurry up and get Mary Anne to a hospital. "Dan, we should go."

Dan was still staring fixedly at the unmasked corpse. He finally turned away, meaning to walk back to the girls. Then he remembered the coffin and the headstone behind it, the headstone that had his name written on it. He looked back over his shoulder at it, with questions running frantically through his mind. Was it really his name? Had he misread it? He had to see it up close and know for sure.

"Hang on, there's something I have to see," he said and walked back toward the headstone. Mary Anne and Denise knelt together in the dark, watching him go. Denise looked at Mary Anne's grimacing face, wishing she could help ease her pain in some way. She had to be aching after falling on her back, then stabbing Charlie Hart like that. Denise hoped the physical activity hadn't made her injuries any worse.

"Hey, it's gonna be okay. We're gonna get you

to a hospital," Denise said. Mary Anne nodded, and gave her a brief glance. "Just hang in there and don't think about the pain. Think about this, you're a hero. You saved our lives." Mary Anne nodded and slipped a hand under her shirt to press against the wound.

Dan shined the light on the headstone. Sure enough, it said *DANIEL PARSONS*.

"We haven't officially met yet. I'm Denise. Denise Simmons," she introduced herself. "What's your name?"

"Mary Anne. Mary Anne Hart."

"Nice to meet you," Denise replied.

Dan delicately picked up the black rose that had been leaning against the smooth gray granite, and stared at it in his hand.

"Why me?" he whispered aloud. He shone the light back on the headstone and saw that the rose had been covering part of the name. It hadn't said *DANIEL PARSONS*, it said *DANIEL PARSONS JR.*

"Junior?" he whispered to himself. He wasn't Daniel Parsons Junior. His father was named Mitchell Parsons, not Daniel Parsons Senior. *Who the hell is Daniel Parsons Jr?*

Just then, Denise made one of her mental connections. "Mary Anne Hart. Like, Hart, as in Hart Street, and the Hart Hill Cemetery?"

Dan heard Denise utter a short strangled cry. He whipped around with the flashlight, dropping the black rose into the soft interior lining of the coffin.

Mary Anne stood behind Denise holding a blood clotted sickle against her throat. In her other hand she tightly gripped a handful of Denise's auburn hair. Denise still knelt on the ground, staring at Dan in frozen terror, pleading with her eyes for him to do something to help her. Mary Anne had an insane grin on her face. The streaks of drying blood on her face now looked like some kind of psychotic Indian war paint. Her pupils were dilated, making her eyes look black.

"Mary Anne?" Dan said slowly. "What the hell are you doing?" Mary Anne breathed hard through her clenched teeth.

"Dan, Dan, Dan," she growled without loosening her tight jaw. "You're still as stupid as ever." Dan's mind spun wildly. It hadn't been Charlie Hart at all, it was Mary Anne this whole time. The girl he had loved, the girl he had lost his virginity to, the girl he had known intimately for two years, at least he *thought* he knew her. He realized that she hadn't even been injured, she must have been holding that sickle blade under her shirt the whole time. He stared at her in slack-jawed shock.

"Wh-- why?" Dan stammered in a breathy exhale. "You killed them. Why would you *kill them?*"

"It's part of *my* New Year's Resolution. You wanna know what *my* resolution is, *Resolution Buddy?*" she spat out Dan and Denise's little pet name. "*My* New Year's Resolution is to pay you, and everyone else, back for everything you've done to me. To make you *suffer.* And when you're all dead and gone, I'll be the hero. Everyone will think it was self defense when I killed my crazy great uncle Charlie Hart. And they'll *love* me!"

"My God, you're insane," Dan said as she began to rant.

"No, I'm *not* insane, *Dan!*" she spat out his name as if it were a dirty word. "You all *hated* me! Everyone in that whole fucking school *hated* me! Your fucking friends hated me the whole time we were together. They tried to tear us apart. Jack Flynn and Mike Cavallo just wanted to use me, like I was their fucking *sex toy!* And you hated me too, Dan, *didn't you? DIDN'T YOU?!*"

"I *loved* you!" Dan shouted at her. "*You* were

the one who turned against *me!* I would've done anything for you."

"*Bullshit!* You didn't love me at all! You *dropped* me! You were looking at other girls in the middle of that contest. You couldn't even keep your mind on me long enough to win it for us. That day could've been the happiest day of our lives and you fucking ruined it!"

"Jesus Christ, Mary Anne. It was just a stupid *contest!* How many times do I have to say it? You killed dozens of innocent people over a goddamn *roller disco contest?!*"

"You still don't fucking *get it!* I was pregnant with *your son!*"

All the fight went out of Dan at that moment. "Wh-- What?" He staggered, his knees felt like they were about to give out. He felt sick with shock and guilt.

"*Daniel Parsons Jr.* That was going to be his name. And I was gonna tell you right after we won the contest. It was going to be the happiest day of our lives! But *you* dropped me, *you motherfucker! YOU KILLED MY BABY! HE WAS MINE! MINE! AND YOU KILLED HIM! YOU DROPPED ME AND YOU KILLED HIM! AND EVERYONE LAUGHED WHILE HE DIED!*"

Everything made sense now. Mary Anne really *had* weighed more when he dropped her, it hadn't been stage-fright or his imagination after all. She had been pregnant, and it explained why she had acted so weird and moody leading up to the contest. And after the contest, she had seemed so irritable, so ready to fly off the handle. It explained why she had been so adamant about him taking her to the hospital that night after he broke up with her, she had been miscarrying their baby.

"Wh-- Why didn't you just tell me?"

"I was about to tell you that day you broke up

with me, but you wouldn't take me to the hospital. You wouldn't take my calls or even talk to me. Because you *hated* me, just like everyone else in that whole school. But you don't hate me nearly as much as I hate you, Dan. *I HATE YOU!* I hate you for what you did to me, and what you did to our baby! And now it's time to finish my resolution. Now it's time to pay you back! No one's gonna stand in my way. Not that old moron who owns this place, I already took care of him. Not the teachers. Not that stupid DJ. Not my disgrace of an uncle. No one. You're the last ones left to die. Just her and *you.*"

In her fury, Mary Anne pulled the sickle blade off of Denise's neck and pointed it accusingly at Dan. With the sharp blade away from her throat, Denise seized her opportunity. She let out a furious cry, and kicked back at Mary Anne with her left leg. Her tennis shoe only clipped Mary Anne's shin, but it was enough to make her bark out a cry of pain and stumble back a step. Denise tried to wriggle out of Mary Anne's grip. Before she could escape, Mary Anne quickly tugged hard on Denise's hair and raked the tip of the blade across Denise's face. A shallow gouge sliced through Denise's cheek, up across her eye, and onto her forehead. She gasped in shock as she felt her soft skin part like butter. Warm streams of blood began to flow down her face like tears.

*"NO! DENISE!"* Dan screamed out.

Mary Anne lifted one heavy, skate clad foot and stomped into Denise's back. She fell forward, slamming hard against the dirt floor. Mary Anne rushed towards Dan. He turned to run and bumped into the heavy headstone, it wobbled precariously. The flashlight slipped out of his hand and fell in the dirt near the tunnel wall. He half-turned to Mary Anne, she was already right behind him. Years of skating had strengthened her legs and given her an eerie speed.

*"Don't move, Dan!"* Mary Anne continued in that growling rage-filled voice. "Don't you move one fucking muscle unless I tell you to."

Dan froze as he watched the sharp, jittering tip of the sickle in her hand, it was dangerously close to his Adam's apple, ready to rip his throat wide open.

"Mary Anne, stop! You're sick," he pleaded in a small voice, trying to remain as calm as possible. He held his hands up defensively. "Listen, I--"

*"Shut up!"* Mary Anne shrieked, the sickle trembled in her hand. "Get down on your knees and turn around."

"Mary Anne, please--"

"Get down on your knees and pay your respects to your son. The son that you *murdered!* You put that black rose down at the foot of his headstone and think about the life he could've lived, the life we could've had together! I want you to think about that before you die!"

"For God's sake, Mary Anne--"

*"DO IT!"* she screamed.

Dan slowly dropped to his knees in the dirt, never taking his blue eyes off Mary Anne's psychotic black ones. She motioned with her free hand for him to turn around. He slowly obeyed and she kept the tip of the sickle at his throat every second. He breathed in shaky little breaths through his teeth and forced himself to look at that name on the tombstone: *DANIEL PARSONS JR.*

"Tell him that his daddy is sorry. Tell him that his daddy is coming to be with him real soon."

Dan hesitated, unable to bring himself to say anything. His mouth simply didn't want to work under the stress of the anticipation of his own death. She kicked his foot with the toe stop of her skate, he gasped and jumped a little.

*"TELL HIM!"*

"I--I'm s-sorry," Dan stammered.

"I'm sorry, *son*," she corrected. She slowly bent down, reaching into the coffin to pick up the black rose. It was two inches to the right of her hand. She took her eyes off Dan just for a second when her fingertips touched down on the coffin's padded velvet lining.

Two hands latched onto Mary Anne's ankles and yanked backwards. She tipped forward as her skates rolled back along the hard dirt floor of the tunnel. She collapsed against Dan and shoved him under the left arm of the cross headstone. The sharp tip of the sickle chipped against the headstone and gave off a bright spark. Her forehead smacked into the hard stone and the rest of her body went limp, partially falling into the open lid of the coffin.

Dan spun around and saw Denise stand up behind Mary Anne's legs. A thick stream of blood ran sluggishly down the right side of Denise's face. Luckily, the sickle had missed her left eye altogether.

"Help me, Dan, while she's still groggy!" Denise shouted.

Dan sprang forward and shoved Mary Anne deeper into the coffin by her shoulders.

"Kill you, Dan," Mary Anne mumbled drunkenly. Together, Dan and Denise got her fully inside and slammed the coffin's lid shut. Inside the coffin, Mary Anne quickly regained her senses. She began shrieking like a banshee and pounding her fists against the coffin lid.

*"Let me out! Let me out goddammit!"*

Dan lay with his full weight against the bouncing, bucking coffin's lid so she wouldn't be able to open it and pop back out again. In her deep rage, she seemed to have a kind of freakish, unnatural strength. Dan thought that it felt more like he was struggling against a big man, than a teenage girl. He reached over with his right hand, hoping to close the hasp and lock Mary Anne in.

"Shit! Where is it? Where is it?" he muttered to himself.

Denise picked up the flashlight and shined it down to help him see. In the light, he could see only a few twisted shards of metal where the hasp used to be. He suddenly remembered that Charlie Hart had broken it off when he burst out of the coffin a few minutes ago.

*"Fuck! It's broken!"*

Denise stared at Dan with horror. Either her panic, or the pain in her cut face was making her mind blank.

*"Let me the fuck out! I'll kill you, Dan! I'll cut your fucking head off!"* Mary Anne shrieked from inside the coffin. Her ravings became garbled and they could barely understand her.

"Just go! I'll hold it down!" Dan yelled to Denise over the pounding and screams of Mary Anne. "Go see if we can even get out of here. See where the tunnel leads and dig your car out of the snow. Bring it around and honk when you get close. I'll follow you."

"Dan, no. Come with me," Denise protested.

"I can't. Someone's gotta hold her here or we won't have time to dig the car out. Just go, hurry!"

Denise slipped past the headstone. Just before she could leave, she turned back and pointed the flashlight down at the coffin. Mary Anne had fallen into a strange silence. It had happened while they had been arguing about whether Denise should leave or not. Dan noticed it too. Neither one of them cared for that silence one bit. Dan lowered his head down to the curved crown of the coffin lid, trying to listen to what she was doing. He could hear Mary Anne shifting and moving around in there.

*What is she planning?* he asked himself. *Does*

253

*she have some kind of trap door in the coffin too? God, please just let me escape tonight. Please, please, just let me make it home.*

The wood underneath Dan's ear began to drum as Mary Anne tapped her fingers against it. Dan pulled his head away from the eerie, bone-rattling sound. Hearing it made him feel like he was listening to an actual dead person under that coffin lid.

"Oh, Daaaannn," she called tauntingly. "Guess what, Dan?" Her voice had taken on an eerie, childish quality that Denise both hated and feared. Neither one of them bothered to give her an answer.

Now there came a muffled, jingling sound from under the coffin lid.

"Guess where I hid the keys, Dan?" she called. "They're all down in here with me. The padlock keys, the front door keys, the skate rental keys, the roof keys, the plow truck keys, the bus keys. Even the keys to the mausoleum are in here. All mine. You two aren't going *anywhere!*" She erupted into a fit of wild giggles that degenerated into harsh, braying cackles. *"You're going nowhere, Dan! You're going nowhere! Nowhere! Nowhere! Nowhere!"*

The sound of the jingling keys and that mad repetition was suddenly too much for Dan, he exploded at her.

*"You're lying! You're full of shit, just like always, Mary Anne!"* he screamed down at the coffin. He slammed his right fist down on the wood, while being careful to keep his left hand tightly clamped down on the edge of the lid. He refused to believe that they had come this far, gotten this close to escaping this hellish night, only to have Mary Anne trick them like this.

"Go into the mausoleum and see for yourself! You think I'd be stupid enough to forget to lock you in with me? *You can't escape from me, Dan! YOU*

*CAN'T!"* Mary Anne burst into lunatic laughter.

*"Fuck you!"* Dan screamed, banging his fist on top of the coffin lid again, this time hard enough to make it bounce briefly. Mary Anne's hyena laughter cut off abruptly. Dan turned to Denise. In the darkness, he didn't see the sickle blade poking out through the tiny crack between the lid and the side of the coffin. Dan's pounding fist had given her the gap she needed.

"Go up anyway. Go check it out," he said. "She could be lying. We have to make su--"

Mary Anne raked the blade down along the crack and ripped through Dan's left pinky finger. With a gout of blood, it tore free and fell to the dirt floor. Dan barked out a scream and jerked backward. He staggered away from the coffin in shock, clutching the bleeding stump of his pinky finger. The color immediately drained out of his face as he stared down at the ragged flesh where his finger had been only seconds ago. He gasped in great gulps of air, looking like he was about to be sick to his stomach.

Denise pointed the light toward him and saw the blood streaming down his arm. *"Oh my God! Dan!"*

The coffin lid instantly banged up as Mary Anne pounded it with both fists. Standing behind the headstone, Denise looked down as Mary Anne propped herself up on her elbows. She was pushing her way up out of the coffin. The sickle blade flashed in her hand, its razor edge glistening with Dan's blood.

Denise didn't have time to think, she immediately barreled into the heavy headstone like a football player. It tipped and fell down on the open lid, shoving Mary Anne back down again. Her head thudded against the lid and she flopped back down onto the soft inner lining. The weight of the cross clamped the coffin lid shut again. They heard her howl in pain and rage inside the coffin.

Dan stood there, staring gape-mouthed at the wound. He made choked little *Ah Ah Ah* sounds as the first prickles of red, roaring pain began to sting his left hand down to the wrist. His own blood continued to ooze down his arm. There was so much of it, he never realized he could bleed this much.

Behind them, Mary Anne was already inching the heavy stone cross off the coffin lid, screaming and straining from inside. Denise grabbed Dan's shoulder and yanked him toward the end of the tunnel.

"Come on, dammit!" she screamed and tugged him along with her. They sprinted down the tunnel, following the bouncing beam of the flashlight in her hand. Within moments, Mary Anne would be out of the coffin and right behind them. Denise led the way, doing the only thing she could think to do, take them back into Rollerville.

As they ran up the old mausoleum steps, they heard the heavy thud when the headstone fell into the dirt beside the coffin. The lid banged open again. The trap door in the roller rink's hardwood floor flung open for the second time that night and they climbed back up among the bodies. Behind them, Mary Anne's shriek of rage echoed up out of the dark.

# Chapter Thirteen:

# Dropped

### 1

Mary Anne was used to the dark, she welcomed it. She wasn't scared or creeped out down here in the tunnels below Rollerville. Even the fact that there were bodies buried down there, didn't bother her at all. Bodies didn't scare her anymore, she had become Death. Besides, most of them were her own family members anyway, her entire family had buried their dead here for over a hundred and fifty years. They had built this town from the ground up, then built this graveyard at its northeast corner as a place where they could be laid to rest.

It was her great uncle, Charlie Hart, that had inadvertently shown her this tunnel. He was crazy, but he was no murderer. She had come out to Rollerville late one night to mourn the loss of her baby. She had been crying, and then heard a man's voice crying as well. Wiping away her tears, she had followed those ghostly sounds down into the main mausoleum. At the bottom, the hole had been crudely cut through the wall, and the tunnel had been painstakingly dug by hand over the last year. She found her Uncle Charlie down there, drunk and raving. When she got him to calm down, he told her all about their family history. He told her about their founding father Elias Hart, and how he had homesteaded this land. He told her about Elias Hart's trouble with the Indians up on Indian Hill, a golf course was there now. He told her all about how his branch of the family had lost most of the old graveyard's land because of unpaid taxes, and how those bastards had come in here and bulldozed over their ancestors graves. He explained how he wanted to save his parents, and grandparents, and great grandparents bodies from the old mausoleum, and give them a proper resting place. Mary Anne told him she wanted to help him, but that hadn't really been the truth at all. She had only wanted an opportunity for revenge.

Now she heard the boom of the trap door slamming shut at the far end of the tunnel as she shoved her way out of the coffin. She crawled out onto the dirt floor and felt around for what had become her three most important belongings. Groping blindly in the dirt, she felt scuffed, filthy work shoes. It was her Uncle Charlie. His slim, bony body was already cool to the touch, the cold air down here had that effect on bodies.

She rolled him over and felt the first item, her long, curvy weapon: the scythe. Wrapping her hands around the long handle, she tried to pull it out of his chest. It was stuck down deep and tight. She had experienced this before with the power company guy she had lured down here, then held hostage for three days. She had locked him in an empty coffin, then let him out at night to fix up the breaker box and give her control over the power to the building from down here. When their business had concluded, she stabbed him in his rib cage, and the blade got stuck for some reason. She figured it must have had to do with the curvature of the ribs or something. Earlier tonight, in the middle of all the midnight chaos, she had been swept up in a psychotic adrenaline rush and knew she would have to work fast to get the job done. So she had elected to slash and cut mostly, she stabbed only when it was necessary.

Mary Anne placed a skate down on Uncle Charlie's chest next to the blade for leverage, and yanked hard on the long scythe handle. It moved an inch, then she yanked again and it squirted free.

Next, she ripped the black cloak off his shoulders. It was soaked with blood and hung down low, but it had been soaked for hours and she was used to it by now. She swung it around over her head and lowered her arms into the sleeves. Its thick black folds covered up her low cut red shirt and high red shorts, but for the moment, she left the hood drooping low down the back.

She bent down again, reached out, and felt Uncle Charlie's stubbly face. Her index finger fell into his soft, sticky eyeball, her pinky went into his bloody mouth. She reached to the left and found the third thing she wanted, her rubber Death's head mask.

She had found it at a party store on the west side of town shortly after Halloween. It had been a few weeks after Dan had broken up with her and she had lost her baby, and a few weeks after she had discovered the tunnel that Uncle Charlie had dug. When she had come to the Halloween mask aisle, she picked up the ugly, decayed-looking thing up and stared at it for a long time. It had completely represented how she felt. Her life had become shrouded in death, and she felt as ugly as it looked. Her baby was gone, Dan was gone, her family could care less about her. One of the employees had finally walked over and asked if he could help her with anything, and she almost put it back. An impulse at the last second made her buy it though. When she finally got home, she closed the curtains and turned on some ABBA records. She laid down on her princess canopy bed, put the mask on, and began thinking bloody, vengeful thoughts. In the darkness under the mask, she could think more clearly. With the mask on and her arms crossed over her chest in an X like a corpse, she formed the entire plan for tonight in her head.

While she remembered these things, she lovingly ran her fingers over the rubber. She came back to the present, and pulled the mask back down over her own head. It didn't really matter whether she wore it in the tunnels or not, down here everything was dark. She had hated to let complete morons like Mike Cavallo and her drunken tosspot great uncle wear it, but they were necessary parts of her plan. The magnified sound of her own breathing soothed her, it felt as if it were the most important sound in the world.

Now she raised the hood up over her mask and stalked toward the rink again. She pictured Dan, remembering everything he had said and done to hurt her. She remembered their baby and how handsome he would have been, how he would've looked just like her, but been tall and strong like his father. Her breathing under the mask roughened as she thought about the family she had lost. It sped up to a ragged pant as she thought about what she would do to the man who had dropped her, and taken it all away.

She walked right past the electric breaker box on the wall, then stopped herself. Even in the dark, she knew exactly where it was. The dirt floor was more compacted here, this had been where the power company man had stood and worked when she unlocked the coffin in her family's mausoleum and let him out. She turned to the breaker box on the wall and considered flipping the switch again, leaving the hateful ones above in total darkness. But by now, her patience was at an end, and her rage was just too uncontrollable.

Mary Anne lashed out with the scythe blade and stabbed into the breaker box. A flash and a burst of blue electric sparks exploded out of the thing like lightning, flickering against the Death mask like a disco light. She yanked the blade back out and spurts of blue sparks began to jump out of the jagged hole in the breaker box like water out of a hose filled with air bubbles.

Mary Anne walked back towards the trap door with bright blue electricity spurting out of the wall behind her back.

## 2

Dan and Denise scrambled up out of the hole in the floor as fast as they could. Denise went first, turning back to Dan to help him up. He held his hand cradled in the blood-soaked bottom of his shirt. He was in so much pain that he could only move stiffly. Denise had to pull him up out of the hole by his belt.

*"Fuck, fuck, my fucking finger. Ahh!"* Dan hissed. *"It hurts so fuckin' bad!"*

He rolled awkwardly onto his side and lifted his legs up out of the trap door, just before Denise slammed it shut again. It came down with a heavy bang, the iron hook bouncing and clanging against the underside. Once again, they could barely tell it was even there.

Denise got to her feet, slipping in the sticky blood puddles on the floor. The rubber soles of her tennis shoes squeaked loudly in it. She grabbed Dan by the arms and yanked him up.

*"Come on! Run!"* she urged.

She tugged him forward two steps and heard a

loud squeak as he slipped in the blood. He fell flat against the floor, his full weight coming down on his injured hand. He screamed out and rolled over, fresh tears streaming down his face. His breath came only in little hitching gasps, his jaw was clenched tight in agony.

She almost tried to force him to get up and run again, but then she stopped herself. Where exactly were they going to run off to? She looked left and right, frantically trying to think of a way to escape from this death trap. They could try the emergency exit doors again, but that would only be a gamble, one that could cost them precious time. She looked toward the front again. Earlier, when they had walked into the front lobby to see if the double doors were locked, they had been trying to be as quiet as possible. Now they could be as loud as they needed to be. The chase was on, and this was a matter of life or death.

*I could break out one of those narrow windows in the front lobby with a fire extinguisher or something,* she thought. There was no guarantee that they would be able to get her car started, or even dig through the snow and lock themselves in before Mary Anne got to them again. It was still a better plan than nothing at all.

She looked down at Dan again, grimacing in excruciating pain and clutching his stump of a finger wrapped up in his shirt. He looked all scrunched up, like his body was trying to fold in on itself from all the pain. His face looked pale and waxy with cold sweat.

*I have to get something for him or he's gonna pass out on me.*

*There's no time*, the voice of reason argued.

*There's a first aid kit up on the DJ booth somewhere.*

*Just get moving. Leave him.*

*You could use first aid yourself. Or have you forgotten that your own face is still gushing blood.*

*She's coming!!!*

Denise knew running might have been the smart thing to do, but it still wasn't an option.

"I'm gonna get the first aid kit," she told Dan. "But get ready to run. Okay?" Dan gave her a quick nod and she ran up onto the DJ booth. He glanced down at his hand and the sight of all that dark blood soaking into his shirt made him feel faint. Clouds of gray were trying to seep into the corners of his vision, so he tried to will them away by staring up at the twinkling disco ball spinning lazily above his head. There was a dark brown splotch of dried blood caked on the underside. Seeing that made Dan feel like he was going to throw up.

*Please God, let me get out of this. Please!* he thought.

Denise flung all the messy debris off of Freddy's desk. She wondered how someone could be such a slob, then she reminded herself that he was dead and felt guilty. She bent down under the desk and searched around in the dark. There were stacks of records, stacks of notebooks, a pair of platform shoes, a wire trash can full of empty Pepsi cups, but no first aid kit.

"Come on, come on. Where the fuck is it?" she muttered to herself.

Then the lights went out again. Denise gasped and pulled her head up from under the desk. She peeked over the edge of the desk with wide eyes, dreading Mary Anne's next attack.

*Fuck! I knew I should've just run for it.*

The lights flickered back to life almost immediately, then dimmed again. All over the rink the bright colored lights began flickering irregularly. Denise watched the weird effect from her crouched position on the DJ booth.

Dan stood in the middle of the rink, spinning around in a circle, also watching the lights flicker on and off. He felt like he was in some strange disco-themed haunted house. Looking at the lights only added to the lightheaded feeling he already had from the loss of blood.

"Oh shit. She's coming," Dan said. He walked toward the booth to stand close to Denise and wait for Mary Anne to come popping out of the floor again. This time there were only two victims to go after, she would have an easier time. He took hurried baby steps over the blood puddles so he wouldn't slip again. His plan was to jump over the empty spot on the floor where he thought the trap door was. He stopped when he reached the trap door's edge, not knowing that his toes and the balls of his feet were already on top of it.

Just before he could jump forward, the door flung open underneath his feet. He was launched backwards and up into the air. The force of the door flying open like that kicked his legs out from under him and made his body tilt horizontally in midair. Only his flailing arms prevented his body from doing a complete back flip.

He came down hard on his back on top of a pile of cold, bloody bodies. They squished and slid apart for him, tangling him up in their sprawled arms and legs.

Mary Anne slammed the scythe flat on the wood floor, planted her hands, and jumped up. Her feet parted as she stomped down on either side of the trap door hole. She rose up in her full death costume, with the cloak's hood pulled down over her rotting skull mask. She loomed above Dan, seething with hatred. She lifted the blade up, dragging its razor sharp tip across the wooden floor. It left a long, curved scratch in its polished surface.

Dan crab-walked backwards. His hands and shoes slipped on cold, wet limbs and organs.

With a flourishing spin of the long-handled

blade, she swiped down diagonally at Dan. The lights above Mary Anne flickered out just before the blade could slice into Dan's chest. He instinctively rolled out of the way, feeling the wind of the blade as it passed inches above his shoulder. If he had hesitated for even a millisecond, he would've lost his right arm. The lights flickered on again.

Mary Anne stepped forward and stabbed down at him again. He dodged out of the way, lifting his arm and turning his body as far away from it as he could. The blade stabbed down into a dead kid's kidneys. Again, it missed Dan by a few inches.

Denise watched it all from the DJ booth in the space of a few seconds. She recoiled at the sight of Mary Anne and the scythe. Her first instinct was to duck down towards the back of the booth in terror. Then, as Mary Anne began swinging the blade down at Dan, she knew she couldn't just stand there.

She began throwing whatever she could down at Mary Anne. She tossed a notebook full of Freddy's old playlists, but it flopped to the ground behind her. She tossed a record, but Mary Anne stepped out of the way to avoid that.

Denise frantically looked for something she could throw that would be more effective. She found her answer sitting right in front of her, Freddy's DJ chair. It was an old rolling office chair with foam bursting out from several rips that had been patched with duct tape. She grabbed the ugly, old thing by the armrests and turned to throw it, but knew she wouldn't be able to heave it far enough with the desk in her way. Dan kept crawling backwards over the bodies and Mary Anne kept advancing on him, they were out of her throwing range.

Denise hopped up on the desk, her feet accidentally hitting the buttons on one of the the record players. She lifted up the chair and turned to throw it just as Mary Anne was rearing back for another stab at Dan. Suddenly, the speakers started blaring out "Auld Lang Syne" by Guy Lombardo and his Royal Canadians again. The power to the speakers and the record player also flickered in and out just like the lights, crackling with static. The sound slowed down, then sped up again with each surge of electricity. It sounded like some kind of other-worldly siren. It caught all three of them off guard. Denise jumped a little as the sound blasted in her eardrums. She almost dropped the heavy chair.

Mary Anne whirled around and Denise seized the opportunity. She heaved the chair at Mary Anne as hard as she could. Mary Anne saw the flying chair careening towards her head and batted it away with the scythe like a weird baseball swing. The chair clattered to the wood floor just in front of Mary Anne. Three of its five wheels and one of its legs snapped off. It left several more dents in the floor.

Without a moment's hesitation, Mary Anne slashed at Denise with a smooth backhanded swipe of the scythe. Denise jumped over the blade unevenly, both legs moving at separate times. It would've cut her legs off at the ankles if she hadn't leaped over it just in time. She landed shakily on her feet, the whole desk wobbled under her weight and the record skipped. Mary Anne stabbed down at the desk again. The blade chopped down between Denise's legs and went right through the Guy Lombardo record. Sparks shot out of the record player, and with a harsh vinyl *rip* sound, it fell silent.

Now Mary Anne was advancing on Denise. She executed a weird spin that sent the folds of her cloak flying out. Denise watched as the handle slid almost all the way out of Mary Anne's hands, extending towards her. She could see that the next slice would be much more powerful and much higher than a slice across the ankles.

Denise glanced up in desperation, saw the dark opening in the ceiling tiles, and took her chance. She launched herself off the desk and up into the ceiling. Her forearms came down on the ceiling grid and she curled her legs up under her. The blade whistled past the bottoms of her tennis shoes. She kicked down and used the momentum to lift the top half of her body up onto the ceiling grid. The whole thing wobbled and bounced unsteadily, she was afraid it would come crashing down.

On the floor, Mary Anne watched as Denise's legs wriggled up into the darkness above the ceiling tiles. Mary Anne grinned under the mask.

*You're not safe up there, Resolution Buddy,* she thought. *I got that idiotic John Travolta wannabe up there, and I'll get you too. But for now....*

Mary Anne looked back over her shoulder at Dan. He was the more important target anyway.

Dan was still crawling away from Mary Anne. He was trying to get past the pile of bodies in front of the DJ booth, and get out to the empty spot in the middle of the rink. He glanced back and saw Mary Anne looking at him over her shoulder, the black empty eye sockets of the skull mask peeking out from between the two folds of the black hood. She eerily spun to face him, subtly moving her legs and rolling on her skate wheels, keeping those black eye sockets fixed on him. She began stomping over the bodies towards him again, using the handle of the scythe like a walking stick.

Up in the ceiling, Denise scrambled away from the opening that she had crawled through, assuming that Mary Anne would continue after her. She waited tensely for the blade to start slicing up through the thin ceiling tiles around her, but Mary Anne had focused her attention elsewhere.

*"No! Mary Anne! Stop!"* Dan pleaded. He tried to crawl backward, but his hands were covered in

blood, they slipped helplessly on the smooth floor. She reared back with the blade for another slash. He screamed and grabbed the only thing he could find for a shield, another body. In one quick movement, he grabbed its cold, limp arms and rolled with every ounce of strength he had. As he pulled the body over him, he looked up into the dead white face and rolled up eyes of Jack Flynn.

The blade slammed down into Jack Flynn's back. He still wore the sash around his shoulder that read *1981*. Four inches of bloody blade ripped through the middle of the word *1981*, and a gout of cold blood sprayed into Dan's face. He winced away from it, holding his lips tightly closed.

Mary Anne tugged on the blade, but it was tightly wedged in Jack's rib cage. The body jerked in Dan's hands, Jack's head and long, dark hair bounced limply with each tug. The blade refused to come free.

Dan gave another great heave and flung Jack's body, along with the scythe, off to his right. The smooth handle slipped out of Mary Anne's hands and she clumsily groped for it in the air. The body rolled away and slid to a stop in front of the trap door. Jack's body lay there, his back arched over the handle, the blade sticking up out of his chest.

Dan rolled away, freeing himself from the mess of bodies. He came to a stop on his back in the dead center of the rink. With a scream of rage, Mary Anne hurled herself after him. As he scrambled to get back up on his feet, she jumped off of a dead kid's back and tackled him on the floor. Her thin, bony fingers slipped around his throat and dug in. He immediately felt his windpipe close up and her sharp nails cut into the skin of his neck. She screamed garbled, inarticulate words from beneath the mask, more ranting about him killing their baby and her New Year's Resolution.

Denise heard both of them screaming down below. It sounded like they were near the middle of the rink. She crawled past Freddy's body lying limply on the ceiling grid, thankful that there wasn't enough light for her to see his face. She worked her way toward the sounds of their struggles below. There had to be a way to get her away from Dan, she desperately wished she had another office chair to throw down at her.

With both of Mary Anne's hands clasped tightly around his throat, Dan's hands were free. He swung a few ineffective punches at Mary Anne's ribs and tried to pull her arms away. In her fury, nothing seemed to affect her, it was like her deep rage blotted out all physical pain. He reached up to her face to try and poke her eyes out, but the rubbery skull mask got in the way. He grabbed the lower edges of the mask and pulled it up. The folds of rubber bunched up below her nose and held tight. Below the bunched up bottom of the mask, she gnashed her bloody teeth and tried to bite his remaining fingers off. She screamed hoarsely and threw her head from side to side in an effort to shake him off. She only succeeded in loosening the mask. He ripped it off her forehead and tossed it aside. It flopped to the floor.

Denise looked down out of the hole in the ceiling tiles that Freddy's head had broken. Twinkles of blinding light shone up at her, making her squint. She was right next to the disco ball, its round shiny curve blocked out a lot of the struggle down below. Peering past it, she saw Mary Anne straddled over Dan's legs. Judging by the harsh gagging and wheezing sounds coming from Dan, she knew Mary Anne was strangling him to death.

Denise reached out to shove the disco ball out of the way so she could see better, and did a double take. She realized what she could do now. She could drop the disco ball down on top of Mary Anne. The thought did occur to her that she might hit Dan, but it was too late to stop that. She had to do something to stop Mary Anne.

Denise bent forward, the top of her head hanging down below the ceiling tiles. She examined the dusty top side of the disco ball. There was a small chain connecting it to the spinning mechanism mounted in the ceiling. The ball itself hung down maybe six inches from the top of the ceiling. Denise reached her arm out of the hole in the ceiling tiles and wrapped her hand around the chain. She began pulling down on it, making the disco ball bounce and sway. Through the chain, she felt something inside the spinning mechanism start to tear.

Mary Anne grinned down into Dan's purple face. His eyelids were beginning to droop and thick veins were popping out on his forehead. She knew he would pass out soon, and then he would be dead, at long last *dead*.

The disco ball hung by a thread, one more tug would do it. Denise figured it weighed forty or fifty pounds, and it would undoubtedly shatter against whatever it hit. Its little mirror fragments would turn into razor sharp slivers of glass. She had to warn Dan before dropping the ball.

Dan could see little pinpricks of colored light blotting out Mary Anne's ugly, insane leer. He clawed weakly at her face and beat at her hands, but she was winning the battle. Just before the darkness clouded his vision, he looked up and saw a twinkling ball bouncing in the air overhead. At first, he thought it was just a trick of his vision. The sounds of the rink were fading out too, but Dan clearly heard Denise's voice call out to him.

*"DAN! LOOK OUT!"*

Denise didn't see whether he looked up of not, Mary Anne was in the way. She gave one last hard yank and felt something finally snap. The chain slipped out of her hand and the ball fell. It spun in midair, casting its bright spots of light all over the rink for the last time.

Mary Anne heard Denise scream out her warning to Dan. She looked up just as the disco ball crashed down onto her head. She shrieked as it crunched and shattered against her upturned face. The weight of it smashed her against the floor.

The disco ball exploded into what looked like sparkly dust from up above. It made a crunchy tinkling sound as tiny fragments of glass and big white chunks of the disco ball's plaster core broke apart and flew everywhere. The entire empty circle in the middle of the rink was completely covered with pieces of broken mirror and white plaster dust.

Dan had watched the ball fall towards them, growing bigger and bigger. He ducked to the left, covering his face with his hands. Mary Anne's hands slipped away from his throat, then her body gave a big jerk when the ball smashed into her head. She fell away from him to the right. He felt the floor vibrate and heard the explosion but didn't see any of it happen. Sprinkles of broken glass rained on him as the ball shattered.

Now he gasped for breath and began to cough. He lowered one hand to massage his aching, bleeding throat, and planted his other hand down on top of shards of glass that crunched and bit into his palm as he tried to sit up and crawl away from Mary Anne.

Denise looked down, horrified at the wreckage of the disco ball. From up above, it had looked like a giant sparkly egg had cracked open on top of Mary Anne's face. She was still lying there under it, her head at the epicenter of the destruction.

*Oh my God!* Denise thought. *I can't believe I did that to an actual person. What have I done?* Logic told her it was self-defense, but she felt sick to her stomach just the same.

Dan slid backwards, his back and butt crunching over broken shards of disco ball. Mary Anne writhed weakly under the mass of broken glass and white plaster. Her bloody hands clawed weakly against the floor, her fingers sliced open on sharp fragments of the little square mirrors.

The bigger chunks of the disco ball shifted and fell away, and Mary Anne's head emerged from under the wreckage. The skin on her forehead, nose, and cheek bones hung in ragged flaps. It looked like her face had been run through a giant cheese grater. Little rivulets of blood were oozing out of every gash. Her dazed, weary eyes rolled toward Dan, her mouth hung open and her lips were also shredded. She muttered something that sounded to Dan like a slurred version of *My baby....* Then she fell face first back down into the glass, her chin crunching in the sharp debris.

"Dan!" Denise called. Dan looked dazedly up at her as if he didn't know where he was. "Don't touch the glass. You'll cut yourself!" Dan held his hands up to examine them. He saw the jagged stump where his pinky finger had been less than an hour ago. With a sour little laugh, he held up the stump to her.

"How much worse could it get than this?" he said dreamily.

"Hang on. I'm coming down," she called.

Dan slowly got to his feet, and a few dozen broken glass shards sprinkled down from his clothes. He lethargically shook his head and another dozen glass shards fell out of his curly mop of brown hair. He avoided looking at Mary Anne's gruesome destroyed face. Carefully stepping over the bodies, he walked towards the DJ booth to meet Denise. Near the open trap door, he stopped and watched as her feet dropped down from the opening in the ceiling tiles.

The lights still flickered on and off in surges of

electricity. It had a weird effect on him, he felt like he was drunk or dreaming.

There was a tinkle of glass from behind him, and Dan looked back over his shoulder. The colored lights flickered out in the middle of the rink, but he saw a movement in the shadows as something rose up from the floor. They came back on and Mary Anne stood there, illuminated in pink and blue. It was almost as if she had sprung back up like a shredded, bloody Jack In The Box. The glass had torn several slashes in her black cloak. Even chunks of her hair and scalp hung down in messy clumps. She stood there grinning at him and raised her arms as if she wanted to run over and give him a hug.

"Daaaaann," she sighed. "I'm so happy to see you. I love you, forever and always."

Dan stood there gaping at her with a horrified look on his face. The thing in the cloak looked like a creature from a horror movie, not the girl he had fallen in love with back before the Year of Blood.

Mary Anne began walking shakily towards him over the bodies. Dan took a few steps back.

"Don't run from me, Dan. I wanna give you a kisssss." She pursed her lips together and blood squirted out of them grotesquely. Dan stared at her in hypnotized horror.

Denise dropped down onto Freddy's desk in a crouched, squatting position. Her mouth dropped open and she gasped as she caught sight of Mary Anne shambling toward Dan.

*"DAN! RUN!"* Denise screamed.

Dan jumped as Denise's cry broke him out of his horrified paralysis. He whirled to look at her, and Mary Anne pounced. Her terrible insane grin widened as she lurched toward Dan. Those weird, dilated pupils widened, blacking out her eyes. Her hands hooked into glass-encrusted claws and she grabbed for Dan's throat again.

Dan caught her by the forearms, and she stumbled forward on the bodies. He pulled her arms in opposite directions, trying to keep them away from his bruised neck, but they came right back. She dug her skates into his thighs, as if she were trying to climb up on top of him. Dan screamed in pain and arched back under her weight. She climbed even higher, crouching on top of him like some sort of predatory gargoyle. She shrieked down into his face.

Dan struggled against her, working his hands up under her ribs. He heaved her forward and up into the air. Her body sprawled out and flipped over in midair, her arms flailing. Dan had a momentary flash where he saw her falling during the middle of their "Dancing Queen" routine back in September.

Mary Anne came down flat on top of Jack Flynn's body, the upturned scythe blade drove deep into her heart. She let out a grunt and a gout of blood spurted out of her mouth. Dan stood watching as she writhed like a bug impaled on a needle, uttering strange gulping sounds. She had fallen facing the DJ booth with her back to him.

Dan watched as she turned her head and looked back over her shoulder at him. She had the same expression of bewilderment and hatred on her face that she'd had after he dropped her that night during the Disco King and Queen competition. Her face was shredded and bloody, but it was the exact same look. Without turning away from him, Mary Anne's head slowly lowered itself to the floor until her cheek lay flat against the smooth hardwood.

There she finally died, with her eyes locked on Dan under the flickering disco lights.

A hand touched Dan's shoulder and he jumped. Denise stood next to him, she held her hands up defensively.

"It's okay. It's okay. It's just me," she said. Dan looked at her without replying for a moment, then turned back to Mary Anne's fixed, dead stare.

"I-- I--," he stammered. He swallowed and found his words. "I dropped her again."

Dan and Denise stood there looking down at Mary Anne for one shell-shocked moment, then Denise turned away.

"Come on," she said. "We have to get out of this fucking place." She held the flashlight in her hand. "I've gotta go down and get those keys. You gonna be okay up here?" Dan nodded without looking at her. Denise looked warily at Mary Anne, hoping to God that she was finally dead. She knew the sooner she got the keys, the sooner they could get to the hospital. She took a deep breath, turned, and dropped down into the tunnel. A few seconds later, Dan could hear her tennis shoes pounding on the dirt floor of the tunnel, echoing up to him. She was sprinting through the darkness alone, but Dan was too exhausted to feel guilty about not going with her.

He knelt down and stared at Mary Anne. One question burned over and over in his mind. He let it linger there, then he finally asked it out loud.

"Why didn't you just tell me the truth?"

She had no answer for him, only a blank, dead stare. Something told him that even if she were still alive and at least halfway sane, she wouldn't have had an answer for him either. Sometimes people did stupid things for no reason, especially when they were young and in love. Sometimes love makes a person crazy. Or maybe she had really been crazy all along, and he had just been too blind and stupid in love to see it.

Dan turned away from her and saw one of those black roses lying near the carpeted wall of the DJ booth.

He figured Mary Anne must have laid it there earlier tonight. At first, he hadn't spotted it because it blended in perfectly with the dark carpeted walls of the DJ booth. He leaned forward and picked it up, careful not to prick himself on the thorns. While staring at it, he thought about what kind of New Year's Eve they would've had if only he hadn't dropped her months ago. He saw them lying on his bunk bed back at home, watching movies, maybe feeling a baby kick inside her stomach, feeling it kick with all five of his fingers. That sentimental image, phony as it was, gave him a weird impulse to lay the black rose against Mary Anne's body. He looked over and saw her ruined, accusatory face among the bodies of all his friends and classmates that she had murdered. That was the real New Year's Eve she had given him. Dan tossed the black rose down into the open trap door, it disappeared down into the dark below the rink.

"Is she dead yet?" a timid voice spoke up from behind Dan. He whirled around and there stood a freshman kid in a Star Wars T-shirt that he had seen every now and again in the halls of DeAngelo High.

"Where'd you come from?" Dan asked.

"I ran and hid under the pinball machine back there." Joe Jacobs looked and sounded as exhausted and haggard as Dan felt. He walked tentatively toward Dan and stopped a few feet behind him.

"I've seen her before, in the halls at school. You're her boyfriend, aren't you?"

"I used to be. I haven't been for a few months now."

"She killed my best friend." Joe's voice cracked, he sounded like he was on the verge of tears. "Why did she do it? Why?" Dan looked down at her abdomen, it was face down against Jack Flynn's body. He imagined the baby that would've been inside there at one point. His son.

Luckily, Dan didn't have to answer the kid's question. He began backing away as he heard footsteps approaching from the dark tunnel under the rink. Denise came back with a handful of keys jingling in her hands. She and Joe were equally surprised to see each other, and they briefly introduced themselves. She shuddered as she climbed up out of the dark.

Denise found a first aid kit behind the skate rental counter and put a temporary bandage on both Dan's missing finger, and her own cheek. Then without wasting any time, the three of them walked quickly toward the carpeted exit doors to the lobby. Dan stopped and almost looked back over his shoulder at Mary Anne one last time, even turning his head slightly to the side. He decided it would be a bad idea though, and continued forward with Denise and Joe.

In the front lobby, Denise tried key after key in the padlock holding the heavy chain together. On the sixth try, she found the right key. The lock snapped open, and with that one almost inaudible click, they were free.

## 3

They decided to take Geno's truck with the plow on it instead of her old Ford Thunderbird. She had grabbed the key out of the coffin, and figured that they'd have less chance of getting stuck somewhere. When the truck finally started, a blast of cold air blew out of the vents, and the radio began to blare out "Stayin' Alive" by the Bee-Gees. Apparently, Geno hadn't bothered to turn either the heat or the radio off before going back inside earlier that night. She turned them both down now.

All three of them sat crammed together in the

truck, with Denise at the wheel, Joe on the passenger side, and Dan in the middle. They were bloodstained, shivering, and covered in chunks of snow. Denise was thankful that Geno had plowed the parking lot a few times, the snow out there was less than a foot deep, even though three feet had fallen since that afternoon. They were all eager to go, so she decided not to wait until the truck warmed up. She popped it into gear, floored the gas, and let go of the clutch. The tires sprayed up snow and they jerked forward out of the parking spot.

They slid forward, fishtailing on ice and slush. Denise let her foot off the gas a little, and they rolled slowly out of the parking lot. The truck's back end slid again as they turned onto the road that ran alongside the Rollerville parking lot and the graveyard. Denise decided that if she wanted to get them home in one piece, she had better take it slow.

Up ahead on the left side of the road, they saw a dark hulking shape jutting into the air. Denise slowed down and swerved slightly to avoid the back end of the crashed bus, the place where Dan's best friends had met their grisly end.

"Holy shit," she whispered at the sight of it.

Dan looked up from staring at his bandaged hand and saw the bus. He wondered who, if anyone, was still inside, then quickly turned away. Seeing the bus's crooked, diagonal position and its mashed front end, made him feel sick. With the graveyard behind the bus, it looked like one giant coffin, a coffin big enough to bury all of his dead friends.

Denise glanced over and saw Dan's grief stricken face as he stared down at the floor mat. She felt like she had to tell him something, had to ease his mind somehow.

"Hey, Dan," she said. He barely looked over at her. On his face was an expression so sorrowful, it hurt her heart. "Don't think about it, hun. Think about something else. Think about...I don't know, our New Year's resolutions. We're both gonna put the past behind us this year, remember?"

Dan looked up in the rear view mirror and saw the winking light of the neon Rollerville sign flicker a little. As he watched, the neon sign went dark. He looked back down at the oncoming snow beating against the windshield.

"I think that's exactly what I did tonight," he said.

She smiled at him, reached down, and gave his hand a light squeeze. Together they sat there, warming each other's hands up for the rest of the ride. Even though her hand was ice cold, he loved the feel of it against his. He regretted the fact that he'd never get to hold her hand with more than four fingers again. Looking up at her filthy, bloodstained face and her ruined white coat, it was now so stained with blood and dirt he could barely see the original color, he thought he had never seen anyone more beautiful. He hoped that they would be able to make good on their New Year's resolutions and help each other forget this awful night.

Denise turned onto Hart Street and headed south. There had to be a fire station along this stretch somewhere. She remembered seeing one on her countless trips to and from work, but she couldn't remember exactly where it was. It was a slow ride and no one said much. "Stayin' Alive," continued to play, and she considered turning it off. More disco music was the last thing in the world she wanted right now, but it was still better than silence.

They drove past a dark, empty park on their left and crossed over a bridge. A wide irrigation ditch ran underneath it. Dozens of drooping, snow-covered trees and bushes lined either side of the ditch. Just beyond the bridge, there was a stoplight locked in the red light position. Denise slowed the truck down and skidded to a stop, pumping the brakes most of the way.

*Why is this stupid light red? There's no one out here, it's three thirty in the morning, for God's sake.* She glanced to the left and jumped. There was a man standing there by the side of the bridge, staring at the truck, staring right at her through the window. Even in the snow, she recognized him. It was the air-guitar man, playing that imaginary instrument in his herky-jerky movements again. She stared at him transfixed as he jammed out on that invisible guitar at the same tempo of "Stayin' Alive." He lifted up a calloused finger and pointed right at her.

That was enough for Denise. She ignored the red light, threw the gearshift into first, and floored the gas pedal. Snow sprayed up behind the car and the tires spun for a second.

The air-guitar man turned to watch her drive, and played on as her red taillights dwindled away in the distance. She went up over a rise, and disappeared farther down Hart Street.

# Epilogue:

Almost everyone in town knew about the bodies lying underneath the old Rollerville skating rink after January 1st, 1981. There were many more deaths throughout that long year of blood, but the New Year's killing spree at Rollerville was the one they would always remember most. As it turned out, nine people survived the mayhem that night. When the authorities arrived they found six more teenagers alive, unconscious, and in critical condition. After surgeries and rehabilitation, all six eventually returned home, and went back to finish the school year at DeAngelo High.

After the news coverage, the candlelight vigils, and the huge funerals ended, people began to talk. Rollerville had become a haunted place. Kids swung by in their cars on Friday nights every so often to vandalize the building. Some threw rocks at it, shattering the windows and the neon sign above. One night in May, a young vandal and troublemaker named Mack Rosenberg and a few of his buddies drove out to Rollerville. They spray-painted the word *ROLLERKILL* in drippy red letters across the side of the building. Egged on by his friends, Mack threw two dozen rocks at the neon sign above the front entrance, demolishing it. As he stood cheering with his friends, he heard a low crying, moaning sound from inside the dark abandoned building. Mack called, "Hello?" His friends dared him to go inside, and after a bit of arguing, Mack slowly began making his way up the ramp toward the entrance. The Plexiglass had been broken, and the doors were haphazardly boarded up. Mack pulled aside a loose board and began crawling into the dusty front lobby. Once his head was inside, he heard a low, eerie chuckling, echoing from somewhere inside the rink. He forgot all about his pride, and sprinted back to his car. With all of his friends on board, Mack burned rubber, tires screaming as he tore out of there as fast as he could.

Rumors spread like wildfire after that. Some people said that that crazy bitch Mary Anne Hart was buried out in the old abandoned, Hart Hill Cemetery. Others said that her body was never found. They claimed that her ghost haunted the old roller disco, with a big grin on her decomposing, shredded face as she skated to "Dancing Queen." Some kid would tell the story to a naysayer, and the naysayer would respond promptly with a *bullshit*, or a *getouttahere*, or a *you fuckin' liar.* But if they ever drove up Hart Street at night and happened to look over at the graveyard and the dark ruined building beyond it, they would wonder.

The only people in town who knew what really happened to Mary Anne's body were the Hart family, and they refused to talk to anyone about her. They kept to themselves. If anyone saw any members of the Hart family out at the grocery stores, or the post office, or the bank, they would stop and stare. Later, they would whisper about how bad they looked, and how that whole roller disco incident had aged them.

Everyone knew that it was best to steer clear of Rollerville, especially at night. They all knew that at night, ghosts skated around on the warped wooden floor in there. Anyone who ventured inside might be dragged away by some dead thing, down into the tunnels that were supposedly underneath the rink, never to be seen or heard from again. No one tried to redevelop the area again, no one tried to bulldoze over it, they just stayed away. Some places just don't belong to the living, some places belong only to death.

*Cameron Roubique*
*Thornton, Colorado*
*December 31, 2014 – April 1, 2016*

# Afterword:

Getting started on this book was particularly hard because it had so much to do with moving on. Not only was I forcing myself to dig up a lot of high school memories that were probably best left buried, but I was also having to force myself to step away from Cyndi and the *Kill River* books. Writing about Cyndi is pretty addictive for me, and it was really hard to try to get going with new characters. I'm not sure if I'll ever create a character that I love as much as I love her.

The initial idea for this story came out of an idea I had for *Kill River 2*. I originally wanted the killer in that story to murder a bunch of lifeguards partying at a water park after hours, but it just didn't make sense for that story. Why wouldn't they just hop the fence and run away? There's no way he could get all of them. So I let that idea just sit on the back-burner. Then one night, I think it might have been my birthday (which is in November), Darla (my wife, girlfriend at the time) and I went to the adults-only-skate-night at Skate City in Westminster. I remember it started snowing when we showed up, and I didn't think much about it. Inside, I was skating around and remembering a scene from a slasher movie called *Curtains* where the killer, in this creepy old woman mask, chases after a girl on ice skates. I pictured that killer coming after me under those colorful disco lights. A couple hours later, we got ready to leave and about a foot of snow had already fallen. I turned to Darla, and in my eloquent way of speaking, said, "Holy shit. Can you imagine if we got snowed in here? Tha'd be fucked up!" We walked past the parked school bus in the parking lot, and my mind went back to that killer from *Curtains* chasing after me on roller skates. Getting snowed in didn't seem like such a funny idea anymore. Later, I made the connection to that *Kill River 2* idea, and came up with a funny, catchy, over-the-top title, *Disco Deathtrap*. By then, I knew I definitely wanted to write this story.

    I'd like to thank my dad, my BFF Tim Taylor, and my wife Darla for helping me edit this book, I really can't thank them enough for all the time and work they put into it. If you notice any mistakes, they are entirely my fault. And I'd like to thank my buddy, and fellow slasher fan, Chris Velazquez for helping me with that line of Spanish in the Prologue. I also have to thank my little sister, Natalie, for playing "Dancing Queen" at her wedding at the Stanley Hotel. Hearing that song over the loudspeakers in that creepy place showed me the way to start my story.

    One last thing I'd like to mention, most hardcore slasher fans like me know that 1981 was a huge year for slasher movies, and it's no coincidence that I set this story at the very beginning of that year. I really like the concept of a whole slew of slasher stories taking place in the so-called "Year of Blood," 1981. So if you liked this book and want to read about more of these "Year of Blood" killers, I've definitely got a few ideas that I think would be a ton of fun. Write me and let me know what you think, I love talking '80s slashers with people.

So next time you happen to go roller skating, go up to the DJ booth, request "Dancing Queen" by ABBA, and while you're out there, think about what might be buried under the floor.

*Cameron Roubique*
*August 20, 2016*

## Soundtrack:

The following is a list of songs that are either prominently featured in this book or inspired me as appropriate background music in some of the scenes. You really don't have to listen to these songs to enjoy *Disco Deathtrap,* but all of them are excellent and if you're not already familiar with them, I highly recommend checking them out.

Cameron Roubique

1. "Dancing Queen" - ABBA
2. "Don't Bring Me Down" - Electric Light Orchestra
3. "Don't Stop Til You Get Enough" - Michael Jackson
4. "All Over the World" - Electric Light Orchestra
5. "And the Beat Goes On" - The Whispers
6. "Funkytown" - Lipps Inc.
7. "Do the Hustle" - Van McCoy
8. "Rock With You" - Michael Jackson
9. "Whip It" - Devo
10. "What I Like About You" - The Romantics
11. "Gimme! Gimme! Gimme!" - ABBA
12. "Happy New Year" - ABBA
13. "Auld Lang Syne" - Guy Lombardo and his Royal Canadians
14. "Stayin' Alive" - The Bee Gees

## About the Author:

Cameron Roubique lives in Thornton, Colorado, with his wife, Darla, cat, Penny, and pug Vader. He is an avid 80's slasher movie, superhero, and water park fan.

You can follow him on his website
at www.killriver.com
on twitter at twitter.com/lil_cam_ron
and on instagram at instagram.com/cameronroubique.

He can also be reached through email at
cameron@killriver.com.

Printed in Great Britain
by Amazon